Kate Sedley was born in Bristol and educated at The Red Maid's School, Westbury-on-Trym. She is married and has a son and a daughter and three grandchildren. THE WEAVER'S INHERITANCE is her eighth detective novel, following DEATH AND THE CHAPMAN, THE PLYMOUTH CLOAK, THE HANGED MAN, THE HOLY INNOCENTS, THE EVE OF ST HYACINTH, THE WICKED WINTER and THE BROTHERS OF GLASTONBURY, all featuring Roger the Chapman and available from Headline.

Kate Sedley lives in Bristol.

The Weaver's Inheritance

Kate Sedley

HEADLINE

First published in hardback in 1998 by
HEADLINE BOOK PUBLISHING

First published in paperback in 1999 by
HEADLINE BOOK PUBLISHING

10 9 8 7 6 5 4 3 2 1

ISBN 0 7472 6128 8

Printed and bound in Great Britain by
Clays Ltd, St Ives plc

HEADLINE BOOK PUBLISHING
A division of Hodder Headline PLC
338 Euston Road
London NW1 3BH

The Weaver's Inheritance

Chapter One

The letter, brief and obviously written with all the difficulties experienced by a person unused to wielding a pen, reached the home of my mother-in-law, Margaret Walker, just prior to the Christmas season of that year of Our Lord, 1476.

For once in my life, I had been looking forward to the cosiness of a winter spent mainly within four walls. I would contribute towards the household expenses by hawking my wares around the outlying villages and hamlets of Bristol, but intended to venture no further afield than a half-day's journey, thus ensuring my return home before curfew and the closing of the city gates. I had also promised myself that those long, dark evenings, when doors and shutters were closed early against the inclement weather and we huddled together around the fire, would be spent getting to know my motherless daughter better.

Elizabeth had celebrated her second birthday in November, and was now a busy, prattling little girl – although it needed Margaret to interpret most of her utterances for me – toddling about the cottage, her hands constantly outstretched and ready to meddle in everything that did not concern her. Her grandmother's spinning wheel held a particular fascination for Bess, as did the cooking crane over the fire, with the big iron pot suspended from its hook. Indeed, the only items in which my daughter evinced no interest were her toys; two wooden dolls named Rosemary and Fleur, a brightly painted wooden spinning top, and an equally garishly coloured wooden ball. These lay neglected and gathering dust in the chest alongside the bed which she shared with my mother-in-law.

Those of you who have read my previous chronicles, will know that Elizabeth's impending arrival was the reason why I had married her mother, Margaret Walker's daughter, Lillis. Our wedded life had been of short duration, Lillis dying in childbirth eight months later; and I had never been able to forgive myself for the overwhelming relief which I had felt at this tragic event. Guilt, as well as the heady sense of freedom which life on the open road engendered, had kept me almost continuously on the move these past two years, abandoning my child to the care of her grandmother.

Watching Elizabeth, that cold, grey December morning, as she sat amongst the rushes on the floor, carefully examining one of her feet, my chief consolation was that she in no way resembled Lillis, or my self-blame would have been compounded by ever-present reminders of my dead wife. But there was nothing small and birdlike about my daughter; she had none of the black-haired, brown-eyed, sallow-skinned colouring which characterized Margaret Walker, and which had betrayed so clearly Lillis's Welsh and Cornish origins. No, my daughter was mine through and through; fair-haired, fair-skinned, blue-eyed and already big for her age, showing every promise of being as tall and well-built as I was myself in those days.

'Yes, she's yours all right,' my mother-in-law remarked, coming in through the street door and slamming it shut behind her. She set down the raw wool she was carrying; wool which she would shortly begin to comb and spin, making the most of the remaining hours of winter daylight which filtered through the oiled-parchment panes of the cottage's only window. 'There's no mistaking her for anyone else's child.'

'You made me jump,' I accused her, smiling. 'I didn't expect you back so soon.' I nodded towards her overflowing basket. 'Work seems to be plentiful.'

She removed her cloak and pattens before seating herself at her wheel.

'And likely to get busier now that young Master Burnett's joined his business with that of his father-in-law, Alderman Weaver. Old Burnett must be turning in his grave. Only three months dead, and already his son is making changes he would never have countenanced if he had lived to be a hundred!'

'Why do you think William's done it?' I asked idly, drawing Elizabeth on to my lap and trying to persuade her to put on her stocking and shoe. The bare foot was like a small lump of ice.

Margaret, busily removing burrs and other foreign matter from some of the wool, shrugged.

'His wife is Alderman Weaver's sole heir. Since her brother Clement's death, the old man has neither chick nor child else, other than Alison, to leave his fortune to. So perhaps it makes sense to combine the Burnett and Weaver looms; the spinning and dying, the fulling and weaving and the tenting. After all, Redcliffe's been fairly divided between the two families for years now. And without Alderman Burnett's steadying influence to guide him, maybe young William feels the need of an older and wiser head in charge.'

I snorted with laughter. 'That I can well believe.'

I had met William Burnett to speak to only once, five years ago, when, fresh from my release as a novice at Glastonbury Abbey, I had taken joyously to the road in my new calling as a chapman – or pedlar, to use the commoner word – and discovered for the first time my ability to solve those mysteries and puzzles which, with God's help, had already brought several villains to justice. William had been a fop then, interested in little beyond his appearance, and still was. I had thought him empty-headed and vain, a rich man's son unchecked and overindulged, and

3

wondered what a spirited girl like Alison Weaver could see in him; for, even though it was doubtless a match arranged by their fathers, I recalled that she had looked at her betrothed with admiration. Women were, and are, and always will be, an enigma to me.

During the intervening five years, I had, on rare occasions, noted Master Burnett walking in procession to the nearby Temple Church, where members of the Weaver's Guild maintained the Chapel of Saint Katharine, ensuring that candles were always kept burning before the altar of their patron saint. Those brief glimpses had convinced me that he had not changed, so overdressed and self-satisfied did he seem.

Alderman Alfred Weaver's appearance, on the other hand, had suffered considerable alteration. When I first had dealings with him, he had been a florid, thickset man with the glow of health about him, but the loss of his only son and heir had taken its toll. Even two years ago, when we had again had some contact, he had begun to lose weight, and the hair covering his bald pate had been thinner and sparser than before. But my most recent sighting of him, leaving his house in Broad Street three days earlier, had shocked me beyond measure. His flesh hung loosely on his bones, a fact which could not be disguised even by the heavy, old-fashioned garments which he always wore. His jowl sagged, his cheekbones were jutting almost through the skin, and his eyes, as he looked at me across the street, were dull and lifeless, holding no spark of recognition. He had been accompanied by Mistress Burnett, and it struck me for the first time that there was a stronger resemblance between father and daughter than I had previously imagined . . .

A loud knock on the cottage door disturbed my reverie. Putting Elizabeth aside, I scrambled to my feet, my mother-in-law being busy with her combing. The man who stood outside was known to me, although we had never spoken, as one of Alderman

Weaver's carters; he was called Jack Nym. I stared at him in surprise, wondering what he could want, and he grinned back good-naturedly, showing a mouthful of blackened and broken teeth.

'I've a letter here for Mistress Walker,' he said, 'and a message to go with it. Can I come in?'

Margaret put down her work and rose, picking bits of wool from her skirt as she did so.

'A letter for me?' she enquired. I held the door wide to allow our guest across the threshold. 'I know no one up in the Wolds.'

'I haven't been up in the Wolds this trip,' Jack Nym answered, adding impressively, 'I've been Hereford way.'

My mother-in-law, whose knowledge of everything to do with the weaving and woollen trade was as great as that of anyone I knew, raised her eyebrows.

'My, my! *March* wool, eh? That's going to set Alderman Weaver and Master Burnett back a pretty penny.' She added for my benefit, 'March wool is superior even to Cotswold wool, which gives you some idea of its price.'

'Fourteen marks the sack,' Jack Nym put in with quiet satisfaction. 'But seemingly it's to be used for a special order.' He held out his hand. 'Here's your letter, Mistress.'

Reminded of the reason for his visit, Margaret took it. 'Who can it be from?' she wondered.

'The name's Adela Juett,' Jack answered promptly. 'Claims to be a distant cousin of yours.'

My mother-in-law gave a little screech of excitement. 'Adela! Adela Woodward that was! Dear heaven! Many's the time I've looked after her when she was young. She used to play with Lillis as a child, but I haven't heard from her in ages. She married a man from up country that she met one time at Saint James's Whitsuntide fair, and went away to live. That must be all of seven years or more ago. How does she go on?'

Jack Nym nodded towards the still-unopened letter. 'Widowed last year and left with a little lad, now two years old, to rear. That's how I came to meet her. I had to stay overnight in Hereford and, in order to earn a crust for her and the boy, she serves at table in the inn where, as chance would have it, I chose to lodge. We got talking. She recognized my accent and told me that she, too, came from Bristol. She mentioned a kinswoman of hers, a Margaret Woodward who had married an Adam Walker a twelvemonth after she was born. When she found I knew you, she asked after Lillis, so of course I had to tell her the sad news.' Jack Nym's eyes flickered towards me for an instant before being hastily lowered. 'Anyway, Mistress Juett asked me to tell you that she wants to come home, and she wondered, if she were to make the journey, could you possibly take her and young Nicholas under your roof for a while, just until she gets settled in. I have to go that way again in two or three months' time. I could give her your answer then, and maybe bring her back with me if you're agreeable.'

My mother-in-law handed me the letter. 'You read it, Roger. You know I've no book learning to speak of.'

The handwriting was almost illegible, and the message would have made very little sense without the carter's explanation. And when I had deciphered it, it added nothing to what we had already been told. Margaret thanked Jack Nym profusely for his time and trouble on her cousin's behalf, and insisted that he accept part of a newly baked batch of oatcakes to take home to his wife.

'Well, don't forget to tell me if you want this cousin of yours fetched from Hereford when next I'm up that way,' the grateful carter said as he departed, carefully depositing the oatcakes, wrapped in a clean cloth, on the floor of his now empty wagon.

Margaret thanked him a second time, closed the door and returned to her combing, a thoughtful expression on her face. I

rescued Elizabeth, who was trying to scale the mound of logs
piled up in one corner of the room, and sat down once more by
the fire, ignoring her wails of protest.

'Will you have your cousin here?' I asked at last, when the
silence became oppressive. 'There isn't much room.'

'Enough,' my mother-in-law replied serenely. 'Adela and I
can share the top half of the bed and the children can sleep at the
foot. You'll have your mattress, as you always do, in this part of
the room, with the curtain drawn between us. It will answer for
a month or two, at least, and it will be a treat for Bess to have
another child to play with, especially one so close to her in age.'
She began winding some of the combed wool around her spindle,
a reminiscent smile hovering at the corners of her mouth. 'Adela
is the daughter of one of my father's cousins. A very pretty girl,
if I remember rightly, who grew into an even prettier woman.
There were plenty of young men hereabouts who would have
been happy to marry her if she would only have had them.'

Margaret spoke so nonchalantly that the hairs started to rise
on the nape of my neck, like those of an animal scenting danger.
I knew my mother-in-law's desire for me to marry again,
recollected her attempts at matchmaking during the past year or
two, and decided there and then that long before Jack Nym set
out again for Hereford, I would be off on my travels.

It wasn't that I didn't want to take another wife, but I wished
it to be in my own time and of my own choosing. Besides,
although my mother-in-law did not know it, I already had a lady
in my eye. She was a certain Rowena Honeyman who lived with
her aunt in the town of Frome, and whom I had met during the
past summer in circumstances which I was not, as yet, prepared
to divulge to Margaret, who was bound to disapprove of them.
In any case, I had no idea what Rowena's feelings were towards
me, and until I did, silence was golden. Our acquaintance had
been brief and difficult, confined to a few days in early

September, and we had not seen each other since. But I thought of her often.

I realized that Margaret was speaking, and was forced to beg her pardon.

'I'm sorry, Mother, my mind was elsewhere. What were you saying?'

She gave me a sidelong glance and cleared her throat, starting to spin.

'I said I thought it was a long time for poor Adela to have to wait for Jack Nym. Two or three months he reckoned, before he gets sent that way again.' Margaret was suddenly very intent on her work, avoiding my eyes. 'I thought that perhaps if you went to fetch her as soon as the Christmas season is over, she and her little boy could be settled in here well before the end of January.'

There was a protracted silence, while Elizabeth escaped my slackened grasp and crawled away, unchecked, to pursue her investigation of the logs.

At last I answered coldly, 'You have begged me, after what happened last year, never to go more than a mile or so beyond the city gates in wintertime. But now you're asking me to travel to Hereford. And what about your cousin and her son? Do you think it will be better for them to walk so many weary miles in the coldest part of the year, rather than ride the whole way with Jack Nym in the spring?'

There was another silence while I waited with interest to discover how my mother-in-law would deal with this eminently reasonable argument. I knew exactly what was in her mind; that this Adela Juett and I would be forced into each other's company for ten or twelve days, in circumstances that could not help but forge some sort of bond between us. I watched, in grim amusement, the various expressions which flitted across her face as she struggled to find an answer, and smiled at her obvious vexation as she came reluctantly to the conclusion that there was none. But Margaret Walker was not a woman to be worsted when she had set her heart on something. She stopped spinning, raised her head, chin jutting belligerently, and looked across at me.

'I want my cousin and her son here, under my roof, as soon as possible. I should have thought, after all I've done for you, that it would be a small repayment for you to oblige me in this.'

I returned her stare, as nonplussed as she had been a moment or two earlier. I was caught, and I could tell by her triumphant smile that she knew it. She had never before reminded me of all that I owed her, looking after Elizabeth for the past two years while I went my carefree, irresponsible way. She wasn't going to pretend that what she was asking me to do had any rhyme or reason to it, except of course to herself. She was simply calling upon me to pay my account. Not to do so would be worse than churlish.

'Well?' she demanded, raising her eyebrows.

I glared back at her, but then my anger evaporated. I had no real objection to being on the road, for I was already growing restless, and I reflected that there was no way in which she could *make* me fall in love, or even contract a marriage of convenience with her cousin. She had no idea that I was already armoured against such a possibility, bewitched by a pair of periwinkle-blue eyes and hair the colour of ripe corn. And who was to say that Adela Juett would wish to have me for a husband even if I were to offer for her?

'If that's what you want, Mother,' I answered pleasantly, 'of course I'll oblige you.' I saw her expression sharpen from triumph to suspicion. 'I'll set out as soon as Christmas is over.'

The mystery in which I was to become embroiled during the next few months, unlike some of my previous adventures, had no connection with the greater happenings unfolding in the country at large; but I was to become a spectator of these events simply because I chanced to be in certain places at particular times. The first occasion was at Tewkesbury sometime around the middle of January, 1477.

I had set out from Bristol as soon as Christmas was done, arriving in Hereford just over a week later and making my way to the inn where Adela Juett lived and worked. Once my mission was explained, she seemed perfectly willing to accompany me, shrugging off the hardships which a walk of so many miles would entail, especially with a young child to fend for.

'We can take it in turns to carry him,' she said. 'I'm strong and used to his weight. Don't think that I shall expect you to be the only packhorse. And no doubt we shall be offered a ride by any carters we happen to meet on the road.'

She was as good as her word, shouldering the burden of young Nicholas as often as I would allow, and coming close to losing her temper on several occasions when I refused to let her take him from me. Whenever we heard the rumble of a cart in the distance, she would urge me into the middle of the track where we could clearly be seen by the driver; and Hereford had hardly been left behind before we were perched somewhat uncomfortably on top of a wagonload of turnips, the first of many similar journeys. The boy's presence also ensured us shelter at any cottage along our route where there was no nearby inn or ale-house to offer accommodation, and some of the goodwives were reluctant to accept recompense for their trouble.

Nicholas Juett was a sweet, sunny-natured child with an endearing smile and the huge, velvety-brown eyes of his mother. He also had Adela's dark wavy hair and soft red lips, which made him the immediate target of almost every female who encountered him; but he suffered the shower of kisses rained upon him with a commendable lack of grievance. In this he again resembled Adela, for she spoke little and never complained; and on an afternoon of lowering skies and gathering cloud, when a light flurry of snow had already presaged the threat of colder weather, we had been on foot for several long and wearisome miles, but still she remained resolutely cheerful.

It was getting dark as we approached Tewkesbury. For the past half-hour, I had been aware of more traffic on the road than might normally have been expected at that season of the year, both coming from and going towards the town. There were a surprising number of men-at-arms, and amongst the badges which had caught my eye were the Black Bull of Clarence, the White Boar and Red Bull of my lord of Gloucester, the Gold Lion of the King's brother-in-law, the Duke of Suffolk, and the White Rose and Sun in Splendour of King Edward himself. Something was afoot in Tewkesbury and curiosity drove me forward, quickening my step in spite of the weight of young Nicholas Juett, who lay sound asleep in my arms.

'Make for the nearest inn,' I advised my companion. 'We're all tired and need rest.'

It had been my original intention to seek shelter in one of the guest-halls of the Abbey, but the town was so crowded that I doubted if the monks would be able to accommodate us. But neither could the first two hostelries at which we applied. I was beginning to feel worried when a hand clapped me on the shoulder.

'Well, fancy seeing you here, Chapman,' said Timothy Plummer.

Chapter Two

A harassed pot-boy brought two cups of wine, one for Timothy and one for myself, before hurrying away to serve other customers in the crowded ale-room.

This inn was as full to overflowing as the others from which we had been turned away, and my travelling companion and I would have been hard-pressed to find any lodging for the night had we not fallen in with Timothy Plummer. But one word from him and a couple of young squires, sporting the Duke of Gloucester's livery, had removed themselves from the merest cupboard of a room, which was now happily occupied by Adela and her son. As for myself, I was invited to share Timothy's bed in an adjoining chamber.

Timothy Plummer was the Duke of Gloucester's Spy-Master, and he and I were old acquaintances. We had first met six years earlier, when I had been enquiring into the disappearance of Clement Weaver, the Alderman's son; since then, our paths had crossed on two further occasions. Each time, through chance or force of circumstance, I had been able to render Duke Richard a signal service, and therefore I had Timothy Plummer's trust.

'Very well,' I said, taking a gulp of wine in order to wash down a supper of rabbit stew, wheaten bread and cheese, 'you know why *I'm* here, but why are you? Why is the town so crowded?'

Timothy choked over his drink. 'Where have you been these

past few weeks? All right, all right! You've been walking to Hereford, I haven't forgotten! But I should have thought you might have heard the news of Duchess Isabel's death somewhere along the way. Indeed, she died on the twenty-second of December, before, according to you, you left home. Did no word of it reach you in Bristol?'

I stared at him. 'I've heard nothing. But . . . Duchess Isabel? Clarence's wife? I saw her at Farleigh Castle only last summer. She looked tired, it's true, but I thought that due to the fact that she was heavily pregnant. Did she die in childbirth?'

'Shortly afterwards. The child died too. And yesterday was the day of her funeral. She's been lying in state here for the past three weeks, before being buried in the Abbey. Duke George, as you may know, holds the Honour of Tewkesbury.'

I didn't know, but neither did I confess my ignorance. 'Poor lady,' I said. A fresh thought struck me. 'Are the Duke and Duchess of Gloucester here? It must be a great blow to the Duchess to lose her only sister.'

Timothy grimaced. 'She's not strong herself, and the news made her too ill to travel.'

'So Duke Richard came alone?'

'No, no!' My companion was growing testy. 'He sent his bastard son, Lord John, to represent him. That's why I'm here – to watch over the boy and make sure he comes to no harm. Duke Richard has gone to London to consult with the King and to set a date for the convening of the Great Council, next month. Duke George rode to join them as soon as the funeral was over.'

I was puzzled. 'Why is a Great Council being called?'

Timothy set down his empty cup and sighed. 'You *have* been out of the world, Chapman, haven't you? The Duke of Burgundy was killed while besieging the town of Nancy two weeks or more ago; before January was a few days old, at any rate.'

I gaped, remembering Charles the Bold as I had seen him the

year before last, in Calais; vibrant with life and putting up the backs of all around him. He was, or had been until so recently, brother-in-law to our own English Princes, having taken as his second wife their sister, the Princess Margaret, by whom he had hoped, no doubt, to have a son to succeed him. But there had been no children of the marriage and now he was dead, leaving as his sole heir his daughter, Mary, who must surely be the greatest matrimonial prize in the whole of Europe.

I was still confused however. 'But why does the King need to convene a Great Council?'

Timothy heaved another sigh. 'Use your common sense, man,' he pleaded. 'What do you think happened the moment the news of Duke Charles's death reached the French court?' When I made no answer, he continued wearily, 'King Louis at once announced that Burgundy had reverted to the Crown of France, and our spies report that he is even now mustering his armies to take possession of it. Surely you understand what that means!'

Of course I did. I couldn't live in a weaving community without knowing the vital importance of Burgundy to the English cloth trade. It was one of our biggest markets.

'Then it's war,' I said slowly, twisting my cup between my fingers. 'This time, we shall really go to war with France.'

Timothy Plummer shook his head. 'It's not that simple, my friend. You've forgotten the pension King Louis pays King Edward.' My companion lowered his voice and took a careful look around to ensure that no one was listening. 'Fifty thousand crowns a year isn't lightly to be tossed aside by a man who has to support a greedy wife and her equally rapacious family.'

'So . . . what's the answer?'

'A strong husband for Mary of Burgundy; someone who will devote himself to her interests and halt King Louis in his tracks. And that's chiefly what's worrying Duke Richard.'

'In heaven's name, why?'

Timothy bent his head closer to mine, and his voice sank almost to a whisper. 'Think, man, think! The Duke of Clarence is now a widower. He's Dowager Duchess Margaret's favourite brother. You've only to note how his retainers and followers are already puffing themselves up with a new-found importance to guess what's in Prince George's mind.'

'But . . . would it be such a bad thing if my lord of Clarence married the Duchess Mary? It would keep Burgundy firmly yoked to England, and surely that's in His Highness's interest. In all our interests!'

Timothy grunted and signed to a passing pot-boy to refill our cups, waiting until this was done before replying.

'Oh, yes! It's what every cloth merchant in the country wants, I've no doubt, as well as more money for his goods; something he's not likely to get if King Louis controls the Burgundian exchequer. The Guilds are always sending deputations to London as it is, to demand that a better price be negotiated for their wares. And, I might add, none are so vociferous as the weavers and fullers and tenters from your part of the world. I had to accompany Duke Richard to London last October, and there was a company of men from Bristol there then, pestering everyone concerned, including the King, with their extortionate demands.'

'Well, there you are then! If the Duke of Clarence were to marry his stepniece . . .'

'Christ's nightshirt!' Timothy interrupted in exasperation. 'Do you really think that the King or any of the Woodvilles would entertain the idea, even for an instant? Do you imagine they'd want Clarence at large in Europe, the possessor of its most s-splendid coronet?' In his excitement, Timothy was beginning to stutter, his voice rising in despair at my lack of political *nous*. In spite of the noise all around us, he was attracting attention and heads were starting to turn. With a visible effort, he took himself in hand.

'Just consider,' he went on more quietly, 'that it's only a little over six years since George of Clarence was at the French court, an ally of King Louis; since he and his father-in-law, Warwick, returned to England to depose King Edward and restore King Henry to the throne; and something less than six years since he again turned his coat to fight alongside his brothers here, at Tewkesbury. The Woodvilles loathe and detest him. He was in Warwick's camp when the late Earl ordered the execution of the Queen's father and her brother, John. They'll neither forget nor forgive. And as for the King, however many times *he* may have forgiven Duke George, he'll never trust him again.'

'But,' I persisted, unable to let the argument rest, 'suppose the Duke of Clarence offers for Mary of Burgundy and is accepted. What could King Edward or the Queen's family do to prevent the marriage?'

Timothy drained his cup and sucked his teeth. 'They'd probably have to use armed force, for it's certain Duke George would never heed any injunction laid on him forbidding the match. It's what's worrying Duke Richard, but he puts his faith in the fact that Duchess Mary, from all that he knows and has seen of her, seems to be an extremely practical and level-headed young woman. He says that if she chooses anyone but the Hapsburg, he'll be very surprised. She needs a great prince to defend her and her duchy against King Louis, not someone who's concerned only with his own interests, and who'll bring her nothing but trouble.' There was a moment's silence before Timothy added ruefully, 'But of course, Duke George won't see it that way.'

'But if the lady refuses him, there's an end to the matter, surely?'

Timothy shook his head. 'Not if he sees her rejection as the result of the evil machinations of the King and the Woodvilles – as he almost certainly will, my master reckons. Duke Richard is

17

fearful that Brother George will do something even more stupid and rash than usual.'

I shrugged, suddenly weary of the subject. A man who could seriously consider taking a second wife almost before the first was decently interred in her vault, did not merit a great deal of thought in my estimation. And most people were agreed that it was only a matter of time before the King's patience with the Duke of Clarence eventually ran out. The quarrels of Princes did not really concern me, but the consequences to the country's cloth trade, should France overrun Burgundy, did. Many livelihoods, including perhaps my mother-in-law's, could be affected if that happened. My own feeling was that England should immediately go to the Duchess Mary's defence; but I could understand that King Edward would be reluctant to oppose King Louis too openly because of that annual pension of fifty thousand crowns.

My worries, however, did not prevent me from sleeping like a log, although Timothy complained the next morning that my tossings and turnings had kept him awake half the night. I retaliated with allegations about his snoring. Nevertheless we parted after breakfast with expressions of mutual goodwill, he to wait upon the Lord John and I to see if I could find a carter travelling in the direction of Bristol. I was lucky enough to discover one carrying a load of sea-coal as far as Gloucester, and before the winter sun had risen very high in the heavens, Adela Juett, a sleepy Nicholas and I were perched up on the seat beside the driver.

We reached Bristol at last somewhere towards the end of the month, the final thirty or so miles of our journey having been hampered by worsening weather and a lamentable dearth of wagons going in our direction. It was almost dusk on a bitter winter's afternoon as we approached the Frome Gate, and the

Porter was just getting ready to close it for the night. I shouted to him to wait and, hoisting Nicholas higher on my shoulder, started to run, urging Adela to do the same. Instead, she slowed to a halt, clutching my arm.

Angrily, I freed myself. 'Come along!' I protested.

She stumbled in pursuit, making a second attempt to detain me.

'Didn't you hear it?' she panted. 'There was a cry, as though someone were in distress.'

'I heard nothing,' I answered impatiently.

We had, by this time, reached the gate, which the Porter was grudgingly holding open for us.

'You're cutting it fine,' he grumbled. 'I'm waiting to get away home to my wife.'

I was about to offer our apologies when Adela cut in, asking the same question as before.

'Didn't you hear it?' She turned to the Porter. 'Did you hear a cry as though someone were in distress? I feel certain it came from one of those houses over there.' And she waved a hand in the direction of Lewin's Mead.

The Porter shrugged. 'Probably some drunk. Or some goodman beating his wife. Or some wife taking a broomstick to her husband. It's always happening round here.'

'But you heard nothing?'

'Not a thing.' The Porter was running out of patience. 'How could I be expected to, with your husband shouting at me at the top of his voice?'

Adela was momentarily diverted from her purpose. 'He's . . . he's not . . .'

Taking advantage of her confusion, I put my free hand under her elbow and steered her forward, wishing the Porter a firm goodnight. As we started to cross the Frome Bridge, I heard, behind us, the bolts of the gate being rammed into their sockets.

'Not much further now,' I said encouragingly. 'We'll soon be home.'

Adela slowed to a halt, leaning on the parapet of the bridge and staring down into the waters of the Frome, as it flowed towards Saint Augustine's Back and its conjunction with the River Avon.

'I did hear something,' she insisted, 'and it wasn't just an ordinary cry. Whoever made it was very frightened.'

'I believe you,' I said, 'and I'm sorry if I implied just now that I didn't. Was it a man's voice or a woman's?'

'It sounded like a woman.'

I sighed. 'Well, I'm afraid there's nothing we can do about it. Try to put it out of your mind. We must get on. I can't carry Nicholas for very much longer.'

She was immediately contrite and tried to take the child from me.

'No, no!' I said testily. 'I can manage well enough for the little distance left. I simply want to get home, that's all.'

We passed under Saint John's Archway into Broad Street where candles were already being lit, their dim radiance piercing the encroaching gloom. Soon, shutters would be closed upon the panes of horn and oiled parchment, but in one dwelling at least, the flicker of flame and candleshine would continue to illumine the darkness. This was Alderman Weaver's house, where the upper windows of the hall were made of glass, a newfangled conceit of the well-to-do to let in more light.

We were abreast of the Alderman's door – Adela gratefully leaning upon my stick, footsore after so much weary walking – when it was thrown violently open and a woman ran out. Her voice was raised in anger.

'You're unjust! You're unjust, Father! You weren't always so, but William's right! Old age has addled your brain!' The wail rose to a shriek. 'You've been deprived of your wits by a conniving, unprincipled rogue! William! William, where in heaven's name are you? I've had enough of this! I'm going home.'

With a shock, I recognized the woman as Alison Weaver, now Mistress Burnett, and remembered how close she had once been to her father. What could have happened to so turn her against him? She was growing hysterical, pounding with her fists against the outside wall of the house and screaming, 'You're a fool, Father, a fool, and I hate you!'

Two men came to the door to reason with her, trying to urge her back inside, and, framed by the light from the hall, I could see that they were the Alderman's servants, Ned Stoner and Rob Short. Her husband, on the other hand, seemed to be ignoring her pleas for support, in spite of her repeated calls for 'William!' Eventually, the two men prevailed, more by dint of brute force than persuasion, and Alison was lifted bodily over the threshold. The door slammed shut.

Adela and I resumed our homeward journey, for both of us had stopped, spellbound by the scene unfolding before us.

'Your return to Bristol is proving to be more eventful than you could possibly have imagined,' I remarked flippantly. 'Cries in the night and now this! There's bound to be a third thing.'

It was a moment or two before she answered, but at last she replied quietly, 'Whatever you may think, I did not imagine that cry. You were shouting to the Porter and might not have been listening. But I heard it plainly. I thought you said you believed me.'

'I've told you I do.' I shifted the sleeping Nicholas to my other arm and quickened my step. She was such a serious woman: there seemed to be no laughter in her. She rarely smiled, although when she did, I had to admit there was great sweetness in it.

As we hurried down High Street, it began to rain, a cold, thin drizzle which cut all exposed flesh like a knife. People that we passed huddled into their cloaks, pulling the collars up around their ears, while the beggars, usually so importunate, slunk away to find shelter in the alleyways between the houses and the doorways of churches. We crossed the bridge spanning the Avon, the shops and dwelling-places on each side affording us some relief from the cold, which was increasing with every moment. Then we were in Redcliffe with its rows of weavers' houses, its tenting fields and rope-walk, and ahead of me, I could see the church of Saint Thomas. A few minutes later, I pushed open the door of Margaret Walker's cottage and ushered Adela and the still-sleeping Nicholas inside.

The cousins embraced, but neither was of a demonstrative nature and the greetings were restrained. On Adela's side, there was no indication that she was delighted to be back in her native city, while my mother-in-law gave no hint of that former urgency which had sent me tramping through the winter countryside to fetch her kinswoman home. Nevertheless, there was an air of quiet satisfaction about both women's demeanour, and to be fair, they had much to occupy them. Margaret had to set about the immediate preparation and cooking of a meal. Adela had Nicholas to attend to, as well as familiarizing herself with the cottage and the location of the outside pump and privy. Afterwards, she unpacked the meagre belongings which she had carried with her, in a linen bag hooked to her belt.

In spite of this seeming indifference however, I was conscious of the covert glances being directed at me by my mother-in-law, and of the scarcely repressed speculation in her eyes. Nor did Adela escape her share of this veiled scrutiny, but to her it meant nothing and she remained unaware of it, so I was able to continue to treat her with the same unaffected camaraderie which had characterized our relationship so far. I noted with amusement Margaret's growing disappointment but, with a sinking feeling in the pit of my stomach, I also saw the stubborn jut of her mouth and jaw. She had set her heart on my marrying Adela from the first moment that Jack Nym had mentioned her name and she knew that her cousin was now a widow. All her previous attempts at matchmaking on my behalf had been as nothing compared with this; and my mother-in-law could be a very determined woman when she wanted something badly enough. Well, I should just have to be on my guard, and prove to her that I could be equally stubborn.

I had received my usual rapturous, and thoroughly undeserved, welcome from my daughter, but the unexpected presence of another child had soon drawn her attention away from me. I discovered to my surprise that I was inclined to be jealous and a little hurt by her desertion, but the sight of her and Nicholas playing so happily together on the floor, soon made me ashamed of such emotions. They took to one another from the first, and I saw the triumphant smile curl Margaret's lips as she, too, observed them. I tried to ignore it, telling myself that the children's friendship would have no influence on my own with Adela, and affecting deafness on several occasions when my mother-in-law directed me, quite unnecessarily, to assist her cousin. Instead, I ostentatiously attended to my own duties of chopping logs and topping up the water barrel.

But at last the meal was ready, stewed mutton and dried peas for ourselves and salted porridge for the children, and there was no longer an excuse for avoiding Adela's company. Happily, there were the details of our journey to be related, plus all the news of great events which I had garnered from Timothy Plummer in Tewkesbury. The report of the Duchess of Clarence's untimely death had reached Bristol during my absence, but the rest of the story was naturally unknown and caused Margaret much excited speculation as to the eventual outcome, successfully taking her mind off more personal plans. Anything to do with the royal family always aroused her interest.

There was much to ask, too, about Adela's life in Hereford and the years of her marriage; there were childhood memories to be recalled and mulled over, old friends and acquaintances to be remembered. And when, finally, these topics were exhausted, it was time to clear the dishes and put the children to bed, amidst much giggling and laughter, at the foot of the goosefeather mattress. Then the curtain was drawn to divide the room in two, and Adela, my mother-in-law and I gathered around the fire to while away an hour or so until sleep should claim us also.

'Well, and how did you both get on together during that long journey?' Margaret demanded, smiling encouragingly at us.

Adela, who had been about to say something, looked slightly bewildered, but she was sufficiently acute to work out the significance of the question for herself if I could not divert her thoughts.

I said quickly, 'I haven't told you yet, Mother, of the strange incident which Adela and I witnessed this afternoon,' and I proceeded to give her an account of the scene in Broad Street.

My recital had an immediate effect upon Margaret. She gave a great gasp and clapped one hand to her mouth.

'How could I have forgotten to tell you! But seeing Adela again after all these years drove everything else right out of my head. What do you think happened, Roger, while you were away? Only a day after you left, as a matter of fact. No, no! Don't bother guessing! You'd never do so in a month of Sundays.' She drew a deep breath and added impressively, 'Clement Weaver has come back.'

Chapter Three

I was certain that I had misheard her. I murmured, 'I'm sorry, Mother, I didn't quite catch what you said.'

Margaret repeated, making each word distinct and separate, 'Clement-Weaver-has-come-back. Or – ' and her head bobbed towards me conspiratorially – 'someone who claims to be the Alderman's son.'

There was no misunderstanding her meaning this time, and besides, in spite of my total disbelief, it made sense of that scene which Adela and I had witnessed in Broad Street. Yet I could not accept so ridiculous a notion without protest.

'How can he possibly have come back?' I expostulated. 'Clement Weaver's been dead these past six years. Who should know that better than I, who was chiefly responsible for bringing his murderer to justice?'

'But you never saw Clement's body,' Margaret objected. 'You only *presumed* him to be among the victims of that evil man. You've told me the story too often for me to be mistaken.'

Of all my whirling emotions at that particular moment, the one suddenly uppermost was resentment at my mother-in-law's implied suggestion that I boasted about my achievements.

'I've never repeated the story unless you asked to hear it!' I disclaimed hotly, and saw by her look of surprise that she had intended no criticism.

'I know you haven't.' She was hurt by my anger, and turned

to her cousin. 'Roger's a very clever man,' she went on earnestly, aware that somehow or other I felt myself demeaned, and anxious to put matters right. Not for the world, I realized, would she consciously denigrate me in front of Adela. 'But he's very secretive. He won't tell you everything. At least, he won't tell *me* everything. All the same, I know by little things he accidentally lets drop that he's been of help to people of far greater importance than Alderman Weaver. If he ever marries again,' she added coyly, 'I suppose it's possible he might confide in his wife.'

Once again, I saw the dawning of suspicion in Adela's eyes and hurriedly changed the subject.

'For pity's sake, Mother! Tell me more about this person who says he's Clement Weaver. Does he look anything like him?'

Margaret pursed her lips, a little annoyed at having been thwarted in her purpose. But she was, after all, in no hurry.

'I can't really remember Clement all that well, and six years is a long time. People alter. But I should say that yes, there is a resemblance. You'll have to see what you think yourself.'

I shook my head. 'I never met him. He'd vanished months before I reached Bristol and was enlisted by the Alderman to help in the search. Where does "Clement" say he's been all this while?'

My mother-in-law rubbed her nose. 'According to Nick Brimble's aunt, Goody Watkins – who, I swear, has eyes and ears at every keyhole in the city – he's been living in the Southwark stews, amongst all the thieves and vagabonds, the beggars and whores of London. His story is that six years back, when he was on that ill-fated trip to London with Alison, he suffered a severe blow on the head and afterwards couldn't remember who he was; not, that is, until before the Christmas just past, when suddenly, miraculously, his memory was restored and he came hurrying home to Bristol. He arrived here, on foot and in a shockingly diseased and filthy state, the day after you left for Hereford. You can imagine! The whole town has been buzzing with rumour and speculation ever since.'

'A severe blow on the head,' I repeated slowly. 'Yes, that could make sense . . . it could be an explanation . . . No, no! I found his tunic. Bertha Mendip told me—' I broke off these musings to ask, 'What of Alderman Weaver? What does *he* say to this unlooked-for resurrection?' Although I suppose I already knew, having overheard Alison Burnett's recent outburst.

Margaret shrugged. 'Oh, the Alderman accepted him straight away. He has no doubt whatsoever that this is Clement. But as you know, he's always found it very hard to accept the death of his son, especially as there was no body, no grave – nothing to prove to him that Clement really had been murdered. He wants to believe, more than anything else in the world, in this young man.'

'But Mistress Burnett and her husband think him an impostor,'

It was not a question. Again, I already knew the answer.

My mother-in-law gave a bark of laughter. 'Of course they do. What would you expect?'

'Yet Alison seemed to me to be fond of her brother.'

'She was. I've seen them together many times, both when they were children and when they were grown up, and there was always a great affection between them. You'll remember yourself how deeply distressed she was by her brother's disappearance. But that doesn't mean she's going to fall on the neck of anyone who bears a passing resemblance to Clement and accept his word that he is who he claims to be, not without proof. Besides,' Margaret added shrewdly, 'Mistress Burnett and her husband have had six years to grow accustomed to her being her father's sole heir. It's impossible that they would happily share her inheritance now, even with someone of whom they were certain. But with a man who could so easily be a fraud . . . Well, that would be asking too much of them, surely.'

'Not necessarily. Not if Mistress Burnett were to be convinced that he really is her brother.'

'But she probably doesn't wish to be convinced,' Adela said quietly, having followed our conversation thus far with interest. 'And most likely neither do you, Roger.'

I looked at her, half in annoyance, half in admiration.

My mother-in-law shifted uneasily. Although an acute woman herself, and inclined, on occasions, to be acid-tongued, she was nevertheless unshakeable in her belief that a single man should be flattered and complimented until he proposed marriage and the knot was tied – after which, of course, there was no further need for prevarication.

'I'm sure Roger is always eager for the truth,' she reproved her cousin. 'Aren't you, my dear?'

I smiled a little shamefacedly. 'I'm afraid that in this case Adela may be right. I've always been so certain that Clement Weaver is dead that I'm not anxious to be proved mistaken.' I added another log to the fire, watching the resin as it caught and spluttered. I sat for a moment or two, staring into the flames, before straightening my shoulders and once again addressing my mother-in-law. 'But there must be something more than his looks to persuade the Alderman that his man is his son. He must know something of Clement's childhood; of the years before that ill-fated visit to London. Has Goody Watkins anything to say on this head?'

'Only that he seems to have enough knowledge to satisfy Alderman Weaver.'

'But not Mistress Burnett and her husband?'

'Ah!' Margaret rose and fetched three wooden cups from a shelf near the door, carefully filling them with ale, milk and spices which she had been mulling over the fire for the past half-hour. 'According to Maria Watkins, there lies the nub of the matter.'

'What nub? What does she mean? And how reliable is her information?'

My mother-in-law answered my second question first. 'In all that relates to the Weavers, I think you may trust her. Haven't you ever noticed that Goody Watkins is very friendly with Dame Pernelle?' When I shook my head, Margaret sighed. 'No, I suppose you wouldn't. You're so often absent.'

'Who is Dame Pernelle?' asked Adela.

'She's housekeeper to Alderman Weaver, and the third such since his wife died, more than seven years ago now.'

Adela sipped her posset. 'It must be,' she agreed. 'I remember you sending me a message that Mistress Weaver had died at Michaelmas, a few months after I married Owen. A kinswoman of the Alderman, Marjorie Dyer, you said, had moved in to take care of him and the children.'

'Of course!' my mother-in-law exclaimed excitedly. 'What's the matter with me? I'm forgetting that you knew the Weavers! You'll be able to give your opinion as to whether or not you think this person really is Clement.'

'No.' The younger woman was emphatic. 'My memory, after all this time, simply isn't good enough. However hard I try, I can't recall either of the Weaver children in any detail.'

'Mother,' I said, interrupting with some impatience, 'what does Goody Watkins mean by "the nub of the matter"?'

Margaret looked confused for a moment, then recollected.

'Well, according to Dame Pernelle, who told Maria, who told me, this young man who says he's Clement Weaver does indeed know quite a lot about the family, and also about incidents in his childhood. That's one of the reasons why the Alderman is so sure he's his son, and accepts so readily the story of the lost memory and its sudden restoration. But Alison and William

Burnett are convinced that he has been well informed by someone with intimate knowledge of them and their history. The question is, by whom?'

'And also why?' The mulled ale and milk slid down my throat like satin, and the aromatic scent of the spices teased my nostrils. 'As Alison became her father's sole heir on the death of her brother, what could anyone else, apart from the young man himself, possibly have to gain from such an imposture? Who would take the trouble to find and prime a stranger in a masquerade that could have no benefit for him – or her? How do Master and Mistress Burnett explain that?'

My mother-in-law stared at me blankly for a moment, then shrugged.

'I never thought to ask, nor Goody Watkins to tell me. You'll have to make those enquiries for yourself – I've told you everything I know. Adela, my dear, you look worn out, not surprisingly after such a journey. We mustn't keep you up talking any longer. Come along, we'll retire and leave Roger to settle himself when he pleases. Quietly now, we don't want to wake the children.'

Adela was only too willing, being more tired, I fancied, than she cared to admit, and both women disappeared behind the faded red and green curtain. I took myself outside for a breath of fresh air after making up my bed on the floor, not too close to the fire for fear of falling sparks. The rain had stopped, but a bitter wind was still blowing across Redcliffe from the Backs which lay either side of the encircling arm of the River Avon. My mind was racing as it struggled to absorb the strange event related to me by my mother-in-law.

I took shelter in the narrow alleyway beside the cottage, which led to the privy and the pump, shared by Margaret and her nearest neighbours. I could sniff the salt smell of the sea and picture the ghostly outlines of ships riding at anchor outside the city walls, moored close to the banks of Frome and Avon. I was glad I had put on my cloak, and pulled it closer around me against the January cold. It was not very late, and although the gates were now shut, people were still abroad, in the ale-houses and taverns or visiting one another in their houses. Someone close at hand was laughing – a high-pitched, exultant peal of feminine glee, joined almost at once by the deeper tone of the man who accompanied her. They passed the end of the alleyway, their forms entwined, two shadows merging into one. I suddenly felt lonely and a little desolate, yearning after a girl with golden hair and soft blue eyes, living retired with an elderly aunt in Keyford on the outskirts of the township of Frome. I promised myself that one day soon I would go to visit her, but not just yet. It would be a while before I was welcome, and not an intruder on her grief.

I wrenched my mind back to the problem of Clement Weaver. Surely this man had to be an imposter, hoping to claim the Alderman's fortune for himself. But who had schooled him in the details of Clement's former life – and why? What could that person hope to gain? The answer, when it came, was simple, as these things so often are. He hoped to gain the same as the pretender; a share of the spoils.

I had no idea how rich Alderman Weaver really was, but I guessed his fortune to be considerable. Not only was he generally accepted to be one of the wealthiest merchants in a wealthy city, but I had reasons of my own for suspecting that he was also involved clandestinely in the illegal selling of slaves to Ireland. This was a trade generally thought by the world at large to have been stamped out several centuries earlier, but which, to my certain knowledge, still throve in secret. It was the way in which Bristolians disposed of their unwanted kinsfolk or enemies, shipping them off to that other island across the water; and it was rumoured to be a lucrative business, for the Irish were prepared to pay well for their servants. Alderman Weaver had once tried to justify the trade to me by claiming that, in general, the Irish treated their domestics as friends, everyone sitting down to meals together and eating from the same dish. He had also claimed that many Bristol men, women and children who had been sold into slavery, found a happiness in Ireland that they had not known at home. Not, he had added hastily, that he could condone something which was a crime against both Church and State, even though its consequences were not always to be deplored.

I had not believed him then, and I still did not. Alderman Weaver was undoubtedly involved in the trade and, consequently, was far richer than he acknowledged himself to be. It was likely, however, that the full extent of his wealth was known to, or at least suspected by, those closest to him. I remembered Alfred Weaver as I had last seen him, in late December; a very sick man, if I were any judge. Perhaps there was someone, the Alderman's brother who lived in London, for example, who, quite by chance, had stumbled across a stranger bearing an uncanny resemblance to Clement Weaver – a poor man, a desperate man, down on his luck, one with no qualms, easy to persuade into wrongdoing – and seen a way to use him to his advantage. All this lookalike had to do was to convince a dying man that he was his long lost son, live in ease and pampered luxury until the Alderman eventually died, inherit his half of the money and then share it with his fellow conspirator.

But would he? How could my mysterious and shadowy villain be certain of getting his slice of Alfred Weaver's fortune? Once accepted and established as the Alderman's son, why should the false Clement be persuaded to part with any of his ill-gotten gains? Because, maybe, his true identity could be proved. Or perhaps because he had been forced to set his name to, or make his mark on, a piece of paper admitting the plot to defraud Alison

Burnett of her rightful inheritance. (I had no doubt that there were plenty of lawyers who, for a sufficient fee, were unscrupulous enough to draw up and witness such a document; for when I was young, lawyers were held in even greater disrepute than they are today.) And it was possible that the man had not known what it was that he was signing . . .

No, I decided, that would not do. The imposter had to be of some intelligence. He had to absorb and remember a vast amount of knowledge concerning Clement's youth. The Burnetts, and maybe others on their behalf, would be waiting to catch him out. And no one, surely, could have foreseen how easily the Alderman would accept the reappearance of his 'son'.

Another gust of wind, tearing down the alleyway between the houses, made me shiver, and I realized how cold I was. My feet were numb and I was forced to stamp the ground in order to regain any feeling in them. It also made me aware that it was high time I was in bed. I let myself back into the cottage, moving softly so as not to disturb the women and children, and while I undressed, I wondered what I had been doing out there, in the freezing weather. This was nothing to do with me; no one had solicited *my* help to determine if this man really were Clement Weaver or no. So what was my interest?

It was twofold. Firstly, I was naturally as intrigued as everyone else in the resurrection of a dead man, in trying to decide if he really was who he claimed to be. But secondly, my pride was touched. I was the one who, six years ago, had assured Alderman Weaver that his son was dead. The possibility that he might have survived had never crossed my mind, and even had it done so, I should have rejected the notion out of hand. Common sense told me that I was not to blame, that my conclusion had been the natural one to draw. Clement had accompanied his sister to London to buy her bridal clothes and had been carrying a large sum of money about his person – a fact his killer had known only too well. And that killer had been a cunning and very thorough man. But could he have bungled the execution of his crime just this once?

I lay down and pulled up the blankets, the fire being almost out. I felt worn to the bone, as though I could sleep for a month without waking; and yet I guessed that my slumbers would be troubled by dreams. I heard Elizabeth cry out, and the immediate, soothing response from my mother-in-law, as though she slept with one ear cocked and one eye open.

My senses began to swim as I approached unconsciousness. Now was the time when all those images would make me toss and turn, disturbing my rest. My lids grew heavy and gradually closed – and I knew nothing more until morning.

I was awakened from this dreamless slumber by something heavy falling on me from a height, and also by a sharp pain in the head. I opened my bleary eyes to find my daughter sprawled across my chest, her small inquisitive fingers stroking the stubble on my chin, while Nicholas Juett continued to tug at my hair. They were fully dressed, as was my mother-in-law, who was busy lighting the newly laid fire.

'You were tired, my lad,' she remarked, getting up from her knees. 'Even all my clattering didn't rouse you. It took these two imps of mischief to do that. Well, we'll leave you alone while you get dressed. There's hot water in the pot if you want to shave.'

She shooed the two children back behind the curtain, following them to make sure that it was decently pulled. I could hear her speaking softly to Adela Juett, and I suddenly felt embarrassed by the proximity of this stranger. I scrambled into my shirt and hose and hurried through my shaving, cutting myself twice in the process. I swore under my breath. The cottage seemed cramped and overcrowded, and I longed for the freedom of my calling, of tramping the surrounding villages, selling my wares. I knew that before I went to Hereford, the stocks in my pack had been running low, and I determined that as soon as breakfast was over, I would visit the Backs to see if any merchant ships were tied up at the wharves. I could often pick up items cheaply before the cargoes were unloaded and carted away to their various destinations. Some Masters and their crews were inclined to be light-fingered with the owners' goods, for their share of the profits was a mere pittance compared with that of the merchants, in spite of the fact that they risked their lives daily on the high seas.

I announced my intention to my mother-in-law while we ate our porridge and oatcakes, but she made no demur. Rather, she approved.

'We could do with the money,' she said without thinking.

Adela spoke up at once. 'Nicholas and I won't be a burden to you for long, Margaret. If you could speak to Alderman Weaver or Master Burnett for me, I should be grateful. The Alderman might even remember that I was one of his spinners before my marriage – although seven years is a fair time. And if there is the chance of a vacant cottage somewhere . . .'

'There's no need for you to be leaving yet awhile!' my mother-in-law exclaimed, dismayed. 'You must get used to being at home again before you think of setting up on your own. Between us, Roger and I can earn far more money than we need to support just ourselves and Elizabeth. You and I still have so much to talk about, and besides, the children get on so well together. They're firm friends already. When I said we could do with the money, I was simply encouraging Roger not to be idle.'

Adela appeared to accept the lie with her usual courteous smile, which gave nothing away as to her true feelings.

'Nevertheless,' she persisted, 'I should be very grateful if you would do as I ask.'

'Roger!' My mother-in-law appealed to me. 'Tell Adela how pleased we are to have her and Nicholas under our roof.'

Before I could answer, Adela spoke again.

'My wishes have nothing to do with Roger, nor are they any reflection on your hospitality, Cousin. It's just that I'm used to my own home and find sharing with other people difficult.'

I glanced gratefully at her, and once more she gave that small, tight smile.

Margaret sighed, acknowledging defeat. 'Oh, very well! I'll speak to Master Burnett if I see him today. But,' she added, brightening, 'I must warn you that I know of no dwelling standing empty at present. You may have to remain here longer than you would wish.'

Adela nodded, reaching across to wipe Nicholas's mouth. Again, there was no clue as to what she was really thinking. A moment later, a knock at the door heralded the arrival of Goody Watkins at the head of a small deputation of neighbours, all anxious to welcome the new arrival home to Bristol. I noticed several of the women giving me an appraising look, and I guessed that my mother-in-law had made no secret of her aspirations. But if Adela was also aware of the glances in her direction, she gave no sign.

'Well,' said Goody Watkins, turning to me when, at last, all the exclaiming was over, the questioning of young Nicholas and his mother finished, 'no doubt Mistress Walker's told you of the goings-on while you've been away; of Clement Weaver's return. If,' she added with a dubious sniff, 'it *is* Clement Weaver! And now, if that weren't enough excitement for one month, Imelda Bracegirdle's been found murdered, strangled, in her cottage on the other side of the Frome Gate.'

Chapter Four

'I told you,' Adela said, addressing me, 'that the cry I heard was made by someone in distress. But you wouldn't stop and go back.'

'How could we have gone back?' I demanded indignantly. 'The Porter was just shutting the gate. Besides, there are so many cries. Who was to say that this one was different from any other? And even so, what you heard may have had nothing to do with the murder of Mistress Bracegirdle.' I turned to my mother-in-law. 'Do you – I mean *did* you – know her?'

'Not very well – only by sight. I don't think we've ever spoken.'

'Nobody knew her well. She kept herself to herself,' Goody Watkins put in with the regretful air of one who had failed in a self-imposed challenge which could never now be met. She added venomously, 'Secretive, that's what Imelda Bracegirdle was. Secretive.'

There was a general murmur of agreement from most of the other women, but one raised her voice in dissent.

'It's true she wasn't one for company. I disremember seeing her at the High Cross or the Tolzey amongst the gossips, but she was always civil if you gave her the time of day.'

'Anyone can be civil if you give them the time of day. Did she ever invite you into her cottage?' Goody Watkins asked belligerently, one wrinkled hand scratching her equally wrinkled chin.

'No.' Her friend was defensive. 'But then there are a lot of people who live outside the walls who aren't well known to those of us living within.' She glanced at the older woman. 'Are *you* on visiting terms, Maria, with anyone dwelling in Bristol Without? Because if so, it's the first I've heard of it.'

'I don't tell you everything, Bess Simnel,' Goody Watkins snapped back, but the spots of high colour in her wizened cheeks told their own tale.

The rest of the women were becoming anxious to get home. They had done what they came to do; they had inspected the new arrival in their midst, and one more death, even murder, in a city where death was commonplace failed to excite more than a passing interest. The Sheriff's men would do what was needed to be done, ask all the necessary questions. A woman whom some of them knew only by sight, and others not at all, was soon forgotten. Someone had a grudge against Imelda Bracegirdle, that was certain, but there were very few people without an enemy or two; and when feelings ran high, animosity now and then turned to murder.

Goody Watkins, sensing her companions' restive mood, said briskly, 'We must be going. It's a pleasure to see you again, Adela, but why you had to marry a "foreigner" from upcountry in the first place, I shall never understand, not when there were plenty of good Bristol men for you to choose from.' She stood on tiptoe and kissed Adela's cheek. 'Well, well. That's all in the past. You're home now where you belong, but next time, pick one of your own kind. Westcountrymen are best. I should know – I've married three of them.'

The beady, bright blue eyes, the only youthful features in her ancient face, flickered from Adela to me and back again. I pretended not to notice and stooped to gather Elizabeth into my arms; but my daughter, formerly so flatteringly eager for my embraces, protested vociferously and struggled to get down

38

again. I had interrupted a game she was playing with Nicholas. My mother-in-law suppressed a triumphant smile as she saw her visitors to the door and closed it behind them. Margaret knew better, however, than to remark on Elizabeth's defection, although she did give her granddaughter an approving pat on the head on passing.

'You'd best be off, Roger,' she advised, 'if you want to get started early.' She seated herself at her spinning wheel. 'Adela, my dear, I shall leave the children and the cooking in your charge today.'

Adela was doubtless only too pleased to be able to repay her cousin's hospitality in this fashion, but she nevertheless looked somewhat resentful at being told what she should do, rather than asked. There was an edginess to the way she responded with, 'Of course, Cousin, anything you say,' which made me glad to escape from the house. In my experience, when women fall out, it's better to be elsewhere. I pulled on my boots, threw my cloak around my shoulders, gathered up my pack and cudgel, and let myself out into the street.

I retraced my steps of the previous afternoon, over the bustling thoroughfare of Bristol Bridge, with its busy shops and elegant houses, up High Street to the High Cross, where the citizens gathered to hear the latest gossip, and along Broad Street towards Saint John's Archway, beyond which lay the Frome Bridge and Gate.

In Broad Street, I paused opposite Alderman Weaver's house, staring up at the three-storeyed building, searching for signs of life. But the door remained firmly closed, and the windows, although unshuttered, had the dead-eyed look of an uninhabited place. Yet somewhere inside was a man either newly reawakened to an awareness of his former existence, or a clever imposter, trained in his deception by one even cleverer than himself. I wished I could get a glimpse of him, thought it would do me little good, for I should not recognize my quarry if I saw him. But no one appeared, not even one of the servants.

As I passed under the Frome Gate, I looked for the Porter, but it was a different man from the one of the previous afternoon. All the same, I gave him good-day and added, 'There's been trouble, I hear.'

He understood me at once. 'Ay! A murder just over the way, one of the houses in Lewin's Mead. Imelda Bracegirdle. She was strangled, so they say. The Sheriff's men are over there now.'

There was a temporary lull in the traffic going in and out of the gate, so I asked, 'Did you know her?'

The Porter shrugged. 'I've seen her about. A widow, but not a woman who mixed much with her neighbours.'

'So I've been told. Was she old or young? Plain or pretty?'

He laughed. 'Neither. Not young, not old. Not plain, not pretty. A well-looking creature, I suppose, but over thirty. Her husband, John Bracegirdle, died some seven or eight years ago. The house was rented by him from Saint James's Priory, and after his death, the Brothers let Imelda go on living there.' The Porter added darkly, 'Her mother was from Oxford, a woman called Elvina Stacey. But her father's name was Fleming.'

I smiled inwardly. Although it was over a century since the last King Edward had encouraged his Flemish wife's countrymen to settle here, and although, in the meantime, Fleming had become a common enough surname, Englishmen in general have never ceased to resent this influx of foreigners who came, as our forefathers saw it, 'to take the bread from out of our mouths.' To my way of thinking, the descendants of the Flemish are usually hardworking, diligent and sober-minded people, not much given to the theory that it is a working man's bounden duty to do as little as possible in exchange for his wages. But in England, both when I was young and still, today, we believe that pleasure is just as important as industry, maybe more so. And who is to say that we are wrong?

According to my mother-in-law, who had it from her father, the Flemings who settled in Bristol had given a great boost to the city's flagging wool trade, so that Bristol's red cloth soon became famous not only throughout the land, but on the Continent, as well. This fact, however, had not made them any more popular, and their progeny were still regarded with a certain amount of suspicion and dislike. Those who lived retired, like Imelda Bracegirdle, would inevitably incur more than their fair share of hostility from inquisitive neighbours.

I went out into Lewin's Mead, once an open meadow but which was now gradually being built over as the town's population steadily increased. (It was no longer possible for everyone to live within the safety of the city walls, as was witnessed to by the number of houses already climbing up the sides of the encircling hills.) Across from where I stood and a little to my right, I noted a great deal of activity around one of the cottages, much tramping to and fro and in and out, and people busily conferring with each other. A Brother from the Priory, his black Benedictine habit flapping about his ankles, was running agitatedly from one person to the next, and it was all I could do to stop myself from going over to join them. But it was not my business; God had not called upon me to intervene here. (Or to poke my nose in, which would, I suppose, be a more honest way of putting it.) So, reluctantly, I turned to my left and proceeded westwards along the northern bank of the Frome.

It was only then that I paused to wonder why I had not turned left after passing under Saint John's Archway, and walked along the river's southern bank. Why had I bothered to cross it at all? The answer, of course, was simple. Because I had wished to see

41

the site of last night's murder. My natural curiosity would not let me rest until I had done so – but did this also mean that God was directing my feet? I was still pondering the question an hour or so later when I said goodbye to the crew of the only ship I had visited that morning, and strolled down the gangplank on to the quay.

My pack was still half-empty, for as ill-luck would have it, most of the vessels moored along the Frome that day were carrying fish; a cargo of dried cod, or stockfish as the locals call it, from Iceland, and from Ireland two more of salted herrings. I had, however, managed to find one merchantman with a lading of caps, combs, silks and suchlike, but the Master was a cautious fellow, prepared to sell only a very few of his employer's goods for fear of being found out and losing his position. I sighed. I should be forced to go to the market after all and pay higher prices, which meant that my profit would be less.

I walked back the way I had come. When I reached the Frome Gate, I saw that only a solitary Sheriff's Officer now remained on guard outside Imelda Bracegirdle's cottage. On impulse, I went across and spoke to him.

'Do you know who killed her?' I asked.

The man, red-haired with bright blue eyes, slowly shook his head.

'Nor never will, I don't suppose. A chance thief, hoping to find some secret store of money, is as good a bet as a person with a grudge against her.'

The house was like my mother-in-law's, one-roomed, one-storeyed with a single door and window facing on to the track which ran past it. I said, 'No one forced his way in. Neither door nor window is broken. Therefore, whoever killed her was known to Mistress Bracegirdle. She must have invited her murderer inside.'

The man's face assumed a look which boded me no good. 'You think yourself a clever sod, and no mistake. Why don't you just push off and mind your own business?'

'There's no need for that,' I protested in an injured voice. 'I'm only trying to be helpful; making you free of my observations.' A thought struck me. 'Do you know what's going to happen to the cottage?'

The Sheriff's Officer eyed me with distaste, not without good reason.

'You don't miss an opportunity, do you?' he sneered. 'And Mistress Bracegirdle not yet laid to rest in her grave.'

'I don't ask for myself,' I assured him hastily, 'but for an impoverished widow and her little son who have just returned to Bristol after seven years in Hereford . . .'

Before I could explain further, the guard interrupted me, his blue eyes suddenly widening with pleasure.

'Adela Woodward! Is that who you mean? She married a Hereford man – I forget his name. Is it her? Is she back at last, then?'

'Adela Juett,' I said, 'cousin in some degree or another to my mother-in-law, Margaret Walker. Yes, I believe her name was Woodward before her marriage.'

'Well!' The round face beneath the red hair beamed with delight. 'Tell her Richard Manifold was asking after her. She'll remember me, I don't doubt.'

I promised most earnestly to pass on his message, and then returned to the subject of the empty cottage without any further resentment on the part of my companion.

'Best go to the Priory and ask,' he advised, adding, 'they've carried the body there already.'

At these words, I hesitated, not hurrying away as Richard Manifold seemed to expect.

'In that case,' I said persuasively, 'might I just go in for a moment or two and look around?'

I could see from his expression that he was about to warn me off, but then he recollected that I was to be the bearer and interpreter of his good wishes to Adela Juett, and thought better of it.

'Very well,' he grudgingly agreed, 'but only for a minute. Leave the door ajar and if you hear me whistle, come straight out. It'll mean someone's coming. Though why you want to look inside beats me. There's nothing to see. Nothing out of the ordinary, that is.'

I thanked him and, after glancing round to make sure that I was not observed by any passer-by, I pushed open the door and went inside.

My informant was right: there was nothing to see beyond the normal paraphernalia of everyday living. The rushes on the floor were several days old, but not yet in urgent need of replacement. When the fire was lit, the smoke rose straight up through a hole in the roof, which, like most of those in Bristol, was tiled with slates. The cottage walls were made of wood and plaster. A bed, covered with a quilt of faded and badly rubbed amber velvet, occupied one wall of the room and appeared not to have been slept in. A stool, a table, a chair and a corner cupboard which held the dead woman's few possessions, made up the remainder of the furniture, except for a carved wooden chest standing beneath the window. This latter, on inspection, proved to be disappointingly empty, but the pot suspended from the crane arm, over the burnt-out ashes on the hearth, was still half-full of what smelled like mutton stew, a crust of congealed fat covering the surface. A clean wooden bowl and spoon were laid out on the table. There seemed to have been no disturbance of any kind, no struggle or scuffle, confirming me in my belief that Imelda Bracegirdle had known her attacker and had felt in no danger from him or her. My guess, therefore, was that she had been strangled suddenly, from behind, with no prior warning.

I said as much to Richard Manifold when I rejoined him outside, but he shrugged and said no doubt his Sergeant had already noted all these things and that they would be included in his report to the Sheriff. As for himself, he held by his opinion that Mistress Bracegirdle had been killed by a thief who was after her money.

'For you must know,' he added, 'that the gossip along the Mead is that she had a secret hoard of gold hidden somewhere in the cottage.'

'Then why didn't the murderer turn the room upside down to look for it?'

But Richard Manifold had his answer ready. 'Maybe it wasn't difficult to find. Maybe she kept it in that chest under the window.'

'And how did the killer get in without forcing an entrance?'

Again, he was ready for me. 'Mistress Bracegirdle had gone to bed and forgotten to bolt the door . . .'

'She hadn't gone to bed. The bed hasn't been slept in. Moreover, her supper is still in the pot over the fire, uneaten. Not even tasted. The spoon and bowl on the table are clean.'

'Very well! She hadn't gone to bed.' My companion was desperately trying to control his temper. 'She was still sitting over the fire but had forgotten to lock the door. Our murderer crept in, strangled her and took the money from the chest. It would be the first place to look, now wouldn't it? And if he found it there, there'd be no need to go ransacking the cottage.'

He hadn't convinced me, but I had to admit that his version of events was plausible enough. It was known that some thieves tried the latches of houses at night on the offchance that a few doors might be left unbolted. I recollected seeing our own latch being lifted on one occasion, when I happened to wake up in the middle of the night. (I scared my mother-in-law half to death by leaping out of bed, yelling at the top of my voice, in order to frighten away the would-be intruder.) So I sighed and conceded the argument.

'You're probably right. I'll be off to the Priory then, to see about the cottage.'

Richard Manifold nodded smugly. 'You do that. Ask for Brother Elmer. And in future, stick to the thing you're good at. Peddling.'

I gritted my teeth, but made no answer.

The Priory of Saint James had been founded as a cell of Tewkesbury Abbey, but at some time in the distant past, an agreement had been reached between the then Abbot and the local people that the nave should be maintained by the parishioners and used for parochial purposes. This morning it had been taken over by the Sheriff and his men in order to hold a brief, preliminary inquest into Imelda Bracegirdle's murder. I wondered whether or not to go in and make them free of my thoughts on the subject. Then I told myself not to be a fool, and went instead in search of Brother Elmer.

The January morning was less overcast than it had been earlier, the threat of rain and sleet receding, but it was still extremely cold and the trees of the orchard stood like skeletons against the skyline. I found Brother Elmer at last, after enquiries at both the brewery and the bakehouse directed me thither; he was closeted with Father Prior, and so I was able to make my request on Adela's behalf to the highest authority. I was promised that the matter would be raised at the following day's Chapter meeting, and with that I had to be content. There would also be, as Brother Elmer pointed out to me, other equally deserving cases to be considered, but the claim of Adela Juett would be borne in mind.

'Do you have any idea by whom, or why, Mistress Bracegirdle was murdered?' I asked as I turned to go.

'Oh, a chance thief, undoubtedly,' replied Brother Elmer, 'who took advantage of an unbolted door. The Sheriff is convinced of it.' He glanced for confirmation at Father Prior, who inclined his venerable head. 'There were always stories that Imelda had a secret hoard of money, though alas, poor soul, I think it most unlikely. But a thief, abroad after dark and who had heard the rumours, finding her door unlocked could have thought it worth the risk, and a sudden evil impulse prompted him to kill her. Or perhaps a man desperate for money, to repay an urgent debt.'

I knew now where Richard Manifold got his version of events, for it seemed to be the Sheriff's version, too. I was half-inclined to pay this worthy a visit and tell him about the scream heard by Adela Juett, with the added information that it had still been only dusk at the time. But what good would it do? The Sheriff already seemed to have decided what had happened, and Adela would not thank me for dragging her into the clutches of the law. Besides, what proof did I have that the scream had been uttered by Imelda Bracegirdle? Neither the Porter nor I could confirm Adela's story. I decided therefore to go about my business and not interfere. With a sigh of relief, I hitched up my pack and bade Father Prior and Brother Elmer good-day.

It was nearly suppertime when I returned to the Frome Gate, and my pack was once again almost empty.

On leaving the Priory, I had decided to visit those remote homesteads and dwellings on the heights above the city, and had walked as far as the great gorge cut between the rocks by the River Avon as it ebbs and flows between Bristol and that narrow sea which divides us Westcountrymen from the wilder shores of Wales. I had done well, parting with such wares as I had for a purseful of money, and I hoped that my mother-in-law would be pleased; for I should need all the goodwill I could muster when she discovered that I had done my best to obtain the tenancy of Imelda Bracegirdle's cottage for Adela, and so thwart her plans for keeping us both beneath the same roof. I felt a little guilty when I thought of my daughter, for Elizabeth was certainly enjoying Nicholas's company, but she had not yet had sufficient time to grow used to it, and would no doubt soon recover from his loss.

As I entered the Frome Gate, I glanced back towards the empty cottage, where it now stood shuttered and silent. Richard Manifold had vanished, relieved of his guard, and there was no longer anyone or anything to single it out from its neighbours. Adela could make herself and her son comfortable there, I reflected, provided that what had happened did not give her a distaste for the place. But I did not think that likely. She was a sensible woman, not easily given to panic, and I sent up a short prayer that the Prior and his monks would favour her claim above the others.

Shops were beginning to close for the night, stall- and booth-holders locking their goods away until morning. The central drain was choked with meat and fish offal, although not so much as in the summer months, and the stench was correspondingly less. I was looking forward to my supper, for it was some hours since I last eaten; a collop of salted bacon between two slices of black bread given me by an elderly woman to whom I had sold some needles. I recollected that Adela was to do the cooking today and wondered what she would put on the table.

As I pushed open the door of my mother-in-law's cottage, a warm, savoury smell stole out to greet me, making my mouth water. But I was also aware that the room was even more crowded than when I had left it early that morning. A woman was seated in our only good chair, a man standing behind her, drumming his fingers impatiently against its back.

My mother-in-law said with relief, 'Ah! Here he is at last. Roger, Master and Mistress Burnett have come especially to see you.'

Chapter Five

William Burnett wasted no time in greetings, but said at once, 'We require your services, Chapman.'

'Indeed?' I answered coldly. I set down my pack and cudgel and divested myself of my cloak without further comment, then went to warm my hands at the fire.

Master Burnett, who had doubtless expected instant acquiescence, was annoyed and showed it. A hot rejoinder was plainly on the tip of his tongue, but his wife held up an imperious finger to silence him.

'If you please, Master Chapman, and if you can spare the time,' she amended politely.

Gone was the screaming harridan of the previous afternoon and in her place was a tired, sad woman in want of help. Alison Burnett had never been what you could call truly pretty; her nose was a trifle too large, her mouth slightly too wide, her jaw a little too determined. But she had always had lovely eyes, soft hazel flecked with green, and a clear, honey-coloured complexion. The eyes, however, with their fringe of long, dark lashes, seemed to have dulled with the passage of time, and her skin was muddied and sallow. In short, the past six years had not dealt kindly with her. Nevertheless, she still had that air of command as of someone accustomed to obedience, and which she almost certainly inherited from her late mother, a member of the de Courcy family. But Alison also had a fair share of her

51

father's guile and his rock-hard determination to get his own way by any means at his disposal. She would pander to my vanity by treating me like an equal if it served her purpose, unlike her husband whose high opinion of himself was too great ever to allow him to employ such a measure.

I had never liked William Burnett. His father, another of Bristol's Aldermen, had, according to my mother-in-law, been a sensible, down-to-earth man who had made light of his kinship with Lord Henry Burnett, a nobleman who lived in the village of the same name, a few miles outside the city. But the Alderman's weakness had been his only son, whom he had indulged and encouraged in every kind of folly from William's boyhood onwards. The result was an empty-headed man of great self-consequence who thought only of his own convenience and pleasure. In appearance, he had changed very little from the young fop I had first encountered in Alderman Weaver's house nearly six years earlier. The pikes of his shoes were perhaps a little shorter than they had been then, and it was no longer necessary to fasten the points to his knees with ornate golden chains. But they were still of a length to set any dandy aquiver with admiration, and the auburn hair which curled fashionably to his shoulders was anointed with a peculiarly pungent pomade. His clothes, too, would not have been out of place at King Edward's court, his parti-coloured, tightly-waisted tunic being almost obscenely short and his cod-piece decorated with dangling golden tassels. His ornamental red velvet cloak was lined with black sarcenet, his sleeves slashed to reveal insets of oyster satin. Beside him, in her dark blue, fur-trimmed gown and white lawn hood, his wife paled into insignificance.

Nevertheless, I addressed myself to Alison Burnett, ignoring her husband. 'What do you want of me, Mistress?'

I already knew what she wanted, but I did not expect it to be expressed with such uncompromising vigour. 'You must go to my father and denounce this imposter who calls himself my brother.'

'Quite so,' her husband put in, adding peremptorily, 'and the sooner the better!'

I heard my mother-in-law's sharp intake of breath and imagined rather than saw the decisive shake of her head. Alderman Weaver was her landlord and employer: she could not afford to incur his hostility, even at second-hand. I gave her a reassuring glance.

'Mistress Burnett, I cannot do that. For one thing, I never met Clement Weaver and so am in no position to say whether this young man is your brother or no. I never even saw the dead body of Master Clement, any more than I saw those of his fellow victims. You know the circumstances as well as I do.'

'How dare you speak to my wife like that—' William Burnett was beginning, his voice shrill with indignation, but once again Alison's raised finger prevented him from saying more.

'That's enough, William. We must respect Master Chapman's scruples. What he says is very true.' She smiled up at her husband to soften the reproof, but William continued to glower like a sulky schoolboy, one hand tugging bad-temperedly at the red and black silk cord which girdled his waist.

Alison turned back to me. 'Nevertheless, Master Chapman, both my husband and I would be grateful if you could call on us tomorrow, so that we could refresh our memories of events now six years distant, and also acquaint you with a few of the facts concerning this man who insists that he is Clement. Dare we presume to make that claim upon your time?'

I appreciated the restraint of this imperious young woman, and there was no denying that my curiosity was getting the better of my caution. What harm, after all, could one visit do – especially if Alderman Weaver remained in ignorance of it? So after a moment's thought for appearances' sake, I nodded.

Mistress Burnett heaved a sigh of relief and rose to her feet. 'Thank you. Do you know whereabouts we live in Small Street? Good! We shall expect you tomorrow morning then, after dinner. We dine at ten o'clock, so shall look for you sometime between eleven and midday. Goodbye, Mistress Walker. We won't trouble you any further.' She inclined her head towards Adela, not knowing her name. William Burnett simply grunted and followed her out of the cottage.

'Well,' said Adela, with the decision of manner I was coming to expect from her, 'I can't say that Alison Weaver has improved with the years. And as for that husband of hers, I never liked him. Now sit down, Roger. You too, Margaret. Supper's ready.'

I saw astonishment followed by anger kindle in my mother-in-law's eyes, but both emotions were quickly suppressed. Nonetheless, the old saw that two women cannot share the same kitchen occurred to me; and in this case they had been cooped up together throughout the day in the same room. My mother-in-law's determination that her cousin should shoulder her fair share of the household chores was having consequences which she had not foreseen, and Adela's quiet assumption of authority obviously displeased her. It salved my conscience, however, for if a mere twenty-four hours could produce this amount of friction between them, how would they get on in the weeks and months that lay ahead?

As I drew my stool close to the table and took Elizabeth on my lap – for there were not enough seats in the cottage to accommodate two children as well as three adults – I said to Adela, 'I have a message for you from someone who, I think, must once have been an admirer, perhaps even a suitor, of yours. His name is Richard Manifold.'

Adela's arm, reaching across me to place a dish of oatcakes in the centre of the table, was arrested briefly in mid-air, and glancing up at her face I noticed a faint flush of colour along the cheekbones. But within seconds she had regained her composure.

'Indeed?' she replied steadily. 'Dick Manifold. Yes, I remember him. A red-haired fellow. You're mistaken, however, if you think he was ever my suitor. I can't imagine what gave you that idea.'

'His delight at hearing you were home again.' I buttered an oatcake and fed a piece to my daughter, whose mouth had opened like that of a fledgling bird. 'Don't you want to know how I came to meet him?'

Adela began ladling fish soup into bowls. 'Not particularly, but I'm sure you're going to tell me all the same,' she said.

'Quite right, I am, because you'll find the circumstances of our meeting more intriguing than you think.'

I then proceeded to relate the details of my encounter with Richard Manifold and had the satisfaction of watching the women's expressions grow increasingly interested, despite a seeming determination on both their parts to demonstrate complete indifference.

Their first questions, when I had finished speaking, naturally concerned the murder, but I was unable to add anything more to what I had already told them, and after a while Adela's thoughts reverted to her former admirer.

'So! Dick Manifold's a Sheriff Officer, is he? I'm surprised, I must admit. He was rather wild in his youth.' She gave a small, reminiscent smile.

'An unprepossessing boy and an even uglier man,' my mother-in-law opined tartly, her eyes snapping with suspicion as she regarded her cousin across the table. 'I'm amazed you can even remember him, Adela, as pretty as you were. A girl who might have had anyone.'

Adela laughed. 'There were plenty of girls after Dick Manifold, Margaret, including your own daughter, even though she was far too young for him.'

My mother-in-law frowned. 'If you're implying, Cousin, that Lillis was flighty, I think it in very poor taste, particularly in front of her husband and child.'

Adela seemed to be holding her temper in check as she answered, 'I meant no such thing, as I think you well know. But if I've upset either you or Roger, I'm sorry.'

'There's no need to apologize to me,' I assured her, and suspecting that this might prove as good a moment as any, I hurried on, 'There may be a chance you could rent Imelda Bracegirdle's cottage. It's in the gift of Saint James's Priory and I've taken the liberty of mentioning your name to one of the Brothers, who has promised to bear it in mind. Unless, of course, you would dislike living in a house where a murder has been committed.'

'Of course she would dislike it!' my mother-in-law exclaimed angrily, seeing all her carefully laid plans being undermined by my action. 'How dared you presume so, Roger, without consulting Adela first?'

Her cousin, who was spooning fish broth into Nicholas's mouth, paused and stared in surprise. 'Don't scold him, Margaret. He has my grateful thanks. I've told you I don't intend being a burden on you for any longer than I can help, and this could well be the answer.' She turned and smiled at me with genuine warmth. 'It was clever of you, Roger, to think of me; and death is death, in whatever guise it comes. Every dwelling has previously been inhabited by someone who's died.'

'And how do you propose to pay the rent?' my mother-in-law demanded waspishly. 'You seem to have very little money of your own.'

Adela replied serenely, 'You've said you'll speak to Alderman Weaver on my behalf, and I know you too well to believe that you'd go back on a promise. I'm sure he'll find me some work to do if you recommend me.'

I smiled inwardly. Adela Juett was an opponent worthy of anyone's steel. It would not be easy to get under her guard.

My mother-in-law hunched her shoulders and continued to eat in offended silence; but as the meal progressed, her mood began to lighten, and I guessed that she had already realized the discomforts entailed in sharing her home. And by the time we had finished the broth and started on the oatcakes and goat's-milk cheese, she had obviously persuaded herself that all was not yet lost.

'Well, if the Brothers *do* rent you the cottage, Adela,' she said at last, 'I daresay there will be plenty of improvements that need doing, so don't hesitate to call on Roger for assistance. I won't pretend he's the handiest of men about the house, but he can put up a shelf that doesn't fall down and he can carry logs and water.' She looked across at me, the creases deepening in her forehead. 'What are you going to say to Master and Mistress Burnett tomorrow? I don't want you siding with them against the Alderman.'

I understood her worry, but I could not promise her *not* to get involved if I should think it right to do so.

'There's no question of taking sides, Mother. This young man either is or is not Clement Weaver. All I should wish to do is discover the truth.'

'I knew it,' she moaned, pushing away her oatcake, half-eaten. 'You do intend poking your nose in.'

'Would you want Alison Burnett to be deprived of half her inheritance by a clever imposter?'

'I know what I wouldn't want,' she retorted harshly, 'and that's to lose my livelihood and home. Alderman Weaver has every right to consider his affairs none of your business.'

'He wouldn't penalize you like that,' I answered gently. 'He's not a vindictive man. He wouldn't blame you for my sins, however much he might resent me.'

She looked almost convinced by this argument, having worked for the Alderman for many years and knowing that he held himself partly responsible for the premature deaths of her husband and young son, but there was still a lingering doubt in her mind, and I was fully aware that she would prefer me not to meddle.

I owed Margaret Walker a very great deal, and I went to bed that night half-inclined to respect her wishes; but when I awoke the following morning, I knew that, once out of the cottage, my insatiable curiosity would direct my feet straight to the Burnetts' house in Small Street.

Small Street runs parallel to Broad Street, and its dwellings, like all the others in the city, are built of wood and plaster with roofs of stone or slate. The Burnetts' house was no exception, and I guessed that inside it followed the same pattern as Alderman Weaver's; hall, parlour, buttery and kitchen on the ground floor, with family bedchambers on the first and an attic for the servants on the second.

I presented myself, as I had been requested to do, between the hours of eleven and noon, and the door was opened to me by the housekeeper whose keys, dangling from her belt, informed me of her calling. She fixed me with a beady eye and seemed none too pleased at having to allow me across the threshold.

'Good-day,' I said, stepping briskly inside. 'Your master and mistress are expecting me. Roger Chapman is my name.'

She made no response other than a quick jerk of the head to indicate that I should follow her. To my relief we crossed the hall, where the draughts seeped under the doors and whispered among the painted rafters, and I was shown into the parlour, an altogether warmer and cosier room. Tapestries hung on the walls and a fire of logs and sea-coal burned on the hearth, keeping at bay the chill of the January morning.

Alison Burnett, in a red velvet gown trimmed with grey squirrel, was huddled in a carved armchair, her hands spread to the flames whose light appeared almost visible through their delicate, blue-veined skin. She turned her head as I closed the door, the ghost of a smile lifting the corners of her mouth. Of her husband there was, for the present at least, no sign.

'Sit down, Master Chapman,' she invited, nodding at a second armchair on the opposite side of the hearth.

I did as she bade me, but I felt uncomfortable at usurping what I was sure was William Burnett's own place. I perched awkwardly on the very edge of the seat, ready to get up at once should he appear.

Alison nodded understandingly. 'It's all right. My husband has agreed that it might be wiser if I see you alone. He gets so angry on my behalf.' She bit her lip and sighed. 'Indeed, his temper has already caused too much harm.'

I relaxed a little. 'In what way?' I asked her.

She buried her face in her hands for a moment before looking up. 'He has quarrelled so bitterly with my father, told him so many home truths about this evil rogue who pretends to be Clement, that my father has altered his will, cutting me out completely.' She drew a long, shuddering breath. 'I don't mind owning to you, Master Chapman, that his action has destroyed my faith in human nature. Never, *never* did I think that he would treat me in such a fashion.'

I was astonished at this revelation, but it could explain the scene I had witnessed outside the Alderman's house in Broad Street. To make certain I asked, 'When did you learn of this?'

'The day before yesterday,' she answered, confirming my suspicions. 'My father sent Ned Stoner round in the morning with a message, requesting that William and I wait upon him some time before supper. We were hoping that he had come to his senses at last, but it was only to tell us that in view of our hostility towards "Clement" and our attitude towards himself, he had that very afternoon made a new will, leaving everything he possessed to his "son"!' She spat the last word so venomously that a few drops of spittle, landing on one of the logs, hissed and sputtered among the flames.

'Do you believe him,' I asked, 'or do you think he just wants to frighten you and force you into accepting this man?'

Alison kneaded her hands together in her lap. 'Oh yes, he's done it! The lawyer was leaving just as we arrived. But he's signed his own death warrant.'

'Oh come!' I protested with more confidence than I felt. 'You mustn't think like that. No one in his right senses would risk doing away with a benefactor who has just left him all his worldly goods. If the Alderman were to die suddenly now, the finger of suspicion would point directly at the one who stands to gain the most.'

Alison glanced scornfully at me. 'Of course he wouldn't do anything immediately! Even I don't suppose the man's that much of a fool. But my father is a very sick man: anyone can see that he hasn't long to live. It wouldn't need much cunning for either the wretch himself or his partner to help my father out of this life without arousing too many misgivings.'

'When you say his partner . . .' I was beginning, but she cut me short.

'He's bound to have one, isn't he?' Her tone was impatient. 'He can't be as well-informed as he is without having been primed by someone who knows the family. It stands to reason.'

'Unless he really *is* your brother,' I suggested tentatively, braving her wrath.

But she didn't fly at me as I had expected. She merely said flatly and with complete conviction, 'This man isn't Clement.'

'How can you be so sure?'

Alison hunched her thin shoulders. 'Clement and I grew up

together: there wasn't a great difference in our ages. We were close.' Her eyes filled with tears. 'I repeat, this man is *not* my brother.'

In the face of such conviction I felt there was probably nothing I could say to persuade her otherwise, but I had to try in case she should be wrong.

'Is there anything you could ask him to which only your brother would know the answer?' I suggested. 'A secret, perhaps, which you and Clement shared as children?'

Her lips curled. 'I have no intention of wasting my time on the creature. As William says, I should demean myself by giving even the slightest hint that I take his claim seriously.'

It was not for me to point out that such blind prejudice had already done her and her husband a great disservice in her father's eyes, probably costing them the remaining half of Alison's inheritance. I also suspected that the greater intransigence they displayed, the more entrenched became the Alderman's belief that Clement had been miraculously restored to him. The Burnetts had mismanaged a delicate situation from the start, with William goading his stubborn wife into direct opposition to her obstinate father, when a little sympathy and understanding might have given them ascendancy over the old man's mind.

'Are you quite sure,' Alison asked me, 'that you never saw Clement's body?'

'As certain as I'm sitting here now.' I leaned forward, my elbows resting on my knees, and stared earnestly into her face. 'I could only guess at the fate of your brother and all the others who had disappeared from that inn, by what happened to myself. But that doesn't mean, of course, that one of the victims couldn't have survived. And this young man, so my mother-in-law tells me, says that a blow to his head robbed him of his memory for the next six years. I suppose that could be possible. I'm not a physician, but the Infirmarian at Glastonbury Abbey did once tell me the Greek word for such forgetfulness. I can't recall it at the moment, but it shows that the condition exists.'

I might as well have talked to the wall: Alison Burnett remained totally unconvinced.

'You found Clement's tunic,' she accused me. 'Some beggar was wearing it. If my brother wasn't dead, how did this man get hold of it?'

I sighed. 'Your brother could have been stripped while he lay unconscious and his clothes sold some time or other to Bertha Mendip . . .'

'Bertha Mendip?' Alison demanded as my voice tailed off. 'Who's she?'

I shook my head. 'It's a long story. I can't go into all the details now.' I straightened my back. 'Mistress Burnett, why have you asked me here? What is it you really require of me?'

It was her turn to lean forward, the hazel eyes with their distinctive green flecks suddenly blazing into life, the light from the fire reflected in their depths.

'I want you to work for me,' she said. 'I'll pay you well, never fear. I want you to prove beyond the shadow of a doubt that this man who says he's Clement is really an impostor. I want him revealed for the rogue that he is. And above all, I want to know the name of his partner in this crime.'

Chapter Six

One half of me longed to accept her offer, but the other urged circumspection. I hedged a little while trying to make up my mind.

'Mistress Burnett,' I said, 'I'm only a chapman. What makes you think I could be of any use to you in this matter?'

She regarded me scornfully. 'Oh, come! Apart from the service you rendered my father, when you discovered the truth about Clement's murder, there have been other instances when you have successfully employed this talent of yours as a solver of mysteries and puzzles. Do you think it remains unknown? Do you seriously believe that you can nose out the would-be assassin of the Duke of Gloucester without a single word of your success being noised abroad? William heard it talked of when he was in London last October, on business; and that was more than a year after the event, if I'm not mistaken. And goodness knows what you've been up to in the meantime.'

'Fr-from whom did Master Burnett get this information?' I stammered.

Alison shrugged. 'He has a friend who has a friend at court, so from him, I would imagine. Is it of any importance?'

'No . . . No, not at all!' I assured her.

But I was astounded by this revelation that what I had done was of sufficient consequence to be a topic of conversation over a twelvemonth later. It also made me uneasy, for I have always valued my privacy as much as my freedom, and even at that comparatively young age, I had discovered that privacy's greatest ally is anonymity. At the same time, I experienced a surge of pride and knew I could be in danger of getting a swollen head. I sent up a hasty, although admittedly half-hearted, prayer for humility.

'Say something, man!' Alison demanded, obviously annoyed by my silence. 'Will you do this for me, or not?'

'On one condition,' I answered, raising my head and holding her eyes with mine. 'That I am employed by you to seek out the truth, whatever that may be, even if it's something you would prefer not to hear.'

Relief made her laugh. 'Oh, is that all? You're thinking what if you should discover that this man calling himself Clement really is my brother?' I nodded and she continued, 'You won't. I've already told you that. I wish I could convince you. However, it's of no moment if you're willing to accept my offer. You'll find out for yourself soon enough. So, that's that.'

'Not quite,' I protested. 'There are some questions *I* want to ask.'

The door opened and William Burnett entered the parlour. 'Is everything settled?' he enquired.

His wife turned towards him, seemingly apprehensive at this unlooked-for intrusion, and said, 'Master Chapman has agreed to help us.'

'I've agreed to try to discover the truth,' I amended. 'With respect, Mistress, it's not quite the same thing.'

I had half-risen from my seat as I spoke, but Master Burnett waved at me to sit down again and began pacing restlessly to and fro.

'Do you mean you believe this man *might* be my brother-in-law?' he asked incredulously.

'I mean I've no prejudice either way.' I thought about this for a moment or two, before honesty forced me to add, 'But I have to admit that I'd rather he was not Clement. Otherwise, I shall always feel guilty that, six years ago, I made a wrong assumption.'

'Oh, it's *your* peace of mind we should be worried about, is it?' William sneered. '*Ours* is unimportant!'

His attitude was becoming objectionable, and I had a sudden desire to wash my hands of both him and his wife. This thought must have shown in my face for Alison said quickly, 'Hush, William! Your ill-humour has already cost us dear. Master Chapman – ' she turned back to me – 'you said you had some questions you wanted to ask me.'

I hesitated for a few seconds longer, but recognized that even if I walked away now, my curiosity would, in the end, get the better of me. I might as well commit myself and be done with it.

'Very well,' I said. 'Mistress Burnett, how like your brother in appearance is this man?'

'Not at all like,' snapped her husband.

Alison drew a deep breath and closed her eyes for the briefest of seconds, before turning them reproachfully in his direction. 'That's not true, my dear, and you know it.' She looked at me again. 'Yes, there is a similarity of feature between Clement and this creature. It would be foolish to deny it, or why should my father have accepted him so readily? Hair and eyes are also of the right colour, and when I first saw him, even I had a qualm of doubt.'

'But not for long?' I suggested.

'Indeed no! Almost at once I knew him for a cheat.'

'May I ask why?'

Alison Burnett frowned as she sought for words to express her innermost feelings. 'I was very close to my brother,' she said at last. 'Clement would . . . would have behaved differently towards me; been more pleased to see me. This man is hostile.

His only concern is to worm himself into my father's favour. It ... It's difficult to explain. It's just something I feel instinctively.'

'What about moles or old scars? Did your brother have any blemishes on his body which this man does not?'

She shook her head. 'None that I recall.' Was she lying? 'But that's irrelevant,' she went on eagerly. 'I keep telling you, I *know* the man is an impostor.'

I guessed that this line of enquiry would produce nothing further, for however stoutly she might deny it, Alison did not wish for her brother to be alive: she had grown too used to being sole heir to a considerable fortune. On the other hand, perhaps that was to do her an injustice. Instinct is a very powerful force, and is undoubtedly given to us by God for our protection.

'Yet this man must know a lot about you and your family,' I said. 'Enough to convince Alderman Weaver that he is indeed his son. They cannot avoid discussing the past.'

'Oh, I don't deny the creature knows a great deal,' Alison admitted. 'That's why I say he must have a partner; someone who knows us all well and who will share the fortune with him after my father's death.' She cast a fleeting, sidelong glance at her husband and could not resist adding, 'A far bigger fortune, in fact, than could possibly have been foreseen at the start of this venture.'

William muttered something under his breath and stalked out of the room, closing the door behind him with a defiant thud. Judging by the tightening of Alison's lips, I guessed there would be recriminations after I had gone, but for my benefit, she put on a brave show of standing shoulder-to-shoulder with him.

'You mustn't think I blame William for the way in which he stood up to my father. My welfare is his sole concern. The outcome was unfortunate, to put it mildly, and it's true that he let his tongue run away with him. What he said was very bad, but then he was extremely incensed by my father's foolish, irresponsible and totally unreasonable behaviour. And no one could have foretold that I would be cut out of the will entirely. Such a possibility was unthinkable and never entered either of our heads. Even the Broad Street servants were horrified when they heard of it. Dame Pernelle, the housekeeper, went so far as to remonstrate with my father, and was threatened with dismissal for her pains.' Tears trickled down Alison's cheeks and she dashed them away with the back of her hand.

'Have you made no attempt at reconciliation with the Alderman?' I asked gently. 'It was my impression, all those years ago, that he was very fond of you and would certainly not wish to do you permanent injury.'

'He has always been very fond of me,' she gulped, 'but this evil impostor whispers in his ear and poisons his mind against us. My father insists that he will not reinstate my name in his will unless William makes an abject, *written* apology to be presented on his knees, in the presence of all who overheard what was said – meaning, of course, the servants. But that is too much to ask of him. I will not, cannot, let him do it. I won't allow my husband to be humiliated in such a fashion.'

The conditions did seem harsh, and I could understand the reluctance of both the Burnetts to comply with them, especially as William was a wealthy man in his own right and could live comfortably for the rest of his days without having to crawl to his father-in-law for money. All the same, a fortune was a fortune; and one as large as Alderman Weaver's was not to be relinquished without a fight, particularly into the hands of an impostor (if that was indeed the truth of the matter).

'Mistress Burnett,' I said, 'if this man is not your brother, he must, as you point out, have been primed by an accomplice concerning everything to do with Clement's past life, with the exception of the last six years. I had already reached this conclusion for myself, because when my mother-in-law told me what had happened – I was absent from Bristol for the first few weeks of this month – I naturally felt a great personal interest in the story and thought about it very carefully. So, who would know your family well enough not only to recognize this man's uncanny resemblance to your brother, but also to be able to instruct him in all the details of its history?'

Alison turned her chair a little more towards the fire and again held her delicate hands towards its warmth. 'The most probable suspects are my Uncle John and his wife, Aunt Alice, who, as you doubtless remember, live in London. Then there are their children, my cousins George and Edmund. Both the boys are married now, and live with their respective wives in the ward of Farringdon Without, not far from their parents.'

'Your Uncle John is your father's brother.'

I had never seen John Weaver in person, but I had met Dame Alice, together with the elder son, George, and his wife, Bridget, during those weeks in London, six years earlier, when I had been trying to find out what had become of Clement. (At that time, as I recalled, Edmund had been unmarried and still living at home.) Alison had been fond of her kinsfolk in those days, and had stayed with her aunt and uncle whenever she had visited the capital. I asked her what had happened in the meantime to make her change her mind about them.

She shrugged. 'Nothing. I'm still fond of them – until I have reason to feel otherwise. But my uncle, although well enough to do, has never amassed as much money as my father. He thought that by going to London all those years ago, he would make his fortune, while his stay-at-home, older brother wouldn't thrive. I know it has always irked him that my father has done so much better than himself.'

'Has he said so?'

'Not directly. At least, not to me. Of course, he wouldn't. But you know how it is: you can sense these things. In recent years

– whenever he and Aunt Alice have visited Broad Street, or when we have stayed in Farringdon Without – his attitude towards my father has been less open and friendly. He frequently makes snide remarks on the subject of my father's wealth, as though the thought of all that money angers him. On the occasions when either Father or I have taken exception to these remarks, my uncle just laughs and claims that they are only a bit of fun. "Can't you take a joke?" he asks. But they're not really jokes; there's something bitter and twisted behind them.' She added rather sadly, 'The two families don't see each other as much as they used to.'

'And your cousins, George and Edmund, do they also feel this resentment towards your father?'

'I'm afraid so. They have always been easily influenced by Uncle John. When William and I went on a visit to London two years ago, we both noticed how distant and cold the boys had become. I haven't seen either of them since.'

I moved my chair a little closer to the fire as the air in the room began to strike chill. 'What about their wives?' I asked. 'Is either of them the sort who would aid and abet her husband in a deception such as the one that we're suggesting?'

'Bridget would,' Alison said, nodding her head decisively. 'That's George's wife. She's the kind of person who loves money, not to spend, but to hoard. I'm sure that just knowing it's there, piling up under the floorboards or wherever they keep it, gives her a glow of satisfaction. She's parsimonious when she has no need to be.'

I still remembered, six years on, the sallop, the 'poor man's beer' made from wild arum, which Bridget had served me instead of decent ale, and thought that Alison was probably right. 'What about Edmund's wife?' I asked.

My hostess gave a dry laugh that degenerated into a cough. 'Lucy is exactly the opposite, as big a spendthrift as Bridget is a miser, and consequently they despise one another. Lucy gets rid of Edmund's money as fast as he can make it. She's so pretty that she can wind him round her little finger, and the poor fool's so besotted, so proud to have her on his arm when they go out together, that he's afraid even to remonstrate with her.'

I stared thoughtfully into the fire, watching a tiny green flame which flickered like a will-o'-the-wisp at the heart of the inferno. Of the six people named by Alison, only Lucy could not possibly have been the instigator of the deception (if deception it was) because six years previously she had not been a member of the Weaver family, and therefore could not have known her husband's cousin, Clement. But any one of the other five might have had a chance encounter with someone who bore him a strong resemblance and recognized the possibilities; although whether or not Dame Alice would have done so, I was unable to decide. My recollection of her was of a stout, pleasant-faced, easily flustered woman of poor intelligence, deferential to the opinions of others and having very few of her own.

After a brief silence, I asked, 'Is there anyone else you can think of who might feel entitled to a slice of your father's fortune, and have the wits to see a way of getting it if he or she met your brother's double?'

Alison gave an uncertain smile. 'I suppose almost anyone who is familiar with us.'

'No. It has to be someone who knows your family history intimately – more intimately, at least, than a mere friend or acquaintance. How long have Rob Short and Ned Stoner been in the Alderman's employ?'

'In Ned's case, only a year or so before Clement disappeared, and Rob perhaps a twelvemonth longer. I can't really remember, but they certainly weren't members of the household when Clement and I were young.' Alison frowned suddenly. 'But I'm forgetting Baldwin Lightfoot.' When I raised my eyebrows, she went on, 'He's a cousin of my mother's. They were the children of sisters, and I think Baldwin has always resented the fact that it was his aunt, and not his mother, who married into the de Courcy family. I remember him saying to me once, when I was a child, that if he'd been a de Courcy instead of a Lightfoot, he wouldn't have married beneath him. "But I've no doubt," he said, "it was for the money." I was too young at the time to realize that he was talking about my parents, but I never liked him after that. Instinct again, I suppose. I could tell that he despised my father as a common man who had made a fortune out of trade.'

I was intrigued by this Baldwin Lightfoot. 'Where does he live?' I asked. 'Here, in Bristol?'

Alison shook her head. 'No, in Keyford, near Frome.'

My heart lurched in my chest, and immediately a face swam before my eyes; the most beautiful face in the world. Eyes the colour of periwinkles, hair the shade of ripe corn, skin as flawless as a peach, lips as red as cherries . . . I pulled myself up short. Surely no woman in the world was as perfect as that! What in heaven's name was the matter with me? Rowena Honeyman had me bewitched. I turned back to my companion.

'Is anything wrong?' she asked. 'You look so strange.'

I managed a smile. 'It's just that I know someone who lives in Keyford,' I answered lamely. 'Tell me more about this Baldwin Lightfoot.'

Alison grimaced. 'There's little to tell. He's a bachelor, some fifty and more years of age. He has property in Keyford, inherited from his father.'

'Does he ever go to London? Would he have had the opportunity to meet this man who calls himself your brother? Would he have recognized a likeness to Clement?'

Alison bit her lip. Her tone of voice when speaking of Baldwin made it obvious to me that she disliked her mother's cousin. All the same, she wished to be fair.

'In answer to your last question, probably not,' she admitted at length. 'It's a number of years now since he last set eyes on Clement, although in our youth, we saw Baldwin often. As for your other queries, I can only say that he used to visit a kinsman of his father who lived close by Saint Paul's churchyard, but whether or not he still does so, I have no notion. If he does, however, then he might have had the opportunity. But that is for you to find out. It is, after all, what you will be paid for.'

'This Baldwin Lightfoot,' I persisted, 'would he know enough about you, your brother and parents to be able to prime a complete stranger with all those little customs and rituals which are peculiar to every family, but known only to its members?'

The hazel eyes, with their strange green flecks, again met mine, and Alison laughed scornfully. 'He'd know enough. But you still don't understand, do you, Chapman? But then why should you? You haven't yet met the creature claiming to be my brother! Whenever he's challenged with some awkward question to which he doesn't know the answer, whenever he makes an error, he blames it on his loss of memory. "The past six years have taken their toll of me," he says. "I've been ill, and I'm still not completely well yet." And he clutches his brow and complains of pains in his head and looks piteously at my father, who roars at everyone to leave the boy alone. So you see, the gaps in Baldwin Lightfoot's knowledge, were he the instigator of this plot, wouldn't really matter.'

'I see.' I stared thoughtfully at her. 'Mistress Burnett,' I said at last, 'I'll try to find out as much as I can within the next few days. But if I am to discover all the truth, I must travel not only to Keyford, but to London, also, and such journeys will now have to wait until spring. The worst of the winter weather is yet to come, and will soon be upon us. There are obligations which must keep me at home, for a while at least; obligations to my mother-in-law and her kinswoman, Mistress Juett, whom you met yesterday, to Mistress Juett's son and also to my little daughter. In which case, it might possibly be high summer before I am able to offer a solution to your troubles. Even then, I may fail. I can't promise you an answer. In these circumstances, do you still wish me to pursue my investigations?'

She frowned. 'Must they take so long?'

'It's probable. Will the state of the Alderman's health allow him to survive the colder months, do you think?'

Alison continued to look worried, but after a little consideration, she nodded. 'I think it more than likely. My father seems to have been given a new lease of life since the arrival of this impostor. At Christmas, I was convinced he could not be long for this world, although William thought I was being unduly pessimistic. He considers my father good for several years yet, and now I am inclined to agree with him.'

'Are you then not afraid,' I suggested, 'that it might hasten your father's end should it be proved that this young man, in whom he places so much trust and who seems to be so necessary to his well-being, is really a villain?'

Something akin to eagerness leapt into my companion's eyes, before they were veiled by decorously lowered lids. 'I don't think that's likely to happen,' she said, now arguing against herself. 'My father is tougher than you think. He's had to be, to weather the tragedies and disappointments of his life, and also to make himself one of the richest men in Bristol.' She stood up rather abruptly, indicating that our meeting was at an end. 'You'll let me know how you go on, Master Chapman. I wish to be kept informed of anything you may discover. Are you in need of money?'

I had risen with Alison, and bowed over her proffered hand. 'I shall render my account when I have an answer to this riddle, and only so long as I am able to reach a firm conclusion. If I am unable to do so, I shall waive my fee. But if I do have the answer, you will pay me regardless of the outcome. That is our bargain.'

'Very well,' she agreed, after the briefest of hesitations, adding, 'what will you do now?'

I had not given the matter much thought, but inspiration struck even while Alison was speaking. 'I shall return to my mother-in-law's cottage to fetch my pack, and then I shall call on Dame Pernelle in Broad Street. There must be something she, or one of the maids perhaps, could usefully buy from a chapman. And while there, I shall try to discover the general feelings of the household with regard to this man calling himself Clement Weaver. I might also, if luck favours me, manage to have a word with Ned Stoner and Rob Short, both of whom are old acquaintances.'

Alison nodded her approval and rang the little silver bell which stood on a table beside her chair. A servant answered the summons and, two minutes later, I was standing outside the house, thankful that William Burnett had not reappeared.

Chapter Seven

I approached Alderman Weaver's house in Broad Street from the back, through the garden gate that opened into Tower Lane.

The garden itself, after I had lifted the latch and entered, was much as I remembered it, except that the apple and pear trees were at present leafless, the bed of herbs and the border of flowers along one wall locked in their winter sleep. A thin layer of frost, untouched by the feeble midday sun, still coated the pathway and the roof of the lean-to privy, a sure indication that the bad weather was tightening its grip; and a sudden sharp intake of breath made me sneeze, as the cold irritated the back of my nose and throat. I knocked on the outer door of the kitchen.

It was opened by one of the maids. 'Yes?' she queried. 'What do you want?'

I pointed to my pack. 'Is there anything you or the housekeeper might be needing?'

The girl looked dubious, but her eyes had brightened at the prospect of some relief in the monotonous routine of a dull afternoon. 'Wait there! I'll ask Dame Pernelle,' she said, and withdrew indoors.

While I stamped my feet and blew on my fingers to try to keep warm, I could not help but recall the first time I had visited this house in the company of Marjorie Dyer, a distant kinswoman of the widowed Alderman, who had then been in charge of his domestic comforts. Three years later, when I again had cause to contact Alfred Weaver, Marjorie had been replaced by a veritable dragon of a woman, and I could only hope that her successor was of a sweeter disposition.

I was not disappointed. Dame Pernelle was a plump, motherly-looking creature, somewhere, I guessed, in her early or middle forties, with large, soft blue eyes and a double chin. The young maid's attitude towards her appeared to be familiar but respectful, suggesting that the housekeeper ruled her little kingdom by persuasion rather than force, by kindness rather than fear. She peered shortsightedly at me, seemed reassured by what she saw, and indicated that I should step inside.

The kitchen, too, was much as I remembered it, with its stone-flagged, rush-strewn floor, its water-butt and ale-vat standing in separate corners, sides of salted beef and mutton and bunches of herbs hanging from hooks in the ceiling. A delicious smell of baking bread came from the ovens.

A second maid joined us at the table as I started to set out my wares. 'I know you,' she grinned. 'You're Margaret Walker's son-in-law. You live with her in Redcliffe. I've seen you when I've been visiting my aunt.'

Dame Pernelle, who had drawn up a stool, regarded me with sudden keenness. 'Aha! You're *that* chapman, are you?' The blue eyes, so guileless a moment before, now twinkled knowingly, as she fingered a carved ivory needlecase. 'This is very pretty – if, that is, you're really interested in selling us anything.'

'Why shouldn't I be?' I asked, all innocence. 'For what other purpose would I be here?'

The housekeeper chuckled. 'It's no good trying to pull the wool over my eyes, lad. I've heard talk of you from some of Mistress Walker's neighbours.'

'And what do they say of me?' I wanted to know.

'Oh, some say that you're far too nosy, always poking and

prying into people's business. Others, that you're very clever at
solving riddles, and that thanks to you, some evil men and
women, who might otherwise have escaped punishment, have
been brought to justice. There have also been whispers of friends
in high places . . . But I can see by the look on your face that
you'd rather I didn't talk about that.'

'The gossip's bound to be exaggerated, anyway,' I answered
curtly, 'Such rumours usually are. Let me recommend to you
this length of blue silk ribbon. Florentine,' I added coaxingly.
'It arrived in Bristol on a merchantman only yesterday morning.'

Dame Pernelle once again gave her rich, throaty chuckle. 'And
what would I do with it, pray? When would I have a chance to
wear it? Or either of these silly girls, here, for that matter? No,
no! Save it for someone young and pretty who can afford it, and
tell me why you've really come.' She lowered her voice and
asked confidentially, 'Have you been sent by Mistress Burnett
to see if you can make head or tail of this strange business that's
so perplexing to us all?'

The housekeeper's appearance was deceptive. Beneath her
plumply soft exterior, and behind the rather vacuous features, a
shrewd mind was at work. It was no use pretending, so I gave
her what I hoped was my most disarming grin. 'You're right,
there is no pulling the wool over your eyes. Although to say that
I was *sent* by Mistress Burnett is perhaps somewhat misleading.
Let's just say that I have agreed to find out what I can.'

Dame Pernelle looked pleased with herself and her own
percipience. She was about to make some further remark, when
she recollected the maids who, their interest in the contents of
my pack temporarily forgotten, were staring at us with a
fascinated, if not entirely comprehending, gaze. 'You're good
girls,' she said, rising to her feet and patting them both on the
head. 'You've worked hard this morning and deserve a treat.
Later on, I'll buy each of you something from Roger's pack, but

for now, I must speak privately with him.' And she gave a slight jerk of the head, indicating that I should follow her.

Dame Pernelle led the way to a small, tapestry-hung closet on the opposite side of the hall, that evidently served as her hideaway. The air struck chill as there was no hearth and therefore no fire; but as there was only one small window, through which the draughts could seep, it was not as cold as it might otherwise have been. She lit a couple of candles before closing the door and waving me to a seat. When I had lowered my bulk on to a bench which ran along one wall, the dame plumped herself down in the room's only chair. 'Now,' she said, 'we can talk without the girls overhearing everything we say. What do you want to know?'

I shrugged. 'That's easy. Do you believe this young man to be Clement Weaver or do you think him an impostor? No, wait! I may be putting the cart before the horse. First of all, were you previously acquainted with Clement?'

'Oh yes! I knew him well. My elder sister and I grew up in the city, and our father, Robin Dando, was a vintner with a shop in Wine Street, close by the castle foregate. When Clement and Alison were young, they used sometimes to accompany the Alderman when he came to the shop to buy wine. You see, my father imported several excellent wines from Bordeaux to which Alfred Weaver was extremely partial. And then, when I was eighteen, my sister Alice married the Alderman's younger brother, John.'

This revelation was entirely unexpected and I exclaimed in astonishment. 'You're Alice Weaver's sister? I had no notion!' I scrutinized her more closely. 'But now that you say, yes, I can see a likeness.'

'You've met Alice?' It was Dame Pernelle's turn to be surprised.

'Six years ago, in Faringdon Without, when I was searching for Clement.'

The housekeeper nodded. 'She and John went to London to live almost as soon as they were married. He had an idea he could make his fortune if he set up his looms there instead of in Redcliffe. Myself, I think it was a mistake; and I fancy Alice does, too, only she's too loyal to say so.' She echoed Alison Burnett's words. 'John's comfortably off, I don't deny that, but he hasn't made the money that his brother has. He should have stayed in Bristol.'

'And what happened to you?' I asked.

'I married my father's apprentice,' she said apologetically. 'It wasn't the match my parents had hoped for me, but we were in love and it worked out very well in the end. My father left us the business when he died, and Henry ran it at a profit for over quarter of a century until he also died, in January last year. After that, I'd no heart for it. We'd no children, so I sold up; and by great good fortune, the Alderman was looking for a new housekeeper as his old one had just been given notice to quit. He and Dame Judith never really got on.'

It occurred to me that not only was my companion sister-in-law to one of the chief suspects in this affair, but also that she had not been long in the Alderman's employ – a matter of months, no more – before the arrival of this man who claimed to be his son. But for the moment, I suppressed the thought: I would take it out and consider it at my leisure, later on. 'Very well then,' I said. 'You are a kinswoman by marriage of the Alderman and his children. You knew Clement Weaver. So, is this man who he says he is? You must have an opinion one way or the other.'

Dame Pernelle shook her head. 'I'm afraid I don't. Yes, there is a look of Clement about him, but six years of hardship and privation can change a man. An impostor would bank on that fact to explain any alteration in his appearance. Yes, he knows a great deal about the family, the weaving business, his childhood with Alison; but, again, his long loss of memory is held accountable for any of the many slips he makes, or for the frequent lapses of recall from which he suffers.' She sighed. 'It's impossible for someone as impartial as myself to judge the truth of the matter, let alone one as blind and besotted as the Alderman.'

The housekeeper was apparently being very frank, and I realized why she had not wished the maids to hear what she had to say; so I decided to take advantage of this privacy to probe further. 'What were the circumstances,' I asked, 'of this young man's arrival? Exactly when and how did it happen?'

Dame Pernelle seemed only too glad to talk. She settled herself in her chair and, without any show of reluctance, embarked upon her tale.

'It was the day after Twelfth Night,' she said. 'Ned Stoner and Rob Short were taking down the evergreens in the hall, and the two girls were in the kitchen washing the dirty dishes used at dinner. Cook was having a well-earned rest, with her feet up on a stool by the fire, and the Alderman had retired to the parlour after we'd eaten. I was on my way upstairs to the linen press to sort out the items which needed mending, because the seamstress was due the following day and I wanted to be sure that she had enough to occupy her time. I'd just reached the bend in the middle of the first flight of stairs, when there was knock at the street door.

'I assumed it was Mistress Burnett come to see how her father was, for he'd not been at all well over Christmas. Ned and Rob were both perched on the tops of ladders, so I said I'd go, and came downstairs again. When I opened the door, however, it wasn't Mistress Burnett but a strange man, wrapped in a very dirty and threadbare cloak, with the hood pulled well forward over his face. There was a grimy-looking bundle on the cobbles beside him, and I was just about to tell him to be off, when he picked up his belongings and shouldered his way past me into the hall, demanding a word with Alderman Weaver. Ned and Rob, seeing what was happening, slid down from their ladders and caught him by the arms, intending to hustle him straight out again. But immediately, the man started to struggle and shout at the top of his voice, which of course brought Cook and the girls from the kitchen and the Alderman from the parlour. Alfred was looking very displeased and demanded to know what was going on.

'As soon as the man saw him, he got an arm free and pushed the hood back from his face. "Father!" he said. "It's me, Clement. I've come home." Well, I thought for a moment that the Alderman was going to faint. Rob must have thought so, too, because he went to stand by Alfred, ready to catch him if he fell. Ned, meanwhile, was still trying to force the man in the direction of the door, calling him all the names he could lay his tongue to, and no one could blame him for that. None of us wanted to see the Alderman upset, especially as he had been so poorly. And certainly no one expected him to do what he did.'

'What did he do?' I enquired, as Dame Pernelle finally paused for breath.

She turned her blue eyes upon me with the same baffled look in them that they must have worn on the day. 'The Alderman just gave a great cry and flung his arms round the young man's neck. "Clement," he said, "I knew you couldn't be dead. I've always hoped that one day you might come back".'

'Just like that?' I asked, bewildered. 'No questions? No initial disbelief? No incredulity?'

'None,' said Dame Pernelle, 'neither then nor later, as far as I know. I don't think any of the rest of us could believe our eyes and ears.' She broke off for a moment, her face puckered in sudden concentration; then she leaned forward and wagged a finger at me. 'And it's just occurred to me, picturing the scene afresh, that no one was more surprised than our visitor. I'd forgotten it until now, but for a second or two he looked totally dumbfounded. It seemed as if he was as amazed as we were at his easy acceptance. How stupid of me not to have remembered that before.'

'You have had too much else to occupy you,' I consoled her. 'But if you're sure of what you saw, it may have some significance. If this man were truly Clement Weaver, I don't think the possibility of not being accepted by his father would ever have crossed his mind.'

But this was going too fast for the dame: she was not yet ready to come down on one side or the other, let alone permit any observation of hers to decide the issue. 'I . . . Well . . . Maybe I was imagining things,' she hedged. 'I can't be absolutely certain.'

It was on the tip of my tongue to remind her that this was not what she had said a few moments earlier, but I could see that she was growing flustered and let the matter rest. 'What did you think when the young man put back his hood?' I asked. 'Did you immediately think, "Yes, it's Clement Weaver!"?'

'Not then, no! I could see no resemblance. But later, when he was washed and wearing a tunic and hose that had belonged to Clement – for my sister told me that the Alderman never threw anything of his son's away, and resisted all Alison's persuasions to give his clothes to the poor – I was struck by a likeness. After that,' she admitted honestly, 'my opinion changed from day to day, sometimes from hour to hour. It still does. On occasions, he seems nothing like the boy I remember, but at other times, I think I can see Clement plainly in him.' She sighed.

'What about his voice? Is that the same?'

Dame Pernelle again shook her head. 'I can't recall how Clement sounded, not after all these years.'

'What about Rob Short and Ned Stoner? What do they think?'
'You must ask them.'
'But the three of you must have discussed the affair during these past few weeks. It must surely be a frequent topic of conversation among you?'

She made no attempt to deny it. 'Oh yes, but Ned and Rob don't know what to think any more than I do. And with the Alderman himself so positive . . .' Her voice tailed away into silence.

I understood. Alderman Weaver's unhesitating acceptance of the stranger was the cornerstone on which all others' belief was necessarily founded, with the exception of Alison Burnett and her husband. I mentioned their names.

The housekeeper instantly threw up her hands in dismay. 'What goings-on!' she exclaimed. 'What quarrels! What terrible things said on both sides that neither will retract! It's tragic. Alison and William are adamant that it's all a plot to deprive her of her inheritance. The Alderman, on the other hand, insists that they acknowledge Clement – for I must call him something and know of no other name to give him – without any reservations whatsoever, which is very unreasonable, to my way of thinking. Indeed, everyone I've spoken to thinks Alfred a fool for not being suspicious of this young man's story; for accepting him as his son with no more proof than his word.'

'And why do you think the Alderman has done so?'

'Because, secretly, he's never ceased to blame himself for Clement's death, for allowing him to carry so much money on that visit to London. In the years following his son's disappearance, whenever Alfred visited the wine shop, he often used to speak of Clement as if he were still alive. Then he'd pull himself up short with a terrible, lost expression on his face. It broke my heart to see it. A doting father.'

'Not so doting,' I answered drily, 'if he can disinherit his own daughter. First he halves her inheritance, then deprives her of it altogether.'

'Oh, he'll change his mind, given time,' the housekeeper assured me warmly, but there was, nevertheless, an underlying uncertainty in her tone. 'He doesn't care for his son-in-law very much, that's the trouble, and takes pleasure in giving him a fright. I think he liked William well enough when Alison first married him, and his father was one of Alfred's best friends; but over the years, he seems to have lost his fondness for Master Burnett.'

I found this understandable, but not to the extent of punishing his daughter for it. However, there was no point in my saying so, and instead I asked, 'Have you had any word from your sister in London on this subject?'

Dame Pernelle smiled. 'Alice can't write and I can't read. We were never taught our letters. I did send word to her of what had happened by a carter who was London-bound, but it's too soon to expect a message in return.'

'Well then, has the Alderman written to his brother?'

'Now that I don't know, nor is it my place to enquire. He may have done, but he won't be bothered with anything that takes him away for long from Master Clement's side.'

There was a knock at the door and one of the maids put her head around it. 'Beg your pardon, Dame Pernelle, but the master wants to see the chapman. He came looking for you in the kitchen, and then realized that Roger was here. He saw his pack on the table.' She glanced towards me. 'He wants you now, at once.'

The housekeeper rose hurriedly and smoothed down her skirts. 'Is he displeased, Mary?' she queried.

'He didn't sound it. He sent Jane upstairs to fetch down Master Clement.' Mary obviously had no difficulty in calling the newcomer by the name he had, rightly or wrongly, appropriated to himself.

'Where is the Alderman now?' I asked, likewise getting to

my feet and straightening my jerkin.

'He said he'd be in the parlour. It's warmer than the hall.' And Mary withdrew her head, leaving Dame Pernelle and me regarding one another thoughtfully.

A moment's delay, however, was all that the housekeeper allowed herself before returning to her duties. 'You'd better not keep him waiting, lad. As for me, I must go and see about the supper. Master Clement's very fond of rastons, and what he fancies he must have, on the Alderman's orders. That's what you could smell cooking in the oven. When they've been hollowed out, he likes the crumbs mixed with butter and honey.' She added thoughtfully, 'It seems that he always has done. They used to be made frequently for him, I'm informed, when he was a boy.'

'Who told you that?' I asked, as we moved towards the door.

'He did, himself, and the Alderman confirmed it. And so did Alison.' Her tone was bland and matter-of-fact, but she could not resist glancing at me as she said it.

I made no comment, but followed her into the hall, where Mary was still hovering anxiously. Dame Pernelle hurried off to the kitchen to attend to her baking.

Alfred Weaver, who rose civilly from his chair as I entered the parlour and held out a hand in greeting, looked a little healthier than he had done when I had last seen him a few days before the start of the Christmas festivities. There was a sparkle in his eyes, and he was a little fleshier about the cheeks and jowl. 'Come in, come in, my boy,' he invited jovially. 'You've heard my good news, I expect? Of course you have! There can't be anyone left in Bristol who's in ignorance of it.' He waved me to a chair. 'Sit down. I've sent for my son.' He uttered the last two words with pride. 'I want you to meet him. After all, who has a better right than the man who brought those murdering rogues to justice?' He dug me playfully in the ribs before resuming his own seat. 'But you were wrong about Clement. Oh, not about what happened to him. They tried to kill him all right, as they killed the others. But in his case, thanks be to God, they bungled it and he survived.'

'You're . . . You're sure of that, sir?'

The Alderman laughed, showing his blackened teeth. 'People have been getting at you, have they? Planting doubts in your mind? Take no notice of them, boy. Take no notice! Give me credit for knowing my own child when I see him.'

I smiled weakly, unsure what to say; unable to share in his certainty, but afraid of causing distress by voicing my misgivings. I tried once again, however. 'Our murderers were very thorough people.'

'They were – I won't quarrel with you about that – in every case but one. But Clement will be here in a moment and then you can see him for yourself.'

'I never knew your son, Alderman. I never saw him, not even in death.'

'How could you, when he was never dead?' He gave a bark of laughter.

I heard the parlour door open behind me and slewed round in my seat. The Alderman surged to his feet again, arms outstretched, a look of utter joy suffusing his face. 'Clement, my boy, I'm sorry to have disturbed your rest, but there's someone here I want you to meet. I've spoken to you at length about Roger Chapman, and now's your chance to shake him by the hand.'

Chapter Eight

The young man who took my hand and gave me a wary smile bore a resemblance to both Alison Burnett and Alderman Weaver, without being strikingly similar to either one of them. The hazel eyes lacked their distinctive flecks of green; his hair, although brown, was of a lighter shade; the mouth, equally wide and mobile, was so thin that the lips almost disappeared, and the nose was less well-defined. Yet these were the normal discrepancies of feature between brother and sister, parent and child, and the most telling impression was of an overall family likeness.

If he were an impostor, whoever had chosen him had chosen well, with a sharp eye for the similarities between him and the two supposed to be nearest him in blood. This was the more percipient because the mantle of the poor, the hungry and the dispossessed hung about him, largely obscuring what lay beneath. The man was plainly in ill-health. The emaciated flesh was loose on his bones, robbing him of his natural bulk; sores and scabs peppered his scalp, and I could see two large weeping pustules behind his left ear. No doubt the rest of his body was similarly marked (although good food and rest should quickly restore him to full vigour). Either this man was Clement Weaver, or I was looking for a puppet-master of some cunning.

'Master Chapman, I've been hoping to meet you.' The voice had an unmistakable West Country burr to it, with the hard 'r's and the diphthonged vowels of our Saxon forebears, but anyone could be taught to speak in such a fashion. 'My father's told me how you went to London, searching for me, and laid those villains by the heels.'

'The credit was not all mine by any means,' I disclaimed hastily. 'Indeed, I was nearly a victim myself. I owe my life to the good sense and watchfulness of another.' I resumed my seat in obedience to a peremptory gesture from the Alderman and the young man sat opposite me, on a joint stool. 'Tell me of your own experience,' I begged him. 'How did you manage to escape with your life?'

Once again came that disarming smile. 'That's the trouble. I've no idea. I remember being given some wine to drink – and I've only been able to recall that in recent months – but otherwise, all's a blank until I came to, lying stark naked on the banks of the Thames, on the Southwark side of the river. I couldn't even remember my name. I didn't know who I was or where I was or how I got there. There was blood oozing from a wound over my left eye – you can still see the scar if you look closely – and my head felt like it was home to a swarm of bees.'

'The wine, of course, was drugged,' I said.

The young man nodded. 'I realize that now, but at the time, I remembered nothing, and assumed it was because of the blow to my head. I'd been struck violently on the left temple, and reasoned that I'd got it from whoever it was that had stolen my clothes. My tunic was of good camlet trimmed with squirrel fur and must have earned the thief a pretty penny. Not, of course, that I knew this at the time, or had any knowledge of ever having owned such a garment. This is one of the things that has come back to me, you understand, over the past few months, as my memory has gradually returned.'

I frowned. 'So can you recall now how you managed to escape from the Thames?'

'Not really.' He glanced at the Alderman, who gave him an encouraging nod, and then went on, 'I can only think that the drug must have begun to wear off sooner than had been intended, so instead of drowning, I recovered consciousness and managed to strike out for the shore. My father tells me that even as a small boy, I was a prodigious swimmer.'

'And you're sure it was the thief who wounded you? You didn't hit your head on something?'

'I can't be certain, but I don't think so. Nor do I think that I was stripped before being thrown into the river.' The hazel eyes met mine with a puzzled stare. 'I have a . . . a sensation, no more than that, of still being fully clothed while I was in the water. So it's my opinion that the thief discovered me lying there and hit me with something. Perhaps I stirred or groaned, and he was afraid that I was about to recover my senses. In his anxiety, he dealt me a blow which not only rendered me unconscious again, but also robbed me of my memory for six long years.'

On the face of it, it was a plausible enough explanation and one with which I could find no immediate quarrel. Everything could have happened exactly as he said it did. 'So where have you been all these years?' I asked curiously. 'Where did you live? What name have you been using?'

'I lived among the beggars and felons of Southwark,' he answered simply. 'I was befriended by a woman called Morwenna Peto, a Cornishwoman by birth who had run away from home when she was young and journeyed to London, where she found work in the Southwark stews. But her whoring days are long past, and nowadays she runs a thieves' kitchen, where those down on their luck or seeking shelter from the law are always welcome. She found me and took me in. She'd had a son once, who'd ended his life on the gallows, and she said that I reminded her of him. So, when she found I had no knowledge of who I was or where I'd come from, she called me Irwin in his memory.' The young man smiled, but there was, I fancied, a hint of defiance in his expression. 'And that's who I've been for the past six years; Irwin Peto, thief, pimp, pickpocket . . . My father knows the whole story.'

'I do indeed,' the Alderman confirmed, 'and I don't condemn the boy. Nor will anyone else in my hearing.' He thrust out an aggressive lower lip.

'And how, finally, did you recover your memory?' I asked this young man who might or might not be Clement Weaver, and who, for the time being at least, I decided to think of as Irwin Peto.

'Strangely enough, by another blow to the head. Several months ago now, one day last October, when it had been raining and freezing both together and the cobbles were very treacherous, I was trying to escape from a man whose pocket I'd just picked, when I slipped and fell heavily, cracking my skull. I was half-stunned, but managed to haul myself to my feet and make off again. I eluded my would-be captor and reached home, where Morwenna bound me up and told me to get some sleep.' Irwin drew a deep breath. 'I did, and it was after I woke up that, very slowly, memories of my past life, my real life, began to come back to me; a little piece here, a brief glimpse there until, at last, by the beginning of December, I knew who I was, where I came from and some of the circumstances which had led me to be cast up, robbed and left for dead on the Southwark strand.'

He sounded like a child, reciting something he had been taught, his intonation unemotional and flat because he was intent only on speaking the words in their proper order and making no mistake.

'So you decided to come home,' I prompted.

'Yes. I had to let my father know that I was still alive. A week or so before Christmas, I said goodbye to Morwenna and set out for Bristol.'

'You walked all the way?'

'I got a lift now and then from a passing carter.'

'You didn't consider going to your uncle in Farringdon Without and asking for his assistance?'

Irwin shoot his head. 'It seemed only right to confront my father first with my story. Until he believed me, and accepted me for who I am, I felt I had no claim on other people's understanding.'

Once more, there was nothing to quarrel with in this answer, and if it again sounded like something carefully rehearsed, perhaps the fault was with me and my unspoken wish – for my own sake as well as Mistress Burnett's – that he should be lying.

'Well, Chapman!' Alderman Weaver leant across from his chair to mine and clasped my shoulder. 'Are you satisfied with my son's account? Is there anything which couldn't have happened as he says it did? Tell me honestly if you think he's lying.' But his glowing countenance testified to his conviction that I could have nothing detrimental to say.

I glanced towards Irwin Peto and detected a look of apprehension in the hazel eyes. Or did I? The expression was so fleeting that it was gone before I could be certain, and the confidence of innocence was all that remained. 'No,' I said, 'it could have happened exactly as Master Pet– as Master Weaver has explained.'

The Alderman clapped his hands to his thighs in a gesture of satisfaction, his face beaming, the years of misery and ill-health seeming to slip away before my eyes. And I realized that if there had been a doubt that this really was his son lurking in any corner of Alfred Weaver's mind, then my admission had laid it to rest. He seemed not to have noticed my slight slip of the tongue, or if he had, he regarded it as being of so little importance that it was already forgotten.

Not so with the younger man. The expression on his face

indicated that he was fully alive to its significance, and his manner was suddenly more reserved, hostile even, as though he recognized me now for an enemy rather than a friend. I decided therefore that it was time for me to leave while my stock remained high with the father at least, and I rose to my feet. My host did likewise and wrung my hand at parting as though I had been his equal rather than a common pedlar of small account. I wished that I could urge something on Alison's behalf, but there was nothing I could say which would not be construed as an unwarrantable intrusion into his family affairs. Besides, I had no desire at this stage to upset Irwin Peto any further.

I said farewell and removed myself to the kitchen, where I collected my pack and Dame Pernelle paid me for the two items – a length of figured ribbon and a carved wooden loving-spoon – chosen by Mary and Jane. The Dame, I could tell, was anxious that I should stay and give her my views on 'Master Clement', but I thought it best not to commit myself to an opinion just at present. Indeed, there was nothing I could say, nothing I could think of to disprove his story; only an intuitive sense that he was not who he claimed to be. So I took my leave and stepped outside into the wintry dusk.

It was almost dark and very much colder than when I had entered the house an hour or so earlier. The garden path was treacherous for the unwary foot, and twice in the first minute after the kitchen door had closed behind me, I slipped and only retained my balance with the greatest difficulty. And when I arrived at the garden gate, its latch was stiff and difficult to lift. I struggled with it unsuccessfully for several seconds until it eventually opened inwards with such force that this time there was nothing I could do to save myself. I went sprawling in an ungainly heap on the ground.

A man's voice said, 'Are you all right? I didn't know anyone was there.' And a hand reached down to help me to my feet.

'Ned Stoner,' I said, recovering my wind. 'It's good to see you again.'

'Roger Chapman,' he answered. 'I'd know you anywhere now that you're upright. There's no other man in Bristol to touch you for height. What are you doing here?' But before I could reply, he went on, 'No, you don't have to tell me! I can guess. In fact, I'm only surprised you haven't been nosing around here long before now. You must have heard about the return of Master Clement.'

'I only came back from Hereford the day before yesterday,' I grinned. 'I got here as soon as I could.'

He laughed. 'With what success?'

'Enough. I've met and talked to the young man – in the presence of his father.'

Ned gave another snort of laughter. 'I might have guessed you'd manage it somehow, in spite of the Alderman guarding that boy like a hen with one chick. But it's too cold to stand talking outdoors on an evening such as this. Come into the kitchen where it's warm and have a stoup of ale.'

Reluctantly, I shook my head. 'I've just taken leave of them all. I can't very well go back again.'

Ned clasped his arms about his body and stamped his feet. 'Tell you what,' he suggested, 'in that case, let's go to the Lattis and get ourselves a drink. I must know what you think of our young master.'

I readily agreed, and we set off along Tower Lane into Wine Street, then turned right and walked as far as the Corn Market. Here, opposite the entrance to Small Street, stands All Hallows Church, and behind the church an ale-house which, even at the time I am writing about, was already several centuries old. Originally known as the Green Lattis, it had been renamed Abyngdon's Inn when members of that family took it over, but, in recent years, it had changed hands yet again. Its new title was, and, as far as I know, still is, simply the New Inn; but to most of the local inhabitants it remains either the Lattis or Abyngdon's.

The place was crowded as always. Ned and I, entering the ale-room from the stone-flagged passage that runs the length of the house from front door to back, were fortunate to find seats at a table close to the fire, grabbing them just ahead of two other customers. We were cursed roundly, but gave as good as we got; and our luck held when a passing pot-boy took our order almost immediately, to the great annoyance of those who had been waiting for some time.

'The angels are on our side this evening,' Ned said, grinning. 'Now, tell me what you think about this business.'

I shook my head. 'Not until you tell me what *you* think. I never saw Clement Weaver, remember, but you knew him well. So, in your opinion, is this him?'

Ned sighed. 'Well, it could be. There's a look of Master Clement about him, allowing for the way he says he's been forced to live these last six years. And he knows a lot about the family and its history. And what he doesn't know is because his memory still isn't quite right. Or leastways, so he claims. And who's brave enough to query it? Who dares to object, "That's very convenient, my lad," if the Alderman accepts it?'

Our ale arrived and was placed in front of us, some of the liquid slopping over on to the board as the pot-boy hurried away to attend to other customers. 'That's what everyone says,' I murmured gloomily.

Ned swallowed a generous mouthful of ale and wiped his lips with the back of his hand. He leaned forward, frowning. 'The way he claims to have escaped from those rogues, well, you'd know more about that than I would. But it seems strange to me that they didn't bind his hands and feet before they threw him into the water. And what about his clothes? Good money to be made from them, surely?'

'Those rogues, as you so rightly call them, couldn't bind their victims' hands and feet without someone, sometime, being alerted to the fact that people were being murdered. If naked bodies kept being fished out of the Thames with wrists and ankles tied together, what would be the conclusion? Even the river scavengers wouldn't stay quiet about that for long: they'd get word to the Sheriff's men somehow. No, money and valuables were sufficient for those murdering thieves. They weren't going to risk the full force of the law being set in motion, because the trail might eventually lead to them. But when a fully clothed, unbound corpse is dragged out of the river, it's naturally presumed to be one of the many unfortunates who drown every day, either by falling in accidentally or at the hands of an assailant.'

Ned rubbed his nose. 'I thought you told me once that they tied you up. I could have sworn it.'

'They did, but that was because I hadn't drunk the wine. Even so, they were going to knock me over the head and untie me before dropping me into the Thames.'

'Oh, well!' He took another swig of ale. 'I reckon that answers my question. I guess things could have fallen out, then, the way this Irwin Peto says they did.'

'Is that how you think of him?' I asked curiously. 'Not as Master Clement?'

'It's not easy to know how to think of him,' Ned admitted. 'To begin with, I was convinced he was an impostor, but after a while, a few doubts crept in. And now you tell me that his story of how he escaped death could easily be true. Moreover, the Master's always believed in him, from the first moment they met.'

'That could be because Alderman Weaver has never wanted

to think that Clement is dead,' I argued. 'He's not going to let himself believe anything different, and woe betide anyone who tries to persuade him to change his mind.'

Ned drained his cup. 'You mean Mistress Alison and Master Burnett? Aye, it's a wicked thing to have done, to have treated her in such a scurvy fashion. And all because Master Burnett had courage enough to voice what the rest of the Master's friends were thinking. Maybe Master Burnett was a trifle heavy-handed. Maybe he could have curbed his tongue a bit more than he did; been a bit more diplomatic. But then, he was angry, and he didn't expect the Master to respond in such a way. Well, who could have foreseen such a thing? I ask you! To halve his daughter's inheritance on account of some stranger who turns up out of the blue and claims to be Clement is insanity enough, but to disinherit her altogether . . . words fail me!'

I sighed. I was getting nowhere. I was hearing the same story, in very nearly the selfsame words, from every person I talked to; and there was nothing of any significance to be gleaned even from those who had known Clement Weaver before his disappearance. So far, apart from Master and Mistress Burnett, no one was prepared to say definitely whether he or she thought Irwin Peto to be an impostor or not. Well, as I had told Alison earlier in the day, all further enquiries on my part would probably have to wait now until the spring.

For the past few minutes, customers entering the New Inn had been muffled in cloaks heavily caked with snow, and there was talk from the wiseacres of a protracted spell of bad weather. All the signs, they said, pointed to a very cold season, and it would be a foolish man who ventured far afield.

The sudden noise of voices raised in altercation sounded from the room overhead, followed by the clatter of feet on the stairs and the violent slamming of the door that opened on to the street. Very few of the New Inn's customers took any notice, but Ned

Stoner did glance up briefly towards the smoke-blackened ceiling.

'Trouble?' I asked.

He shrugged fatalistically. 'Where there's gambling there's always trouble sooner or later. Too many young cocks nowadays, all swaggering and fighting with one another. They win money at dice or some such game of hazard, fill their bellies with cheap wine instead of decent ale, and think they're lords of the dunghill – until they sober up again and find themselves locked in the bridewell or the castle dungeons. The youth of today have it too easy,' he grumbled.

I hid a smile, for I knew him to be only a year or so older than myself. But I let it pass. 'Do you think it could be one of these young bravos who was responsible for Imelda Bracegirdle's murder?'

Ned grunted. 'More than likely. But I doubt if he'll ever be brought to justice. His friends'll protect him. Swear he was in their company, whenever it happened. Another cup of ale?' But his offer was half-hearted.

I refused and got to my feet. 'I think we'd both best be off home before the weather gets any worse.'

Ned agreed, although our caution did not seem to be shared by the rest of the customers. The ale-room was just as crowded and noisy as when we arrived, and our seats were taken almost as soon as we vacated them. We threaded our way between the tables and out into the passageway, where two young men were just mounting the stairs to the upper room. A third stood inside the street door, stamping the snow from his boots, the light from a torch, in a wall-sconce above his head, illuminating his face.

Ned paused in surprise. 'Hello, Master Clement! Been let out on your own, have you? And not before time if you ask me!'

Irwin Peto started at the sound of Ned's voice, and I noticed that the hand which was fumbling with the strings of his cloak, was shaking badly.

'Are you all right, Master – er – Weaver?' I enquired solicitously, and received a black look for my pains.

'I'm well enough,' he snapped, and turned back to Ned. 'My father doesn't know I'm here. He thinks I'm asleep in bed, so I'd appreciate it if you didn't mention seeing me.' He added on a note of desperation, 'He keeps me like a prisoner, he's so afraid of losing me again.'

'I shan't say anything, you can be sure of that,' Ned answered cheerfully. 'Enjoy your freedom for a while. Goodnight.'

'Goodnight,' I echoed, and followed my drinking companion outside.

It was a fairy world. All Hallows raised a ghostly head, and every contour was rounded and softened by a mantle of glittering white. There was already a hint of frost in the air and, later on, it would freeze; but for the moment, Ned and I were almost blinded by a curtain of whirling snowflakes. As we emerged into the Corn Market, we could just make out, on the opposite side of the thoroughfare, the entrance to Small Street, and the church of Saint Werburgh standing sentinel on the corner. All sound was muffled, and we had taken several steps in the direction of the Tolzey, where Ned and I would part company, when we both stopped and glanced enquiringly at one another.

'Did you hear someone groan?' I asked.

My companion nodded. 'I thought I did.' We listened carefully and the sound came again. 'Back there,' he said, indicating the way that we had come.

We retraced our steps, the noise guiding us to the church, where, in the porch, a man lay huddled on the ground. I went down on one knee, gently turning him over so that we could see his face in the light from the lantern hanging from the ceiling.

Ned gasped. 'It's Master Burnett,' he said. 'And he's been pretty badly beaten, by the look of him.'

Chapter Nine

William Burnett was unconscious, but beginning to rouse a little, groaning and mumbling broken words. I bent lower, hoping to catch some of them, but they were too jumbled to make any sense. The weather was worsening and he must be got under cover as soon as possible.

I looked up at Ned Stoner, who was peering anxiously over my shoulder. 'Run and get two of the Burnetts' men to bring a litter. Meantime, I'll get him into the church where he will at least be out of this bitter cold.'

Ned said, 'Right!' and sped off down Small Street, while I pushed open the door of Saint Werburgh's and lifted Master Burnett inside. I hadn't long to wait. Indeed, I had only just laid my burden down again, when the door burst open and Alison appeared. The hood of her cloak had fallen back unheeded, and her hair was wet with snow. She was still wearing her velvet house shoes, not having paused either to change them or to strap on her wooden pattens. They and the hems of her gown and cloak were sodden.

'William!' she cried, crouching down beside her husband. She raised her eyes to mine. 'What's happened?'

I had no time to answer then, as the arrival of the Burnetts' menservants, carrying a hastily improvised litter of a blanket knotted between two poles, precluded any further conversation until we had William safely within doors. Once in the candlelit

101

warmth of the Small Street house, it was easier to ascertain how badly he was hurt. No bones appeared to be broken, but he was, nevertheless, severely bruised about the face, with a swollen and bloody nose, one eye half-closed and the other already beginning to discolour. The women of the household fussed and clucked about him, and Alison Burnett sent one of the maids to rouse the physician who lived nearby, in Bell Lane.

'And don't come back without him,' she instructed the hapless girl. 'The old charlatan won't want to come out on a night like this if he can help it. And you!' She rounded on one of the men. 'Go and inform the Watch what has happened. As for you, Ned Stoner, you can be off and take the news to my father. Not that I suppose he'll care!'

As she addressed no remark to me, I lingered, hoping that when William Burnett recovered his wits, he might be able to say who had attacked him. I suggested, therefore, that I carry him up to bed, an offer which was gratefully accepted. So, with the assistance of the other manservant, who took his feet, I manoeuvred William's inert form up the narrow, twisting stairs to the bedchamber he shared with Alison, and laid him tenderly on the red damask silk coverlet. As I did so, he stirred and opened his eyes.

'William! What happened?' his wife demanded, bending over him. 'You've been badly beaten. Who did it?' William stared blankly at her for a moment, then turned his head restlessly on the pillows. 'Who did it?' she repeated.

I was standing in the shadows, unnoticed by the injured man, but able to see him quite clearly in the light from the candle placed near the bed. His eyes opened again, but this time to full consciousness and, I could have sworn, to complete knowledge of what had befallen him. There was the sudden intake of a short, painful breath, and an awareness in every line of his face which told its own story. I felt sure that William Burnett knew who had set upon him and why . . .

His eyes glazed over, his features grew slack and his head rolled back towards Alison. 'Someone attacked me,' he muttered.

And very little more could be got from him in spite of her persistent probing. He had, as he reminded her, been on his way to the New Inn for a rummer of ale when, as he turned the corner of Small Street into the Corn Market by Saint Werburgh's church, a man with his hood drawn forward over his face had waylaid him, demanding money. When he had refused to surrender his purse, he had been beaten about the head and body until he lost consciousness, and knew nothing further until this minute.

I said quietly, 'Ned Stoner and I saw Irwin Peto in the Lattis, a few minutes before we found Master Burnett.'

William jumped at the sound of my voice as I stepped forward into the circle of light. 'Who . . . who's Irwin Peto?' he quavered.

I explained. 'Surely you must have been told the name by which Clement Weaver says he was known during all those lost years,' I added.

Alison snorted. 'Maybe we were informed of it, but we took no notice. We're not interested in the creature and his lies.' Her eyes kindled with sudden anger. 'William, do you think *he* might have attacked you? Perhaps he saw you, quite by chance, and decided to take his revenge because we refuse to acknowledge his claim.'

'Well, yes . . . I suppose it could have been him,' her husband admitted slowly. 'But I've no proof. And why should he demand money from me?'

'To throw you off the scent, of course.' Alison's face set in rigid lines of disdain. 'If Master Chapman and Ned Stoner hadn't seen him in the Lattis, we shouldn't have known that he was anywhere near at hand.'

'When the man hit you,' I put in, 'the strength of the blow might well have caused his hood to fall back from his face. Think,

103

sir! Do you recall getting a glimpse of his features?'

William shook his head. 'The first blow knocked me clean out of my senses.' He looked at his wife. 'But you may well be right, my love. It could have been the creature.'

I was puzzled. I remained convinced that William Burnett had recognized his assailant, and that it was not Irwin Peto. And in any case, why was it necessary for him to put a name to his attacker? Every town and city in the kingdom, then as now, is full of these birds of prey who haunt the streets after dark, robbing, maiming and murdering. If William insisted that he had been set upon by a common cutpurse, no one would think to query it. But if Alison carried an accusation against Irwin Peto to her father, as she was very likely to do in her present mood, it would only give the Alderman greater cause for offence than already existed.

The thought seemed to strike William at the same moment that it occurred to me, and he roused himself in sudden agitation, clasping his wife's arm. 'No, no! It wasn't the creature! I'm sure of it now! Alison, I forbid you to go to your father with this story. The man who set upon me was an ordinary footpad. You must believe me.'

His tone was urgent. Obsessed with keeping his secret, he had foolishly allowed himself to implicate another man, and he was now likely to rue this deception unless he could convince his wife of his change of heart. But it was obvious to me that Alison now considered the situation between herself and her father to be as bad as it could get, and she seemed to have abandoned all hope of a reconciliation. Her one pleasure, henceforth, would be to prove to the Alderman, as often as possible, the depraved nature of the man who claimed to be his son. It was also obvious that Alison regarded her husband's sudden retraction as no more than a ploy to curb her animosity; her soothing reassurances that of course she believed him, only serving to underline her incredulity. William must have realized this, too, for after a time, being in considerable pain, he gave up the struggle to convince her and lay back against the pillows, closing his eyes.

I decided, reluctantly, that I must take my leave. There was nothing more that I could do, and I was beginning to feel like an intruder. Besides, it was high time that I returned home. I had been absent for some hours and should no doubt be greeted with reproaches. And as neither Mistress Burnett nor her husband uttered a word to hinder my departure, I murmured my farewells and went downstairs and out into the street.

I can't pretend that my return was rapturously received by either my mother-in-law or my daughter, but I was used to Margaret's disapproving silences, and was growing accustomed to Elizabeth's indifference to me now that she had a playmate of her own age. Not, it appeared, that Nicholas Juett would be her companion for very much longer, a fact which explained his mother's smiling countenance.

'We've had a visit from one of the Lay Brothers of Saint James's Priory,' Adela said, almost before I had closed the door on the bleak scene outside. She rose from her stool, where she had been doing some mending, and took my wet cloak, shaking it so vigorously that the drops of melting snow hissed among the logs and sea-coal burning on the hearth. 'I can have temporary use of Imelda Bracegirdle's cottage, and maybe permanent tenancy if all goes well.'

'That is good news,' I said, a shade too heartily to please my mother-in-law, who looked sourly at me.

But I suspected that Margaret was not too unhappy at the prospect of her cousin's leaving. Two days had been ample time to prove to her that she did not care for sharing her home with another woman.

'When do you go?' I asked Adela.

She began shepherding the two children towards the bed and making preparations to wash them. 'Tomorrow. I wondered if I might count on you to help me with my things?'

'Of course you may,' my mother-in-law answered for me. 'You'll be happy to do anything you can, won't you, Roger?'

'Of course.' I sat on Adela's vacated stool to pull off my boots. 'And to lend Mistress Juett any money she may need until she finds employment.'

'Thank you, but that won't be necessary.' Adela poured hot water into a bowl, then added cold from the barrel in the corner. 'I have a little of my savings left, and tomorrow, Margaret has promised to speak to Alderman Weaver about me.'

'You'd do well to visit him early then,' I advised my mother-in-law, 'before his daughter has time to get to him.' And I related the events of my day whilst helping myself to some bread and cheese from the various food crocks that had been placed ready on the table against my return.

And later, when the two children were safely in bed – although not anywhere near asleep, judging by the chattering and giggling which reached our ears from behind the drawn curtain – I was forced to go over it all again as we ate our supper of dried salt beef and such stewed root vegetables as were obtainable at this season of the year.

'And you think Master Burnett knows who set upon him?' queried my mother-in-law, adding with a shrug, 'Well, he must have made plenty of enemies in his time. He's never been as popular as his father. He gives himself too many airs and graces. Thinks himself superior to his workmen. People resent that. But he's foolish if he drives a bigger wedge between his wife and father-in-law than exists already. According to what you say, that seems to have been your fault, Roger. Opening your mouth too wide as usual. If you hadn't mentioned seeing this Irwin

Peto, or whatever his real name is, entering the Lattis . . .'

The subject occupied us comfortably until bedtime, smoothing over any little awkwardness which might otherwise have arisen from Adela Juett's determination to quit her cousin's roof after less than three days. And I could still hear the two women discussing this latest piece of gossip long after they had retired for the night, their voices muted for fear of waking the now-sleeping children at the other end of the bed. I laid my own pallet as close to the dying fire as it was safe to do, took another blanket from the press, and hoped that not too much snow would drift through the smoke-hole in the roof. And the next thing I knew, it was morning.

It had stopped snowing, but was freezing hard, making conditions underfoot extremely treacherous. On inspection, the handle of the local pump was found to be immovable and the well water inches deep in ice. As soon as it was light, therefore, the men of the surrounding houses, including myself, were set to shovelling frozen snow into iron pots, which the women of the household then heated over the fire. I was thrown into the company of Jack Nym and Nick Brimble, both of whom were already in possession of the story concerning yesterday's assault on William Burnett.

'You and Ned Stoner discovered him, so I'm told, Chapman,' Nick Brimble said, pausing to wipe the moisture from his face, for, in spite of the cold, the exercise was making him sweat.

'And went home with him,' I agreed.

'They're saying – ' this was Jack Nym – 'that Mistress Burnett is laying blame for the attack on this fellow who claims to be her brother, and that Master Burnett also believes it might have been him.'

I wondered how, in the name of Saint Michael and all the angels, had he got hold of that piece of information? However dark the night, however appalling the weather, there must be constant communication between one household and the next, from one side of the bridge to the other. I hastened to set them straight on the matter.

'Master Burnett, it's true, did at first encourage her in that belief, but only for a moment. When he had had time to think about it properly, he denied it utterly and has forbidden her to spread the rumour. The misunderstanding was, according to my mother-in-law, in some respect my fault,' I admitted, and explained what had happened. 'My own feeling, for what it's worth, is that William Burnett knows who his attacker is, but isn't saying.'

Nick Brimble and Jack Nym glanced at one another and guffawed. 'Daresay he does know,' said the former.

'One of Jasper Fairbrother's men, no doubt,' agreed Jack, stretching his arms with the air of a man who had done quite enough shovelling on an empty stomach.

I knew of this Jasper Fairbrother by repute, and he had been pointed out to me on several occasions. He was a master baker who constantly flouted the law – in particular a city ordinance made four years earlier, protecting the livelihoods of the women hucksters whose right it was to sell loaves and pastries – but who escaped punishment by threatening his victims with condign retribution if they laid a complaint against him. He employed three or four hefty young bravos solely for this purpose, and had once, in a very roundabout fashion, tried to recruit me, but I had given his messenger extremely short shrift.

'What would Jasper Fairbrother have to do with William Burnett?' I asked, puzzled.

Nick Brimble grinned. 'They both like games of chance, dicing and suchlike. And they also share the shortcoming that afflicts a lot of rich men: they resent parting with their money when they lose. Word at the Lattis is that William Burnett has had a run of bad luck in recent months and owes Jasper

Fairbrother a goodly sum, so I reckon Jasper has at last lost patience and given him a warning. And if I'm right, it wouldn't be surprising if William wanted to keep Mistress Burnett in ignorance of what really happened.'

I grasped my shovel in one hand and picked up the iron pot full of frozen snow with the other. 'It would explain a good deal,' I admitted. 'I didn't know William Burnett was a gambler.'

'Always has been, like his father and grandfather before him,' said Jack Nym. 'They were rich men and could afford it, and so can William. It's just that he has this mean streak which makes him reluctant to discharge his debts until forced to do so. He's the same with his taxes, by all accounts. Mind you, he's generous to himself; never stints on any item of his dress or comfort for his home. Keeps a good table.'

'Simply doesn't like paying out money for anything that doesn't show a return,' added Nick Brimble.

I returned to the cottage, where my mother-in-law was waiting impatiently for the pot of snow, which she immediately placed on the fire. I retired to a corner, out of the women's way and until Margaret was ready to dole me out a measure of hot water for shaving, to mull over the information just imparted by Nick Brimble and Jack Nym. I had no doubt that what they had told me about William Burnett was true, for Bristol was their city and they were more attuned to its gossip than I was; for although I had lived there now for over three years, I was absent for long periods and had not the interest of a native in my neighbours. All the same, I had the temerity to question their judgement. On the face of it, it explained satisfactorily all that had happened; it made sense of my conviction that William Burnett knew his attacker – or at least understood the reason for the attack – and was therefore anxious to divert his wife's suspicion into a different channel. And yet, I could not bring myself to believe that this was really the answer. I felt there was a deeper mystery that I had not yet fathomed.

My mother-in-law's voice cut imperiously across my reverie. 'Roger! Here's some hot water and your razor. Get shaving, for heaven's sake! If you want to see Adela settled in during the best of the morning's daylight, you'll have to bestir yourself.'

Her words recalled me to my more immediate duty and I hastened to comply. Adela sent me a small, half-apologetic smile, which Margaret intercepted.

'I hope you're happy with what you're doing, Cousin,' she scolded, ladling oatmeal into the remains of the boiling water, 'taking a child of Nicholas's tender years to a cottage where there's been a murder only three days since.'

'Why should that bother me?' Adela enquired placidly, setting spoons and bowls on the table. 'Nick is too young to know what happened there, or to be disturbed by it if he did. As for myself, I can see no danger. Lightning rarely strikes in the same place twice, and I shall be very careful to bolt and bar the door and window at night.'

And with this, my mother-in-law had to be content. No doubt, she felt, virtuously, that she had done all in her power to persuade her cousin to stay, and was secretly pleased that her efforts had been resisted, provided that the two households remained in close touch. The one thing she obviously feared was that Adela and I would foil her plans for our marriage.

'You mustn't be afraid to call upon Roger whenever necessary,' she insisted at parting. 'And the children must spend some time together each day. They're fond of one another.' This was so indisputably true as to require no answer. My mother-in-law continued, 'I shall speak to Alderman Weaver about finding you work as a spinner this very morning.' She turned to me. 'Roger, it will be your job to purchase a spinning wheel for Adela, which will be our gift to you, my dear, in your new home.' And as her cousin started to protest, she lifted an admonitory finger. 'We shan't be denied, shall we, Roger?'

As we walked up High Street some twenty minutes later, Adela carrying her bundle of worldly possessions, I with Nicholas in my arms and both of us struggling to keep our feet on the hard-packed snow, my companion said quietly, 'You need not think that I'm unaware of Margaret's hopes and plans for us. Indeed, I think I guessed them before ever we reached Bristol, your manner was so distant and cautious towards me. And why else, I asked myself, had she sent you now, instead of waiting for Jack Nym to fetch us in the warmer weather?' Adela drew a deep breath. 'What I'm trying to say is that these schemes for our future are no more welcome to me than they must be to you, so please have no fear that I expect anything other than friendship between us.'

I turned my head and smiled at her. 'Thank you for being so frank. It clears away all constraint, and I hope that from now on, we shall indeed be good friends.'

She made no reply, but none was needed. We understood one another.

We made our way first to Saint James's Priory, and afterwards to the cottage in Lewin's Mead. One of the Brothers accompanied us as far as the door, his presence putting the seal of authority on our right to enter, in case any zealous neighbour should challenge it. No one did, however, although I had the impression of being watched by half a dozen or more curious pairs of eyes.

'Are the Sheriff's men any nearer to discovering Mistress Bracegirdle's murderer?' I asked the Brother.

He shook his head. 'The Sergeant is as certain as he can be that it was a passing thief, who tried the door, found it open and chanced his arm. When Mistress Bracegirdle confronted him, he killed her.'

'I can see you find it hard to accept that explanation,' Adela remarked when our escort had departed in the direction of the

Priory, huddled into his cloak against the bitter cold. 'May I know why?'

'Because,' I answered, ushering my charges into the cottage, 'it seems far more probable to me that a thief would have turned tail and run. Or if he were determined on violence, he would have used his fists or a stool to bludgeon her to death. Or even a knife to stab her, if one had happened to be lying handy on the table. But strangle her? No! It doesn't make sense. To do that, he must have taken her from behind, and surely she would never have turned her back on an intruder.'

'Maybe you're right,' Adela answered thoughtfully, and began to inspect her new home.

All was much as it had been, except that a three days' coating of dust now covered everything, and the remains of the murdered woman's last meal were beginning to smell. The dead ashes of Imelda's fire still lay on the hearth, and the cooking utensils that stood on a long shelf just inside the front door, proved, on inspection, to be none too clean. There was much to be done before the place could be rendered truly habitable. 'What do you wish me to do first?' I asked.

Before she could answer, however, there was a knock on the door and, being nearest, I opened it. Richard Manifold stood on the threshold.

Chapter Ten

'I've come to pay my respects, Mistress Juett,' he said, remaining outside the door, as though unsure of his reception. 'I heard that the tenancy of the cottage has been granted to you, and I want to say how pleased I am. Welcome home.'

Adela went forward, hands outstretched. 'Richard Manifold! I'm happy to see you again after all these years.'

I had never see her so animated, not even when greeting my mother-in-law, and I felt a small stab of irritation. Surely her cousin deserved a warmer response than a mere friend, however close to one another Adela and the Sheriff's Officer might have been in the past.

'Come in,' she invited, 'and shut the door. The weather's bitter.'

'I can't stop but a moment or two,' Richard Manifold protested, but doing as he was bidden. 'I'm on my way to Master Burnett's house. It seems he was attacked last night.'

Adela nodded, pushing forward one of the chairs, which she dusted with a corner of her cloak, and seating herself on the other. 'I know. It was Roger, here, and a man of Alderman Weaver's who found him and helped carry him home.'

Richard Manifold turned his head to look properly at me for the first time since his arrival and gave me a nod of recognition. '*You* found him, eh? Did Master Burnett give any indication who he thought might be responsible for the assault? Did he mention a name?'

I hesitated a moment before answering. 'There was some talk of this young man who claims to be Clement Weaver, but . . .'

The Sheriff's Officer cut me short. 'That accounts for it, then.' In response to our raised eyebrows, he went on, 'One of our Sergeants was called to Alderman Weaver's house in Broad Street earlier this morning to deal with a disturbance between Mistress Burnett and two of her father's servants, who had been ordered to remove her bodily from the premises. She was in a great sweat, my friend said, pouring out a torrent of abuse on the Alderman's head, and calling him by names which no respectable matron should even know, let alone make use of.'

Adela gave a little snort of laughter. 'And did they manage to remove her?' she asked.

Richard Manifold shrugged. 'As far as I can gather, Mistress Burnett was eventually persuaded to let one of her father's men take her home, before she was charged with causing a public affray.' He shook his head sadly. 'A bad business, that. A very bad business. She's been a good daughter to the Alderman, and for the old fool to take against her in such an unreasonable fashion is a great shame. But she's just as pig-headed. She won't consider for a minute that this man who says he's her brother might be telling the truth.' He waved a dismissive hand. 'However, I didn't come to discuss the affairs of my neighbours, but to welcome you back to Bristol, Mistress Juett. Though I must say,' he added, 'that that name sits uneasily on my tongue, for Adela Woodward you've always been to me, and always will be.'

'That was a long time ago,' she smiled. 'I'm the Widow Juett now with a two-year-old son, and no doubt you're a father yourself, Richard.'

'I've never married,' he answered simply, looking at her with a soulful expression which, for some unknown reason, deepened my irritation and made me long to knock both their heads together.

My companion, however, suddenly seemed to sense danger in the situation. 'It was kind of you to call,' she said hurriedly, 'but as you can see, there is much work to be done here if I'm to make the cottage habitable by Nicholas's bedtime.' And suddenly recollecting her son, she looked around to see what mischief he was up to, only to discover him sitting on the floor at the back of the room, quietly playing among the rushes.

Richard Manifold, with a sigh and a thought to his own duties, took the hint and also his leave, but not before promising to return later in the day to see how she was faring. 'For there's still a deal to talk about,' he added comfortably. 'No doubt you'll want to know what's become of your old friends and neighbours.'

Adela could have said that her cousin had already told her all that she wished to know, but she didn't, increasing my festering annoyance yet further. She was so calm, so self-contained, so self-possessed. It surely must be as obvious to her as it was to me that the Sheriff's Officer was presuming on what I guessed to have been an unequal friendship in order to renew their acquaintance, and to ensure a comfortable billet for his bachelor evenings during the long winter months ahead. Why then did she not send the fool packing with a flea in his ear? Why encourage a man who, I arrogantly concluded, was not worthy of her notice?

Not, of course, that it mattered to me who Adela Juett chose as her intimates, but, I told myself, I was indignant on my mother-in-law's behalf. Margaret had set great store by her cousin's return, and I resented anyone who might deprive her of Adela's wholehearted attention and company.

'What do you wish me to do first?' I asked when the door had finally closed behind Richard Manifold, repeating my question of half an hour earlier.

But once again the reply was delayed as Adela cried sharply, 'Nicholas! What are you up to?'

She went across to her son and fell on her knees beside him. I followed suit, and was interested to discover that the cottage floor, when swept clear of rushes – Nicholas having busily created a space all round him – revealed stone flags, and not the beaten earth that I would have expected. But this was not all. With his strong little fingers, and at the cost of a broken fingernail or two, the child was trying to prise free one of the flags which stood proud of its fellows.

'Nick,' his mother scolded, 'just look at your hands! They're filthy. And we've no water as yet to wash them.' She glanced frowningly at me. 'I shall have to get that slab hammered down. It could be dangerous. One of us could easily trip over it.'

'Undoubtedly,' I agreed. 'That's probably how Nicholas discovered it. I'll secure it for you before the day's out, but first let's see if there's anything underneath which might have caused it to rise.'

I was able to raise the flag, which was some nine or ten inches square, with surprising ease, disclosing a shallow cavity cut into the earth in which it was bedded; a cavity about three inches deep and slightly smaller in area than the stone, which normally fitted comfortably on top of it. I put in a hand and felt all round.

'The bottom of the hole is lined with a thick waxed cloth,' I said. 'Feel for yourself.'

Obediently, Adela did so. 'A hiding place, evidently and recently disturbed. What . . . What do you think it was for?'

I pursed my lips. 'Your friend, Richard Manifold, told me it was common gossip that Mistress Bracegirdle had a hoard of gold secreted somewhere in this cottage. He thinks it's what her murderer was looking for, and hazarded the opinion that she kept it in that chest under the window. But if she did have any such hoard, this would have been a much better hiding place for it.'

Adela raised thoughtful eyes to mine. 'And the fact that it's now empty would suggest that whoever killed her knew exactly where to look for the money. Not a chance thief, then, but one with a fell purpose in mind. Maybe even someone she knew and to whom she had entrusted her secret.' She nodded solemnly. 'You were right. Imelda probably did know her killer and let him into the cottage. And after the robbery, he was in too much of a hurry to put the stone back properly.'

I replaced the flag and it fitted snugly between its fellows, removing any necessity to hammer it down. But this very snugness presented a problem of its own: how was it normally lifted?

This part of the room, furthest from the window, was gloomy, and I asked Adela to see if the cottage boasted a tinder-box and some rushlights. She discovered the former on the shelf alongside the pots and pans, together with a lamp, and when this was lit, she carried it over and set it down beside me on the floor. In its pallid glow, I could just make out a deep notch chiselled into the flagstone.

I raised the lamp and looked around the room. 'There must be a lever somewhere which is inserted into this groove and lifts the slab. Can you see anything anywhere of that description?'

'There's something over there, lying among the rushes,' Adela said. 'I noticed it earlier and wondered what it was for.' She got to her feet and took several paces across the room, returning with a hooked iron bar, somewhat rusty and beginning to flake along the shaft. 'Could this be it, do you think?'

'Yes, indeed. Well done!' I said approvingly. I took it from her and fitted the hooked end into the groove. The flagstone lifted with very little exertion on my part and was as easily lowered into place again.

'Should we tell the Sheriff's Officers of our find?' Adela asked me.

'I think we must, although I doubt if it will alter their opinion that the murderer was a passing thief. Officers of the law can be very thick-headed sometimes,' I added nastily.

She knew at once that it was a sneer at Richard Manifold's expense, and looked puzzled, as well she might. I had no clear idea myself what it was that I had against the man. I rose to my feet and was about to put the lever under the bed, out of the reach of Nicholas's questing little fingers, when I became conscious of two or three fine silk threads caught on a patch of the rusting metal. I must have exclaimed, for Adela asked excitedly, 'What is it? What have you found?'

For answer, I carried the iron bar over to the window, Adela following me, and opened the casement slightly to let in more light. It had begun to snow again, and a few flakes drifted through to settle on our shoulders.

'Look here,' I said, 'at these strands of silk. They must have come from the clothing of whoever last used the bar.' And, very gently, I detached them, laying them across my outstretched palm.

My companion put out a cautious hand, and they stirred in the current of air cased by her movement. 'Two black and one red thread,' Adela remarked thoughtfully, 'and of a very fine silk. I don't know much about Mistress Bracegirdle, but I should doubt she owned a gown as good as this.'

I wound the threads around my forefinger, and handed them to her. 'Give these to your friend, Richard Manifold, when he returns tonight, and explain how you came by them. And now,' I went on, without giving her time to reply, 'for the third time of asking, what do you wish me to do first?'

When I finally set out for my mother-in-law's house in Redcliffe, darkness was already closing in and it was almost the hour for curfew. I was bone-weary, for this was by no means the first time that day that I had traversed the Frome Bridge. I had crossed and recrossed it on various trips to and from the market; for as well as fetching water and chopping firewood, spreading fresh rushes and helping to make up the bed, there had been food and other necessities to buy. And it seemed to me that each time I returned, Adela had thought of something else she needed, but which she had previously forgotten to mention.

In the end, she had been forced to borrow some money from me, for her meagre funds were running dangerously low. While we ate our dinner – some eel pies that I had bought from a pie-maker's stall near the Tolzey – she had told me a little more about herself and her marriage to Owen Juett. I gathered that it had not been a happy union, and suspected that she had regretted it almost as soon as she had arrived in Hereford. Owen had been a poor man, a cooper's assistant, who had never acquired the necessary skills to set up on his own account, and whose untimely death had left her with nothing. Such money as she had, had been earned by her own efforts at the inn where Jack Nym had met her.

'You mustn't pity me or feel sorry for me,' she had added. 'I knew my husband's circumstances before I married him, and was headstrong and foolish enough to despise the advice of friends and kinsfolk. Also, to make matters worse, Owen and I were inclined to blame one another for our childlessness. Then when, after five years, we finally had our longed-for son, Owen only lived just another twelvemonth. He died during an outbreak of the plague last spring.'

In spite of my earlier determination not to become involved in Adela's affairs, I had found my sympathy and interest beginning to be engaged to an alarming degree. I had therefore been extremely relieved when the reappearance of Richard Manifold put a period to my stay. I had taken my leave with an alacrity that had been almost offensive, and had turned a deaf ear to Adela's invitation to visit her the following day, if I could spare the time. I had left her to her admirer's company and thankfully made my way home.

Margaret was awaiting my arrival with impatience, and wanted to know every detail of the day; while Elizabeth, robbed of her playfellow, climbed on to my knees and vied for my attention with an incomprehensible spate of childish babble. I answered their demands as best I could, hoping that my replies to my daughter would make more sense than her questions – if that was what they were – did to me. As for my mother-in-law, I was able to satisfy her curiosity, although the information that I had left Adela in the company of Richard Manifold greatly displeased her. And when I added that it was his second visit of the day, she folded her lips and did not speak again for several minutes.

However, my revelation, which I had saved until last, about the secret hiding place under the floor, jolted her out of her sulks and rekindled her interest.

'What do you think Imelda used it for?' she asked, dipping salted herring in oatmeal and beginning to fry it in a pan over the fire.

'The obvious answer, in view of what happened to her,' I said, 'is money. But another question is: Did Mistress Bracegirdle make, or have made, the hiding place, or did she inherit it along with the cottage? Did a previous Priory tenant dig it out of the floor beneath the flagstones? And if so, did Imelda Bracegirdle even know that it was there?'

'But you said the flagstone had recently been lifted,' my mother-in-law objected, pausing in the act of turning the herrings.

'Yes. But while it's possible that the person who killed her might have known of the hiding place, she might not have done,' I suggested.

Margaret immediately, and quite rightly, scouted this idea. 'Nonsense! John Bracegirdle rented that cottage from the Priory for many, many years, long before he married Imelda Fleming. Indeed,' she added, warming to her theme, 'it's more than likely that he was the one who had this safe place made. Or, rather, dug it out himself, for it's doubtful he'd have trusted anyone else to do it and keep the secret. He had the reputation of being a miser. Whether it was deserved or not, I've no idea; but for whatever reason the hiding place was created, there can surely be no argument that Imelda would have known of its existence. Therefore, if she did indeed inherit money from her husband, that's where she would have put it for safekeeping. Not,' she went on, placing the herrings in a dish which she then handed to me, 'that there was ever any sign of Imelda being a wealthy woman. If she had money, she must have been as great a miser as John.'

'And there seems to be no proof for that rumour,' I said, setting Elizabeth on the floor and beginning to eat my belated supper.

'True. It's all conjecture.' My mother-in-law removed the empty pan from the heat and laid it to cool on the hearthstone. 'Nevertheless, Imelda Bracegirdle has been murdered and this hiding place, according to you, has been disturbed. I should say that there's only one conclusion to be drawn from those two facts.'

'Not necessarily,' I objected, but more for argument's sake than from conviction. Imelda Bracegirdle must have known what the iron bar with the hooked end was for, or she would never have kept it all those years. And more than ever, I felt certain that my theory that she had known her murderer was the correct one. I could not believe that a chance thief would have known where to search for her gold; and I wondered what Richard Manifold had made of this additional information that Adela must, by now, have laid before him. And that thought, in its turn, reminded me of what he had told us concerning Alison Burnett.

My mother-in-law, however, was already in possession of the facts, having been paid a visit by Goody Watkins.

'I should have got around to telling you eventually,' she said, 'when I remembered it.'

She sat down suddenly on a stool, and I thought how uncommonly pale she looked. Margaret, it was true, never had many roses in her cheeks during the winter months, but today her complexion was the colour of chalk.

'Are you feeling ill?' I asked her.

'A little light in the head, that's all,' she answered. 'If you'll draw me a cup of ale from the barrel, I'll do well enough.' And when I had fetched it for her and she had sipped a little of it, she did indeed seem better. 'Now,' she went on, setting down her cup, 'what were we talking about?'

I returned to my herrings. 'You were saying that you already knew about the scene between Mistress Burnett and her father this morning.'

'Ah, yes! Goody Watkins paid me a visit sometime after dinner.' Margaret smiled faintly. 'Presumably, by then, all her army of spies had reported back to her.' Encouraged by my snort of laughter, she continued, 'Someone had met Ned Stoner by the High Cross and been told that Mistress Burnett had come ranting and raving to the Alderman's door almost before it was light, accusing her self-styled brother of attacking her husband last night by Saint Werburgh's Church. Ned Stoner claimed she was well-nigh hysterical, and that having gained entrance to her father's house, and the two gentlemen not being out of bed, she went rushing upstairs and set about the younger man like an avenging fury, tearing out tufts of his hair and scratching his face until it bled. The Alderman tried to intervene, but got the same treatment for his pains, and had to send one of the maids to fetch Rob Short and Ned to remove her from the house. He also sent for one of the Sheriff's Officers to enforce the law and threaten her with causing an affray. According to Ned, she went in the end, in floods of tears and shaking all over, as though she had an ague.'

I finished my herrings and pushed my plate to one side, before starting on the oatcakes and cheese that my mother-in-law put in front of me. I recalled Richard Manifold's words. 'A bad business,' I said. 'A very bad business.'

Margaret sighed and rose wearily from her stool to put Elizabeth to bed. 'It is that,' she agreed. 'Alderman Weaver looked very ill to me when I called on him this afternoon, to beg a place for Adela among his spinners. That girl of his will be the death of him if she's not very careful.'

'They'll be the death of each other,' I said. Evidently Mistress Burnett disbelieved her husband's denial that Irwin Peto was the one who had attacked him. What a fool the man was ever to put the notion into her head. Unwisely, I spoke my thought aloud.

'By your account, it was you who first mentioned the impostor – if indeed he is that. *You* told Master Burnett that you and Ned Stoner had seen him in the Lattice,' my mother-in-law chided me.

I should have remembered that Margaret had a good memory, particularly for those details one would prefer her to forget. I changed the subject. 'You haven't yet said what Alderman Weaver's response was to your request about Adela. Was he agreeable?'

'He was graciousness itself, and asked me to tell her to present herself at the baling sheds to collect her wool as soon as she liked, and he would see that word was passed along to the overseer by this evening. We must buy a spinning wheel for her, Roger, as we promised. Tomorrow morning, you must go to the carpenter's in Temple Street and get her the best one that he has in his shop. And I'll go to Lewin's Mead and give her the news. Elizabeth can go with me. She'll like to see Nicholas again.'

She was as good as her word, and set out immediately after breakfast the following morning, although she looked so unwell that I begged her not to go. There had been yet another severe frost during the night, and now it was snowing once more.

'Stay here in the warm with Elizabeth. I'll visit Adela as soon as I've been to Temple Street,' I added.

But my offer was spurned. 'The fresh air will do me good,' was her only answer.

I could do no more and completed my errand at the carpenter's before returning home to collect my pack. I had no intention of going far beyond the city walls in such weather, but I needed to make some money, and people reluctant or unable to go out in the snow welcomed goods brought to their doorsteps. It was well past dinner-time when pangs of hunger sent me back over the bridge to Redcliffe, my mouth already watering in anticipation of one of Margaret's winter stews.

But when I pushed open the cottage door, there was no savoury smell to greet me. Instead, I found my mother-in-law slumped down beside the bed, unconscious, while my daughter sat beside her, sobbing with fright and clutching her grandmother's arm.

'Granny ill,' Elizabeth informed me, raising her tear-blotched face.

Chapter Eleven

By the evening, my mother-in-law was in a high fever which lasted several days and which, at one point, I thought would be the death of her. As it was, it left her debilitated and bedridden for weeks afterwards, and she did not fully recover her health and strength until the beginning of April.

Adela came daily to the cottage and nothing was too much trouble, either for her or for our neighbours. Mistress Burnett, on hearing of our difficulties, sent and paid for the services of the physician from Bell Lane, who dosed Margaret with lozenges of dried lettuce juice, in order to reduce the fever, and a distillation of rosemary and rue which, he assured me, had a purging effect upon the body. All in all, I was the recipient of more kindness that I would have thought possible, and probably of far more than I deserved. Even so, a great deal of extra work fell upon my shoulders.

I had previously had no notion of how demanding, and what hard work, a child of two years old could be. My mother-in-law had seen to all Elizabeth's needs, and when my daughter woke in the night, which seemed an all too frequent occurrence, had roused herself to dance attendance. Now it was my turn, and I was no longer assured of unbroken sleep. In addition, during the early stages of Margaret's illness, she was in need of constant nursing, and there were no willing helpers during the small hours on whom I could call. I often started the day as tired as I finished it.

As I said, Adela came every morning to see how the patient did and to perform those more intimate female tasks which delicacy forbade me attempting. Nevertheless, she could not stay longer than an hour or two, for she now had a living to earn for herself and Nicholas, and was unable to neglect her spinning. This also applied to those other neighbours who dropped in and out during the short winter afternoons; but one or other of these good women would arrange to sit with my two womenfolk, so that I was able to get out of the house and peddle my wares from door to door.

I could not go far, however, even had I wished to. The weather was equally as bad, if not worse than, the preceding winter, with hard night frosts freezing the closely packed snow, and then more snow falling during the day. The dirty white mounds at the roadside grew steadily higher, wells froze over (including the great Pithay well near Christchurch with Saint Ewen), and, worst of all, the great cistern of the Carmelite Friars, filled by a stream which flowed downhill from the heights above the city and which was now reduced to the merest trickle, began to dry up. Water from this cistern was piped across the Frome Bridge and fed the conduit by Saint John's Arch, so it meant that yet another burden was added to the hardships of the season with the necessity of melting lumps of frozen snow before anyone could wash or drink. Even the rubbish set solid in the open sewers, but at least it did not stink so much as usual.

In these circumstances, my life was reduced to getting through each day as best I could, with no spare time to pursue my promise to assist in the mystery of Clement Weaver.

'When my mother-in-law is well again and the better weather comes and I can travel abroad once more,' I assured Mistress Burnett, meeting her by the High Cross one bleak morning in late February, 'then you may be certain that I shall resume my enquiries.'

Her nostrils were pinched, her lips blue with cold and she was shivering uncontrollably in spite of her fur-lined cloak, but she paused politely to hear me out. 'I understand,' she said, adding that she had no expectations from me as matters stood at present. Greatly daring, I asked her how her father was faring in these icy conditions, only to be fixed with a basilisk stare. 'I neither know nor care,' was the embittered answer.

'And Master Burnett,' I continued hastily, 'has he quite recovered from the attack?'

'He is perfectly himself again, thank you, Chapman,' she said and walked on down High Street. After a few paces, however, she stopped and glanced over her shoulder. 'But I shall expect to see you, and hear of your plans, when it grows warmer and Mistress Walker has regained her strength.'

I reassured her for a second time, and went on my way along Broad Street and across the Frome Bridge to Lewin's Mead, to see if Adela had enough wood chopped to last her for the next few days. It was no surprise to discover Richard Manifold there, for he was to be found visiting the cottage as often as not. I had become inured to his constant presence, and no longer resented it as I had done in the beginning. Nothing had been made by him or his fellow officers, or even by the sheriff himself, of the secret hiding place under the floor and the silk threads caught on the iron bar which lifted the flagstone. They had all settled it in their minds that the murderer of Imelda Bracegirdle was a chance thief who was unlikely ever to be brought to justice; not, that was, unless some other villain, jealous of his friend's sudden wealth, revealed his name and whereabouts to those in authority. As for the unknown's knowledge of the hiding place, Richard Manifold had argued that those kind of secrets were bound to reach somebody's ears eventually. So interest in the mystery had gradually dwindled from being a nine days' wonder to being no wonder at all, and by the beginning of March the killing was rarely mentioned.

I saw Irwin Peto once or twice around the town, and a couple of times drinking in the New Inn, but for the most part he kept within doors and the shelter of the Alderman's house, not even emerging for the great Candlemas procession. He needed no further excuses, of course, for this shadowy existence than the atrocious weather and his own impaired health; and I guessed he was relying on the fact that by the time spring arrived, people would have grown so used to the idea of Clement Weaver still being alive that all speculation concerning him would have ceased. I should have liked to speak to him again, but in spite of calling at the Broad Street house on several occasions to sell my goods, I saw neither hide nor hair of him, nor heard even a distant echo of his voice. I had the impression that Dame Pernelle had been told to confine me to the kitchen quarters, so that there was little danger of our meeting. I had served my purpose by confirming to the doting Alderman that the young man's story of his survival could be true.

By the beginning of April Margaret was fully recovered, putting the lethargy of the past six weeks or so firmly behind her and bustling about the cottage as though she had never been sick, in full command once more of her own domain and resentful of any interference, however well-intentioned. Neighbours were discouraged from doing anything other than enquiring after her health, and I was given to understand that, during the day at least, my absence was preferred to my presence. I was only too happy to oblige; and now that I was a free man again, I could turn my thoughts to Alison and William Burnett and my promise to them.

A sudden thaw, mid-March, had brought heavy flooding in its wake, causing the Friars' cistern to overflow and several of the pipes conveying the water to Saint John's Conduit to burst, but it had also been the harbinger of sunnier, milder weather. By the beginning of April, trees were a haze of green, primroses starred the woods with constellations of creamy-yellow blossoms, and purple-veined, honey-scented white violets trembled at the ends of their fragile stalks. Wild arum was starting to thrust its hooded head above the earth, dwarfing the wood sorrel and ground ivy, while along the river banks, the marsh marigolds' great golden cups were reflected in the rippling water. And as the hardships of winter receded and the balmier weather of spring brought the long-delayed promise of summer, my dreams were once again haunted by a vision of two blue eyes set in a delicate, tragic face, surrounded by an aureole of pale, corn-coloured hair.

'Can you and Elizabeth manage without me for a night or two?' I asked Margaret one morning at breakfast.

'I should think so,' my mother-in-law answered drily. 'We've managed without you for years. Why should it be any different now? I'm fully recovered.' She eyed me thoughtfully across the table. 'When you say a night or two . . .'

I tried not to look guilty. 'Maybe a week. I have to go to Frome on business for Mistress Burnett. The Alderman's cousin-by-marriage lives at Keyford.' I knew I must sound self-conscious when I said the last word.

Happily for me, the name of the village meant nothing to Margaret, for I had made light of the events of last summer when recounting them to her after returning home. Indeed, I doubted if my story had lodged in her memory for the length of time that it had taken me to tell; and I had not dwelt on the fact that I had delayed my return still further in order to escort Rowena Honeyman from Keynsham to her aunt's house at Keyford, for fear of giving myself away. For until I had set eyes on this beautiful girl, robbed of her father in such a painful and tragic fashion, I had never believed in love at first sight, nor had I had much interest in romances and the great lovers of history; Tristan and Isolde, Lancelot and Guinevere, Abelard and Eloise. Now, however, their stories were meat and drink to me. I lived, when left to myself, on what seemed a higher plane than the rest of my unfortunate fellow beings; I dreamed of doing impossible feats of chivalry which would win me the love and adoration of this lovely creature. In short, I was behaving like the most callow of youths, although at the age of twenty-four I should have known better.

Over six months had passed since I had last clapped eyes on the lady, and I hoped that sufficient time had elapsed for her to have put behind her the sad circumstances of our first and, so far, only meeting. If the coincidence of Baldwin Lightfoot also living in Keyford had not occurred, I should soon have made an excuse to visit the village. As it was, I could, with a clear conscience, combine my own most fervent desires with my promise to the Burnetts; and I set out at the beginning of April, in the direction of Frome, with a light heart and a spring in my step.

I have already written, earlier in this history, that while I was to play no active part in the political events which were unfolding in the country at large, I was, nevertheless, to be a close spectator and to have an intimate knowledge of them, simply because I chanced to be in the right place at the right moment. I had been at Tewkesbury in January, where I had learned from my old friend, Timothy Plummer, of what were thought to be the Duke of Clarence's marital intentions, now that both his wife and Charles of Burgundy were dead; but after reaching Bristol, the gossip had gradually faded from my mind, there having been too many, and more personal, matters to absorb my attention. And as I approached Keyford on a seemingly quiet and uneventful morning, some three days after leaving home, nothing could have been further from my expectations than to witness another chapter in this sorry saga of royal brother versus royal brother.

My chosen route had eventually brought me out on to the high ground south-west of the old Saxon settlement of Frome, where the village of Keyford looks down on its larger neighbour. I had spent the previous night very comfortably on the kitchen floor of Nunney Castle, where I had begged admission just as it had been growing dark. Sir John Poulet, its present tenant, was from home, at his principal seat of Basing, in Hampshire, and the servants left to man the castle in his frequent absences had welcomed me in with open arms, glad of a fresh face and voice to break the monotony of existence. This morning, I had been up betimes and, fortunately for me, so had the cook. I had been feasted on buttered eggs, wheaten – not oaten – cakes and small beer flavoured with honey and cinnamon. Long before sun-up, I was walking steadily north-east to Keyford which I reached round about midday, having stopped for my dinner at a wayside cottage, where the goodwife, as well as feeding me, had also bought some things from my pack. Added to all this, I had the prospect of seeing Rowena Honeyman again. Small wonder then that I was whistling as I approached the huddle of houses whose roofs I could just make out ahead of me.

'You're very cheerful, Roger,' a voice said reproachfully out of this seemingly empty landscape.

I nearly jumped out of my skin and whirled around, raising my cudgel, ready to strike.

'For God's sake, softly, man! Softly!' urged the voice, which I now recognised as that belonging to Timothy Plummer.

A moment later, I saw him sitting beneath an ancient oak, some of whose branches reached out to spread across the road.

'By the Virgin, you gave me a fright,' I protested, clambering up a little knoll to join him and throwing myself down by his side. 'What on earth brings you to this part of the world?'

'You're a great gawky fellow,' he complained, forced to shift himself so that I could lean my back against the tree trunk. 'What did your mother have in her milk to make you so big?'

'Never mind that. You haven't answered my question. What brings you here?'

'Information,' was the uninformative reply.

'All right,' I said, gathering up my cudgel and pack. 'If you don't want to tell me . . .'

He pushed me down again. 'Don't get offended.' He nodded towards the sleepy houses, basking quietly in the sun, and I realised that from this vantage point, we could plainly see the whole of Keyford laid out before us. 'It looks peaceful enough, doesn't it? I'm beginning to wonder if I'm not here on a wild goose chase, after all.'

'What are you expecting to happen?' I asked curiously, adding, 'Nothing much ever does here.'

The Duke of Gloucester's Spy-Master rubbed the tip of his nose. 'I don't suppose much news of what's been going on in the outside world has reached you in Bristol, has it? No, I thought not,' he continued sourly, when I shook my head. 'I never knew such a city for being so engrossed in its own petty affairs or in those of its immediate neighbours. The inhabitants always know more about Wales and Ireland than they ever do about London, let alone France.'

'Tell me, then,' I invited. 'What *has* been happening in this great outside world of yours that's so important?'

Timothy Plummer grimaced. 'The Duke of Clarence, my boy! He's what's been happening.'

'Brother George?' I frowned. 'I remember now that when we met in Tewkesbury, you told me that Duke Richard was afraid he'd offer for Mary of Burgundy's hand in marriage . . . He didn't, did he?'

'Almost at once. And, of course, Dowager Duchess Margaret

132

lent him all her support. But by God's grace, and as Duke Richard had predicted she would, Mary refused him.'

'But that wasn't the end of the story?'

My companion shrugged. 'Knowing Clarence, would you expect it to be?'

I reached into my pack and produced two apples that the goodwife had given me from her winter store, to sustain me during the remainder of my journey. I handed one to Timothy and we munched for a moment or two in silence.

'I also seem to remember, ' I said at last, 'that at that same meeting, you prophesied Duke George would blame the Queen and her family if Duchess Mary did refuse him.'

Timothy took another bite of his apple and nodded gloomily. 'Which is precisely what he has done. But then, you don't need to be an astrologer to forecast Clarence's reactions. All his life he's been like a spoilt child, stamping its little feet and screaming, "Look at me! Look at me!"'

'I know he's always hated the Queen and the rest of the Woodvilles. But be fair! The marriage must have come as a nasty shock to him.'

'It came as a nasty shock to everyone,' snorted Timothy. 'Duchess Cicely ranted and raved at the King for days, and even went so far as to hint at his bastardy. But it's all a long time ago now; thirteen years since the wedding, and everyone has learned to make the best of it. Or, at least, to dissemble their feelings.'

'Except the Duke of Clarence,' I murmured. 'So, what has he been up to?'

Timothy shrugged. 'So far he's contented himself with being as unpleasant as possible. He's absented himself from court without the King's permission on a number of occasions. Then, when he does deign to put in an appearance, he makes his Chief Taster taste every morsel of food and drop of drink before it passes his lips, the inference being, of course, that the Queen and her relations are trying to poison him. His manners, even towards his elder brother, are atrocious, while he treats Earl Rivers as though he isn't there at all. Still, the King must take some share of the blame for that. His Highness put the cat among the pigeons as far as his brother-in-law's concerned.'

I was intrigued. 'What did he do?'

Timothy regarded me in exasperation.. 'You really don't hear anything down here in this western fastness, do you? Or is it simply that any news that doesn't concern trade and market prices isn't interesting to the people of Bristol?'

'Just tell me a plain story,' I begged. 'I must move on soon.'

'The King,' Timothy explained, and grinned with sudden pleasure at the recollection, 'offered Earl Rivers as England's official candidate for the new Duchess of Burgundy's hand. He guessed, naturally, that Mary would refuse Anthony Woodville – which she did, even more peremptorily than she had Clarence – but he knew how the offer would infuriate his brother, and I suppose he couldn't resist cutting George down to size. The trouble is,' my companion added, the grin fading, 'there was an almighty row, and Duke Richard is being forced, as usual, to play piggy-in-the-middle. His health is suffering accordingly, and he looks thinner and more careworn than ever.'

This I could well imagine, for the Duke of Gloucester seemed to have spent the whole of his adult life acting as peacemaker between his two remaining elder brothers. That he appeared to love them both equally was his misfortune, for his loyalty still lay as it always had done, with King Edward.

'So, what has all this to do with your being here, in this out-of-the-way spot?' I asked yet again.

Timothy took the last bite from his apple and threw away the core. 'This out-of-the-way spot,' he reminded me, 'is part of Clarence's holdings in this county, and Farleigh Castle can't be many miles distant. One of my spies in Duke George's household thinks mischief may be brewing here, but he's unable to discover exactly what. All he's heard so far is the merest whisper, the merest breath of rumour. He's one of my very best men, which means that if there is any truth in the story, the Duke must, for once, be keeping the details extremely close – which in itself is a worrying sign. Clarence usually can't keep his mouth shut.'

I was still nonplussed. 'But there's nothing and no one of any importance here,' I protested. 'What harm could he – or she or it – possibly do either to His Highness or to the Woodvilles in Keyford?'

'It might not necessarily be physical harm,' Timothy demurred. 'Insult, insinuation, both are grist to Clarence's mill in trying to stir up popular support and sympathy on his own behalf. Howbeit, I'm here to keep watch for a day or two. If nothing comes of it . . .' Once again, he shrugged. 'Like you, I'm baffled by my man's report, but I trust him enough not to ignore any of his information.' He glanced along his shoulder at me. 'Now it's your turn to tell me what brings *you* here.'

I knew he would be interested in my tale, for our friendship – if that is not too strong a word for it – had started during my hunt, six years earlier, for the missing Clement Weaver, and to some extent the search had involved both him and his master, the Duke of Gloucester.

He heard me out in silence and then laughed. 'Come and work for His Grace, Roger, as he's asked you to do on more than one occasion. You'd be invaluable to him – and to me. Your nose leads you straight into the thick of any mystery that's in the offing, and your natural curiosity won't let you rest until you've solved it.'

I scrambled to my feet, tossing my apple core into his lap, which he brushed clear of his excellent woollen hose with an exclamation of annoyance. 'No, thank you,' I said. 'I'm happy as I am, being my own master. I must be going. How long do you intend to remain here?'

'Until tomorrow perhaps, but no longer. Whereabouts does this Baldwin Lightfoot live?'

I nodded towards the scattering of buildings. 'Mistress Burnett says his house stands a little apart from the others, with a high-walled orchard adjacent, and I can see only one that answers that description. In any case, if I should prove to be wrong, an enquiry or two should soon locate him.'

I did not add that a cottage in the foreground, with pens for hens and geese, and a small pond behind it for ducks, was the most urgent object of my attention. However, I had already decided that pleasure must come after business, and therefore, with Timothy's eyes still upon me, I made my way along the street, pausing only to confirm from a passing stranger that Baldwin Lightfoot's was indeed the house with the orchard.

My informant was a local man, a woodsman judging by the billhook that dangled from one hand and the axe slung across his opposite shoulder. 'Ay, that's where Master Lightfoot lives all right. And next to him is the Widow Twynyho's, she as used to be one of the ladies-in-waiting to the poor young Duchess of Clarence, God rest her soul.' There was evidently some pride in this royal connection.

I thanked the man and walked on through the quiet of the afternoon towards Baldwin's house. As I approached it, I heard, very faint and as yet some miles distant, the rhythmic pounding of horses' hooves; and, every now and then, so still was the air, the jingle of harness.

Chapter Twelve

Baldwin Lightfoot's house was solidly built of local stone, too small to be a manor, but a substantial dwelling place, nonetheless. There was a capacious undercroft for storage, a paved courtyard in front and a garden behind. Alongside was the orchard, the tops of the trees just visible over the high wall that enclosed them.

I crossed the courtyard and knocked at the door. It was answered by an elderly woman in a gown of dark blue homespun and a bleached linen hood and apron, both of which were slightly soiled and crumpled. The bunch of keys jangling at her belt proclaimed her Baldwin's housekeeper.

'Is your master in?' I asked.

She took one look at my pack and said, 'Not to pedlars he isn't. But the girl and I might be interested if you'll come through to the kitchen.'

'I'm not selling anything,' I answered. 'I've been sent with a letter to Master Lightfoot from his cousin, Mistress Burnett of Bristol.'

The housekeeper eyed me doubtfully, disinclined to believe my story, but at the same time recognizing a certain ring of truth about it. 'Why would she send a chapman?' she demanded.

Fortunately, before it became necessary for me to embark on any sort of explanation, I heard a door open somewhere, and the next moment a man strolled into view. 'Who is it, Janet? Who is this person?'

He was tall, almost certainly over fifty, heavily built with what had once been a well-muscled frame now running to fat. In his younger days he had probably been very handsome, but his face had grown soft and flabby, melting into a travesty of its former good looks. The thinning brown hair, liberally streaked with grey, had receded far enough to reveal a high, domed forehead, and only the eyes, a clear, curiously light grey, retained any spark of youth. There were food stains on his clean-shaven chin, and an unpleasant, faintly sourish odour emanated from his clothes. Yet in spite of all this, he had a cocksure bearing and an air of self-satisfaction that instantly conveyed to the onlooker his pleasure in himself and in all his works.

'This pedlar claims he's been sent to you with a letter from Mistress Burnett, Master,' the housekeeper said, confirming, if confirmation were necessary, that this was indeed Baldwin Lightfoot.

'From my Cousin Alison?' He frowned, unable, in common with Dame Janet, to understand his kinswoman's choice of messenger. But the next moment, his attention, the attention of the three of us and indeed of the whole of Keyford, was distracted by what was taking place less than a hundred yards from his door.

While I had been standing there, the pounding hoofbeats had been growing ever louder, the jingle of harness more intrusive upon the ear, until now, suddenly, riders and mounts burst into view and were all about us in a flurry of plunging, rearing horses and shouted orders. Within moments of dismounting, armed men in the livery of the Duke of Clarence were smashing their way into a nearby house, not bothering to knock or wait for an answer to their summons, dealing summarily and brutally with anyone foolhardy enough to get in their way. From inside the walls there arose a terrible screaming, a female voice, hysterical with fear. A few minutes later, a woman, her arms pinioned, her face bleeding, was dragged outside and thrown across a saddle-bow with no more consideration than if she had been a sack of grain. Neighbours, lured from their houses by all the noise, stood petrified with terror by what was happening; by that constant and unseen danger which lurks in wait for all of us, and comes out of the blue to shatter our peaceful lives, even on the sunniest and quietest of days.

I turned, horrified, to Baldwin Lightfoot. 'What are they doing to that woman? Who is she? What has she done? For pity's sake, we must try to stop them!' I gripped his arm.

'Leave well alone, man! Leave well alone!' He dislodged my hand from his sleeve. 'It's none of our business. Come away! Come indoors!' And he fairly dragged me across the threshold, displaying an unexpected strength when roused.

It was my turn to fight free of him as I made once again for the door. 'We can't let her be abducted without raising a finger! If you and I and the rest of the men in this village stand together . . .' I did not stop to finish the sentence, but lifted the latch and ran across the courtyard, heading for the street.

But Baldwin Lightfoot lived up to his name. He was nimbler and speedier than I would ever have credited him with being, and was after me in a trice, throwing his arms around me in a vice-like grip. 'These people mean business,' he hissed in my ear.

I struggled furiously. 'Let me go! If you won't come with me, let me do what I can on my own. No need for you to be involved.'

'You've involved me already by being within my pale,' he retorted, his arms tightening about my waist. 'It will be noted that you came from this house and that will stand as a mark against me. Besides,' he added on a triumphant note, 'you're too late. They're on their way.'

He was right. The men-at-arms, having securely bound and gagged the unfortunate woman, and one of the bravos having mounted behind her, were off down the street as fast as they could gallop, and were soon nothing more than a cloud of dust on the horizon, a thudding of hooves growing ever fainter as they receded into the distance . . .

Silence seeped back again into Keyford, birds resumed their singing, sunlight dappled the grass and the rutted track, the delicate scent of apple blossom drifted over the orchard wall. The recent violence might have been no more than a bad dream but for the shattered door of the neighbouring house. It had all happened so fast and so unexpectedly that the inhabitants were wandering about in a daze, unable at first to speak. But gradually, they began to gather in little groups, muttering to one another, embracing one another for comfort, trying to make sense of what they had witnessed. Baldwin, releasing me, joined a knot of people gathered outside his gate.

'Why,' he asked no one in particular, ' would the Duke of Clarence send to arrest Widow Twynyho? She was lady-in-waiting to the late Duchess and a member of his household.'

There was a mumble of agreement, and one of the women added, 'Ankaret's such a gentle soul. What can she possibly have done to incur the Duke's displeasure, let alone be treated like that?' She shuddered. 'And we all stood by and did nothing.'

'What could we have done?' someone else demanded angrily.

But it was becoming obvious by the way in which people suddenly avoided one another's eyes, that a feeling of guilt was beginning to plague them. Yet it was sadly true that there really had been nothing that any of us could have done against armed men, not even if we had all banded together and acted in unison; and the element of surprise had robbed us of even that forlorn hope. Who, in any case, would dare to brave the wrath of the mighty Duke of Clarence, when his retribution was so terrible and swift? Whatever it was that Ankaret Twynyho had done to offend Brother George, nothing, surely, merited the sort of treatment meted out to her.

Brother George . . . The slightly derogatory title brought Timothy to mind, and I realized that I had, for the last fifteen minutes or so, completely forgotten his presence here. I glanced around, hoping to catch a glimpse of him, and was rewarded by seeing him skulking on the fringes of the crowd. I left Baldwin Lightfoot, still talking in low, incredulous tones to his neighbours, and made my way to his side. Timothy, however, saw me coming and withdrew even further apart, as though hoping to deter me. But I was not to be put off.

'Well, is this what you were waiting for?' I asked. Taking his silence for assent, I went on, 'What can it mean? I understand that the poor creature arrested, the Widow Twynyho, was lady-in-waiting to Duchess Isabel, and therefore presumably trusted by both her and the Duke. And why use her with such violence? Why does it need God knows how many armed men to arrest one defenceless woman?'

Timothy shrugged. 'To impress the incident on people's minds, maybe. To make sure it's talked about, that it's heard of well beyond the confines of Keyford and Frome. To publish the fact that this woman is a dangerous criminal. To make the world aware that George of Clarence is a very important person and that no one lightly invites his displeasure. Your guess is as good as mine at the moment, Chapman, but time will very quickly tell. In a week or two, probably less, we shall have the answer to this riddle. And now I have to return to my inn and collect my horse. I must be on my way to London within the hour. Duke Richard has come down from the north again to try to keep the peace between his brother, and I was ordered to report to him there as soon as possible should anything happen.'

He moved off briskly, not even pausing to say goodbye, and I stared after him for a moment or two before rejoining Baldwin Lightfoot. The latter seemed not to have noticed my absence, so engrossed had he and his neighbours been in a discussion of the last hour's events. An air of unreality still hung over them like a pall; their eyes and movements were those of sleepwalkers, but sleepwalkers who were afraid to wake up. Their small, cosy world had been shattered by a terror they did not understand, and it would never be the same again.

I had been looking for another face in the little knots of people that had gathered, but could not see it, although I fancied that one of the elderly dames was Rowena's aunt. I could not be sure, however, my memory of her being unclear; and in any case, I had promised myself to complete my business with Baldwin Lightfoot before seeking her out. I touched him on the arm and he jumped as though I had pricked him with a knife.

'Good God, man, don't do that!' He was white and shaken, his face the colour of uncooked dough. He added defensively, 'I didn't see you there. You startled me.'

'I'm sorry, but I have to be leaving soon, and I still have to deliver the letter from your cousin.'

For a moment Baldwin looked bemused, recent events having driven everything else from his mind, but then he recollected and nodded. 'Come inside,' he said. 'We need some wine to settle our stomachs.' He glanced towards his housekeeper, but she was so deep in conversation with two other women that he shrugged and obviously decided not to disturb her.

The house struck chill after the warmth of the April sun outside, and we both shivered. My host ushered me into a parlour hung with tapestries, all of which had seen better days. One, depicting the Judgement of Paris, had a great rent in it, while another was so faded that it was almost impossible to determine its subject matter without closer scrutiny. The room's one armchair had a broken leg that was propped up by a block of wood, and a carved chest, ranged along one wall, was badly splintered around the lock. An air of poverty and decay was all-pervasive.

Baldwin, who had briefly disappeared into the back of the house, returned with two beakers of wine, one of which he handed to me with the loud-voiced assurance that it was a good Bordeaux. I knew as little then about wines as I do now, but I had sufficient knowledge to recognize an English verjuice when I tasted it, and to be certain that its grapes had never been ripened by the hot southern sun. I took one unwary sip, almost choked and put the beaker down on the window seat beside me. Baldwin, happily, was still too bewildered by recent events to take much notice.

'Too potent for you, eh?' he asked. 'I thought it might be.' He sat down in the rickety armchair, passed a hand across his sweating forehead and took a gulp of wine. 'Ah!' he breathed. 'That's better.' He looked at me. 'Now, where's this letter?'

I took it from the pouch at my belt and handed it to him, observing him closely while he broke the seal and began to read. But if he was already aware of what it might contain, he gave no sign, and his amazement when he had finished it seemed genuine enough.

'Mother in Heaven!' he muttered, taking yet another swig at his cup, like a parched soul desperate for water. He got up and started pacing up and down the room. 'What a day this is turning out to be! First Widow Twynyho arrested and now my cousin writes to tell me that Clement has reappeared.' He sat down again abruptly and referred once more to the letter. 'No, that isn't exactly what she says . . . She says it is someone pretending to be Clement, and that Alfred has cut her out completely from his will . . . I'm at a loss. I don't understand it . . . Ah! But she does write that you will explain everything to me.' And he glanced up expectantly.

143

I did my best to satisfy his curiosity, and to do him justice, he was a good listener, such questions as he asked being both pertinent and necessary. Nor did I need to repeat myself, for he had a ready grasp of all the details, surprisingly so, perhaps, for one who had just suffered a severe shock and was now consoling himself with an ample draught of wine. When I had finished, he drained the dregs from his beaker, stared regretfully for a moment into its depths and then sat back in his chair, folding his hands over his paunch.

'A sorry affair! A sorry affair, indeed, and I don't wonder that my cousin is suspicious of this – what did you say his name is? – this Irwin Peto! But what help she thinks I can be to her in the matter is beyond my comprehension. My interference would only make things worse. Alfred never liked me, nor I him. I always thought the man a fool, and his present actions only serve to confirm my opinion. No one but an idiot would have accepted this young man at face value, simply because he bears a passing resemblance to Clement.'

I took another sip of verjuice, but its sharpness set my teeth on edge and I hurriedly put it down again. 'You think then,' I suggested, 'that Mistress Burnett might be right in considering it a plot to rob her of her inheritance?'

'I should say it's more than likely, wouldn't you? But what a couple of crass blunderers Alison and that husband of hers must be to make bad worse! Between them, they seem to have ensured that she'll get nothing at all, when she might at least have hung on to half of Alfred's money. Half a loaf is better than none. But there!' he added bitterly. 'I've no doubt that William Burnett really has no need even of that, being the sole inheritor of his father's fortune. "To those that hath shall be given . . ."' His voice tailed away, and he sat, staring before him, wrapped in thoughts of his own.

I was at a loss how to break the silence, for the purpose of my visit – to see and talk to Baldwin Lightfoot – had been accomplished; and I thought it unlikely, were he the instigator of the plot, that he would give anything away. He was a much shrewder man, with a much sharper mind, than first impressions had led me to believe, and he had obviously seen better days. It was a combination to make me pause and wonder if he were indeed our man – always provided, of course, that Irwin Peto really was a fraud.

Baldwin's voice, cutting across my thoughts, echoed them uncannily. 'Has my cousin considered,' he asked, tapping the letter, 'that this man may, after all, really be her brother? As far as I can tell from your story, while there's no proof that he *is* Clement, there's no proof either that he isn't. And you haven't answered my other question yet. What help does Alison imagine that I can be to her? And why does she feel it necessary to write to me with this news when we've neither seen nor communicated with one another for years!'

I feigned ignorance. 'Mistress Burnett didn't confide in me, sir. She knew I was visiting an acquaintance in Keyford and merely asked me to deliver the letter.'

It was a mistake. Baldwin shot upright in his chair, fixing me with those pale grey eyes, which were now as cold as steel.

'Do you seriously expect me to believe that? According to what you've just told me, you've been a part of this business from the very beginning. Alfred himself, you say, has turned to you for assurance that this Irwin Peto's story could be true. And you want me to believe that you're not deep in Alison's confidence?' He gave a mirthless smile. 'Do you think me so stupid?'

There was nothing left of his earlier geniality, no trace of the bonhomie with which he had treated me in the beginning. The flint-like eyes were brimming with hostility, and I cursed myself for having made such a silly mistake.

He went on, leaning forward and stabbing the air with his forefinger, 'I know why my cousin sent you! So that you could probe and pry into my doings in the hope that I might reveal myself as the instigator of this plot to defraud her of half her fortune. Well, I'll tell you something, Chapman! Even if I'd met someone who resembled Clement, and even if I'd recognized the likeness after all these years, I doubt if I have sufficient cunning to have seen how to turn the opportunity to my advantage. I may be poor, but I'm not a rogue.'

His scorn was lacerating, but although it made me uneasy, I was not convinced by it. My feelings about Baldwin Lightfoot was that he was perfectly capable of concocting such a plot, and that if he was not the culprit, then his anger was directed more against a fate which had denied him the challenge than against me for suggesting it. But I had handled the matter badly and should get no more from him now.

I stood up. 'I'm sorry to have offended you, Master Lightfoot, and I assure you that Mistress Burnett had no thought but to apprise you of what had happened. She felt that as a kinsman you had a right to know.' This was to a certain extent true, for Alison had never seriously regarded Baldwin as a villain, and would have dissuaded me from wasting precious time visiting him if she could. She would have preferred, once the warmer weather came, that I should set out straight away for London, being convinced that that was where I was most likely to discover the truth. 'I must be going now, if you'll forgive me. I'll see myself out.' And I picked up my pack and cudgel from the floor.

He heaved himself to his feet, but his aggression seemed to have abated. 'I daresay I've been over-hasty,' he said. 'If so, I must apologize. The day's events –' he waved a hand towards the window – 'have been most upsetting. Widow Twynyho was an excellent neighbour.' Tears welled up, and I had no doubt that his distress for her was genuine.

146

But that didn't mean he was incapable of trying to cheat his cousin. I asked abruptly, 'Were you in London, sir, at any time last autumn?'

I half-expected another spurt of anger, but although his eyes regained their steely expression, he answered mildly enough, 'I haven't been to London for nearly four years. The last time I was there the Archbishop of York had just been arrested, and there was a great deal of speculation as to what would happen because the Earl of Oxford had landed on the Essex coast. So you can tell what a time it's been.' He added, in a bid for my sympathy, 'I don't get about as much as I did once. Old age, you know. I'm not as spry as I used to be.' He smiled ingratiatingly, showing the gaps in his teeth.

I found myself wondering about this abrupt change of mood. Why was he so anxious to placate me all of a sudden? I let my glance stray to my surroundings. Baldwin Lightfoot could certainly do with money. I asked as casually as I could, 'When did you last see your Cousin Clement?'

He answered, equally casual, 'Not for a decade or more. He may have been – oh, let me see! – fourteen, fifteen years of age when I last clapped eyes on him. Alfred brought Clement with him when he attended my mother's funeral. I used to see a lot of both children when they were young, but after my mother died we somehow lost touch. The Alderman and I never cared greatly for one another. So, I repeat, I doubt very much that I should have recognized Clement, even at the time of his disappearance. Boys can alter a lot between fifteen and twenty. I heard that he'd vanished, of course, but only by roundabout means. There was no word from Alfred. Later, it was reported to me by an itinerant friar from Bristol that Clement had been murdered, and that the rogues responsible had been brought to justice. Since then, there has been little news. I was told that Alison had married, and the name of her husband, but again, not because of any direct communication from Alfred. You can understand, therefore,' he added with a mocking smile, 'how surprised I am to receive a letter from my Cousin Alison now.'

His version of events tallied with what Mistress Burnett had told me, and I felt that there was nothing more to be gained by staying longer. But I had at least met Baldwin Lightfoot for myself, and was able to form some sort of judgement concerning his character and circumstances; and I thought him quite capable of alleviating his poverty by underhand methods should the chance present itself. But had that opportunity occurred?

I took my leave of him, promising to convey his spurious condolences to his 'dearest cousin' and to assure her of his constant goodwill. He would pray, he said unctuously, for a happy outcome to her present dilemma. I thanked him, tongue in cheek, on behalf of Mistress Burnett and hastened on my way, free at last to seek out that other dwelling where lived the most beautiful creature on earth.

People were still standing around in little groups, their heads turning every now and then in the direction of the Twynyho house with its shattered door. But I hurried past them, intent only on reaching a cottage at the end of the street which I remembered from my visit the previous autumn. I could see it. I was almost at the gate in the paling which surrounded its modest plot. I was there and, miracle of miracles, a girl with brilliant blue eyes and a thick mass of fair hair was walking down the path from the cottage door towards me. My heart gave a great leap – before I suddenly realized that she was not alone.

Chapter Thirteen

The young man who accompanied Rowena was a mere half a head taller than she was, stockily built, brown-haired and freckle-faced. His skin had the leathery appearance of the countryman who is out in all weathers, and his clothes were made of grey homespun. He had broad, placid features, blue eyes and a grin which spread almost from ear to ear. Place him, I thought bitterly, among a crowd of other country yokels, and he would never stand out from the ruck. As far as I could tell, seething as I was with jealous disappointment, he had nothing whatsoever to recommend him to a beauty such as Rowena Honeyman, yet twice, before they even reached the gate, she lifted her face for his kiss.

'Mistress!' I said, blocking her path and hoping against hope that her eyes would light up when she saw me.

Instead, she looked puzzled as she tried to remember who I was. 'Your face is familiar,' she smiled. 'Have we met?' But as recollection crowded in on her, the smile faded and she shrank back into the crook of the young man's arm. 'My aunt's not in,' she said coldly, and turned her head towards the reluctantly dispersing knots of people, some of whom still found it difficult to resume their normal tasks. 'I don't think she'll wish to buy anything today, but if you want to ask her, she's over there talking to the woman in the blue dress and the linen apron and hood.'

I recognized the description of Dame Janet and, with a sidelong glance, verified that the woman in question was indeed Baldwin Lightfoot's housekeeper. In that brief moment, however, Rowena and her escort slipped past me and started off down the street towards the open countryside. I half-raised my hand to detain her, to grab at her sleeve, her skirt, any part of her within my reach, but thought better of it and slowly allowed my arm to drop back again to my side. What was the point in trying to claim her attention when she so plainly wanted as little to do with me as possible? In her eyes, I was still the man who had been partially responsible for her father's death. I had been living in a fool's paradise all these months, imagining that she would have forgiven me by now; exonerated me from any blame. How self-deluding I had been!

I stared after her as long as she was in sight, then heaved my pack on to my back and turned in the opposite direction. I felt winded, as though I had been dealt a heavy blow to my stomach, and I walked blindly, looking neither to left nor right. I had treasured up the memory of Rowena Honeyman for so many long months, that there was nothing now to take its place. It seemed as if a huge, gaping hole had been torn in my heart and that my life's blood was slowly seeping away. It was not a sensation that I had ever experienced before and I had no idea how to cope with it. I had never been in love, although once, just over three years ago, I had come close to it – and had married someone else instead! But anything I had ever felt for Cicely Ford was as nothing to the emotions which Rowena had stirred within my breast; and my present dejection was not improved by the knowledge that I had been both arrogant and presumptuous in believing that during our short acquaintance I must necessarily have favourably impressed her. I realized with shame that I was so used to the admiration and friendship of women that I was in danger of taking them for granted and not valuing them as I should. If I was wise, this experience would be a salutary lesson to me.

In this humbled mood, and lost in my own unhappy thoughts, I was not at first aware of someone shouting after me. But suddenly a hand seized my arm, and a breathless voice said, 'Chapman! Why are you hurrying off without letting me take a look at your goods? I'm in want of needles and thread and also a wooden spoon, if you have one.'

It was Dame Janet, flushed and indignant, and I stammered a half-hearted apology. 'I – I'm sorry, but I did tell you that I wasn't selling today. My visit was simply to deliver his cousin's letter to your master, which I've done.'

She snorted angrily. 'Well, if your business with Master Baldwin's finished, what's to stop you doing a little business on your own account? I never knew a pedlar yet who wasn't anxious to sell the nose off his face if the opportunity should offer.'

I had never felt less like hawking my wares, but Dame Janet was an elderly woman in need of commodities which she might otherwise have to go a mile or so to buy. I therefore urged her to the side of the road, on to the same grassy knoll which I had earlier shared with Timothy Plummer, and spread out the contents of my pack in the shade of the oak. As luck would have it, I was carrying several wooden spoons, from which she was able to take her pick, as well as some good bone needles and a quantity of the best linen thread. She haggled over the cost of every item and patently enjoyed the little concessions she obtained on each, but in truth, I was in no mood for bargaining and was content to let things go for whatever she was willing to pay.

'You charge near enough London prices,' she grumbled as she stowed her purchases in the capacious pouch hanging from her belt.

I was no more in the mood for arguing than I was for

chaffering, but something about the accusation stung me on the raw. 'I can assure you that I don't,' I snapped, adding ungraciously, 'and what would you know about London prices?'

'Hoity-toity!' Dame Janet, by the look on her face, was about to score yet another triumph. 'I know what Master Lightfoot pays for the things he brings back from his London visits, for he tells me. "I'm a fool, Janet," he says to me. "You see this leather girdle that I've brought you? I could have bought it in Frome for a fraction of the cost I gave for it, but I know you'll like to boast that it's London made." And he had a silver-gilt cup and some other trinkets that he told me the price of. Extortionate, all of them. But that's London for you!'

In spite of my private misery, my attention was arrested, and as I fastened the buckles on my pack, I asked casually, 'Master Lightfoot often journeys to the capital then, does he? I wouldn't have thought he had the means for so much gallivanting about.'

'Well, you'd be wrong,' she retorted, raising her chin and squaring her jaw. 'He was there only last November. That was when he bought me the girdle from a booth in Cheapside. Oh, I admit he doesn't go often nowadays, but when the fit comes on him, he's off to visit his cousin who lives near Saint Paul's.'

'And he was there sometime last November, you say? You're sure of that, Mistress?'

Dame Janet was suddenly uneasy, the first inkling that she might have said more than she should have done beginning to trouble her mind. But she had been too positive to retract her statement: she could only affirm what she had already said.

'Yes, I'm sure. What's it to you? Why do you want to know?'

'No reason at all,' I lied, and changed the subject. 'The woman to whom you were talking just now – I forget her name – has a niece, Rowena. Is – er – is the young lady betrothed to that youth I saw her with a few moments ago?' I tried to sound as casual as I could.

'You know Mistress Coggins?' Dame Janet enquired, surprised. Then, without waiting for an answer or an explanation, she carried on, 'Yes, Rowena's been promised to Ralph Hollyns these two months or more. Didn't take him two shakes of a lamb's tail, once he'd clapped eyes on her, to know what he wanted. The only surprise is that she feels the same way about him. With looks like hers, she could have had the pick of any man for twenty miles around. Mind you – ' the housekeeper was warming to her theme and growing confidential, her earlier suspicions of me forgotten – 'there's something a bit mysterious about her. She doesn't say much concerning her life before she came to live here with her aunt last year. Talks occasionally about her mother, but clams up when her father's name is mentioned.' The eyes grew bright with sudden hope. 'If you're acquainted with her, maybe you can tell me something of her past. There's a lot of people hereabouts who'd like to know.'

But I shouldered my pack, said an abrupt goodbye and strode off along the road, heading back the way I had come. Rowena Honeyman was promised to a young man with a freckled face called Ralph Hollyns, and had been for the past two months while I was living with my hopeless dreams. Well, it served me right! I was growing too vain and was in need of a set-down. I hoped I should be able to learn from it.

I did not return to Bristol until the end of the following week, partly because I had felt it necessary to make some money by selling my wares, and partly because I needed to be by myself for a while, before returning to my mother-in-law and daughter. As I must have mentioned before, without seeming to pry, Margaret had an uncanny knack of searching out the truth if I appeared in any way unhappy or distressed, and I had no wish to discuss Rowena Honeyman with her. I therefore took my pack into the remoter communities of north Somerset, and, in my idle hours, tried to concentrate on what I was going to report to Alison Burnett.

Baldwin Lightfoot had lied to me about the length of time since he had last been in London. According to Dame Janet, he had visited his kinsman near Saint Paul's churchyard sometime the previous November, and at the beginning of January, Irwin Peto had turned up in Broad Street claiming to be Clement Weaver. Was there a connection here, or was it simply a coincidence? But if the latter, why should Baldwin have tried to conceal his visits? Why had he not been open with me? It seemed suspicious, but I decided, nevertheless, to reserve judgement on him until I had seen and talked to the rest of the Weaver family.

Mistress Burnett was of the same opinion when I went to see her in Small Street a few hours after my return home.

'This visit of Baldwin's may be of some significance,' she conceded, 'but my instincts tell me that the real instigator of this wicked plot is either my uncle or one of my cousins. Or maybe all of them are in it together. Indeed, I should have preferred you to go straight to London, once the good weather was upon us, rather than waste your time going to Keyford.'

We were seated in the same parlour where she had received me on that earlier occasion, and in spite of the warmth of the April day, a fire had been lit, a great pile of logs, the flames leaping and curling up the chimney. The heat was searing, and I had to move my stool back a foot or two from the hearth to escape being scorched. Alison, however, did not seem to be affected by it; so little, in fact, that she wore a woollen wrap over her gown. She looked even thinner than when I had seen her last, and it was obvious that the quarrel with her father continued to take its toll on her health.

'When *will* you go to London?' she asked.

I hesitated. 'In a week or so. I have responsibilities here, in Bristol, which I cannot ignore. I must set my own affairs in order first.' The words rang hollowly in my ears: when had I ever worried about my responsibilities? And why did they weigh so heavily upon me now?

The truth was that for these past few days I had been moving in a kind of dream, where nothing was real except my own emotions. I had temporarily lost interest in the mystery of Clement Weaver, although I understood myself well enough to know that this feeling would not last. I could never resist a challenge nor the lure of London, particularly if someone else was paying for my sojourn there. In the meanwhile, some time was necessary to allow me to pull myself together and accept the situation as it was.

Alison Burnett shrugged. 'I suppose another week or so will make little difference in the end, but I need your solemn assurance that it will be no longer than that. I want this man proved an impostor as quickly as possible, and it is already well over three months since his arrival. Every day sees him more firmly entrenched in my father's affections. Dame Pernelle, when I saw her yesterday, told me that the creature feels confident enough now to override the Alderman's orders where he deems it necessary, and substitute his own. Ned Stoner and Rob Short in particular deeply resent this, and are talking of looking for work at other houses within the town.'

Even this worrying piece of news did not immediately spur me into action. 'I shall be off as soon as I can,' I promised. It was time to go and I rose to my feet, anxious to be away. 'But I shall come again to see you before I leave.'

As I moved towards the parlour door, it opened and William Burnett came in, wearing a very short satin doublet in what seemed to be his favourite colours, black and red. I could smell the highly scented pomade on his long auburn hair and the faint scent of musk that hung about his clothes. I knew that he did not altogether approve of his wife's decision to employ me in this matter of determining Clement Weaver's true identity, and was expecting no more than a bare acknowledgement of my presence. Instead, he shot out a hand and gripped my arm.

'You've been in Keyford recently, haven't you?' he demanded. 'Alison told me you'd gone to visit her cousin, Baldwin Lightfoot. So did you hear anything of any trouble there? A woman, they say, was arrested. A woman who had once been in the employ of the late Duchess of Clarence.'

'I not only heard of it, I saw it happen,' I answered, and immediately captured both his and Mistress Burnett's undivided attention. 'The lady was the Widow Twynyho, formerly attendant upon Duchess Isabel. A number of the Duke of Clarence's bravos hacked down the door of her house, arrested her and carried her off in the most brutal fashion. Why, and what has since become of her, I've no idea, although I've wondered many times in the past nine or ten days.'

'Then I can tell you,' William said, pleased to be as well informed as myself. 'She was taken to Warwick, where it seems Clarence was in residence, and summarily hanged, along with another erstwhile retainer of Duke George. There was a trial of sorts, but it would appear that the Duke had both the Justice of the Peace and the jurors in his pocket. These worthies are now saying that they feared for their own lives if they failed to deliver a guilty verdict.'

While I was struggling to come to terms with this hideous sequel to the events that I had witnessed, Mistress Burnett demanded of her husband, 'How do you know all this?'

'A party of travellers arrived at the Green Lattis shortly before I left. They were full of the story, and presumed that we would wish to hear all about it, this – this what did you call her? – this Widow Twynyho being a Somerset woman.'

'But what was the charge against her?' I asked. 'Did your travellers happen to mention that?'

'Oh, yes!' William Burnett laughed shortly. 'That's the crux of the matter. Both of the accused were said to have poisoned the Duchess of Clarence at the instigation of the Queen's family.'

Alison echoed my gasp of astonishment and horror. 'The Woodvilles will be up in arms,' I said. 'This could lead to civil war if King Edward isn't careful.'

William nodded. 'That's the opinion of these Warwick men. They're predicting trouble. No one, they say, can take the King's justice into his own hands like that. Not even the King's own brother.'

I grimaced. 'He might if that brother is George of Clarence. King Edward seems to have an infinite capacity for pardoning him.'

Master Burnett shook his head. 'These men are unanimous in insisting that, this time, the Duke has gone too far. Well, Chapman,' he added, with an abrupt change of subject, 'when are you off to London?'

'In a week or so,' I answered absently and took a hurried leave of husband and wife, eager to get into the fresh air and cool my head, which was throbbing from the heat. In addition, my mind was reeling from the news of Ankaret Twynyho's vicious and brutal end. Although I had only glimpsed her that once, I felt a personal anger at her death, and also a terrible guilt. I should have tried at least to stop Clarence's men abducting her, but, instead, I had played the coward's part, and it was no consolation to remember that so had every other man in Keyford.

Outside the house, I hesitated, knowing full well that I ought to visit Adela to thank her for all that she had done for my mother-in-law and daughter during my absence. The former had been lavish in her praise almost before I had crossed the cottage threshold.

'How Elizabeth and I would have managed without my cousin's attentions, I really don't know, for I haven't properly recovered from my illness,' Margaret had proclaimed, standing there, hands on hips, and looking the very picture of health and strength.

But instead of turning towards Bell Lane and the Frome Bridge, I walked up Small Street into Corn Street and crossed over to the New Inn (alias the Green Lattis) behind All Hallows church. Once in the tap-room, it wasn't difficult to identify the strangers in our midst by their accent, so different from our own West Country burr, and I approached the four men to ask for more details of Widow Twynyho's death, explaining my personal interest in their story.

They were friendly men, pausing for a night's rest and refreshment on their way to Glastonbury, the elder of the four (father, he explained, to the other three), expressing his wish to see the tomb of King Arthur and Queen Guinevere before he died. They identified the man executed along with Mistress Twynyho as one John Thuresby, but the name meant no more to them than it did to me, except that he, too, had been employed in the ducal household.

'What was the exact charge against them?' I enquired, for although I had heard it from William Burnett, I wished to have it afresh from the strangers' own lips.

'Why, that they had poisoned both Duchess Isabel and her newborn child,' the older man answered, handing me a pot of ale which he had generously ordered and paid for on my behalf. 'And if you're going to ask me why two apparently faithful and loyal retainers should do such a wicked thing, what advantage they gained by these murders, don't bother, for I'll tell you. The implication is obvious to the meanest intelligence. They had been suborned by those who wished to be revenged upon the Duke of Clarence, and had been bribed by them to kill his wife and child.'

'In short, it was a Woodville plot,' I said, sipping my ale.

'What else? But there's more to it than that,' my new-found friend continued, while his sons nodded in agreement. 'Duke George is out to prove himself King in all but name. And King in name sooner or later, if he can manage it. He's never forgiven his brother for spoiling his chances of marriage with the Duchess of Burgundy, and there have been rumours in our part of the country for months that Clarence is arming his retainers like a man ready to rebel.'

'But on what grounds could he possibly take up arms against the King?' I demanded. 'Even if Edward were killed in the conflict, he has two sons to succeed him.'

My acquaintance from Warwick hunched his shoulders. 'If Clarence were successful, I wouldn't give a fig for the lives of any of the Woodvilles, including those of the little Prince of Wales and Duke of York, for they're both half Woodville, after all.'

'They're also Clarence's nephews,' I protested.

'Maybe,' put in one of the sons, 'but there have been odd stories floating around Warwick for some time now. We've a kinsman who is one of the Duke's Yeomen of the Chamber, and he talks of messengers who come from parts hereabouts, from Robert Stillington, the Bishop of Bath and Wells. It would seem that the Bishop and the Duke have much to say to one another.'

At his words, I was transported back in my mind to the previous August, to Farleigh Castle on the other side of Bath, and to the almost royal reception accorded by Clarence to Robert Stillington. I remembered, too, thinking it more than a coincidence that the Duke should be spending twenty-four hours in Somerset at the same time that the Bishop was visiting his diocese; and I had also wondered why, with such little time at their disposal, they had found it necessary to spend it together. Afterwards, I had considered myself unduly cynical, but here was proof that I had been right to be suspicious. However unlikely an alliance it might seem, something was being hatched between those two.

We talked a little longer about the possible future intentions of the Duke of Clarence, then I finished my ale, thanked the men from Warwick for their time and patience and wished them God speed on the final stage of their journey to Glastonbury the following day. The late April afternoon was already somewhat advanced when I emerged from the inn, and my womenfolk would be on the lookout for me, for I had promised my mother-in-law that I would not stay long in Small Street. And I had still not visited Adela to tender my thanks. I debated for a moment or two whether or not to leave my call on her until the next day, but conscience won and I walked down Broad Street, under Saint John's Arch and across the Frome Bridge to Lewin's Mead.

As I approached the cottage, I saw Adela framed in the doorway, talking to someone. It was not, as I had half-expected, Richard Manifold, but a stranger, a thin wisp of a man with greying hair, bandy legs and clothes which were clean and carefully mended, but which had seen better days. He had a slightly bewildered air, staring around him in confusion and biting his nails as though he didn't quite know what do to. Just before I reached the door, he finally shuffled off, with a number of backward glances over his shoulder.

'Who was that?' I asked, stooping to give Adela a brotherly kiss on the cheek.

'A kinsman, or so he claimed, of Imelda Bracegirdle. He'd come from Oxford, looking for her,' Adela said thoughtfully, 'and at first refused to believe that she was dead. The news appeared to distress him, and he kept saying, "She can't be. What's he going to do?"' She smiled up at me. 'I'm so pleased to see you, Roger. Don't stand there on the doorstep. Come inside.'

Chapter Fourteen

I stepped inside a little warily and was immediately embraced about the knees by Nicholas, who seemed as delighted as his mother at my unexpected reappearance. I swung him up into my arms and returned his embrace, but something must have shown in my face, for Adela laughed.

'Set your mind at rest,' she said bluntly. 'As I've told you before, a woman can be pleased to see a man without expecting a proposal of marriage.'

I could feel the colour rising in my cheeks. 'I . . . I didn't imagine . . .' I began, but being unsure how to proceed, I gave Nicholas a hearty kiss and lowered him gently to the floor.

The brown eyes mocked me. 'No, of course you didn't.' Adela motioned me to a stool and busied herself fetching me a cup of ale from the barrel. 'How was your journey? What did you discover in Keyford? Is Mistress Burnett's cousin behind this plot to defraud her, do you think? Or are you still as much in the dark as ever?'

The awkward moment passed, her deliberate spate of questions allowing me time to recover my composure, and I settled down to give her all my news, and to thank her for looking after Elizabeth and Margaret during my absence. This last she dismissed with a wave of her hand and an exhortation not to be so foolish. But for the rest of my story, it was perhaps natural that the arrest and subsequent execution of Ankaret Twynyho should claim the largest share of her interest, for its consequences might well plunge the country into another bout of civil war.

I tried to reassure her. 'The King has never rounded on Clarence yet, however often Brother George has betrayed him.'

'But according to you, the men from Warwick think that the Duke is plotting open rebellion, and planning to take the crown for himself.'

I leaned forward and squeezed her hand. 'In my opinion they're being unduly pessimistic. King Edward has always been more than a match for his brother. He's always been able to mollify Clarence before matters went too far, and he'll do so this time, mark my word. Forget it, and tell me about this man who came looking for Mistress Bracegirdle.'

'There's nothing to tell,' she protested. 'He was only a minute or two before you, and when I answered the door, his surprise at seeing me was obvious. He asked for Imelda. When I said she was dead, murdered last January, he at first refused to believe me and declared I must be mistaken. Finally, when he'd accepted that I was speaking the truth, he just kept repeating, "She can't be! What's he going to do?" Then he saw you coming and moved away. Poor man! I should have invited him in. He seemed completely broken by the news.'

'And you say that he's a kinsman of Mistress Bracegirdle?'

'I think that's what he said. I can't really remember now, the whole conversation was over so quickly, but I'm almost sure he claimed to be a cousin of her mother's. Oh, and he was holding a bundle of something under one arm, wrapped in sacking.'

Now that she mentioned it, I, too, recalled noticing the bundle, although the fact had made little impression on me at the time. I wondered where the stranger had gone and if I could search him out. But the effort of enquiring all over the town and its suburbs for a man whose name I did not even know suddenly proved too much for me, as the lethargy that had held me prisoner for the past ten days renewed its grip.

'Are you feeling well?' Adela was regarding me with concern. 'You seem out of spirits.'

I denied the imputation vigorously, but then, somehow or other – and I still, to this day, have no idea how it came about – I was pouring out the whole sorry story of Rowena Honeyman; my part in her father's death; how, before he had died, he had charged me with taking her to her aunt's house at Keyford, my passion for her, which I had nursed all winter; my arrogance in assuming that she could ever return my affection; her patent dislike of me and her betrothal to Ralph Hollyns. Adela let me talk, hearing me out in silence, but when I had finished, she came to kneel beside my stool, putting a friendly arm around my shoulders.

'You'll recover,' she said gently. 'Believe me, people often do, however heartbroken they may feel at the time. I know that my words sound callous, but unrequited love is very difficult to keep alive.'

I smiled thinly. 'Do you speak from experience?'

'As a matter of fact, I do.' She rose from her knees and fetched me another cup of ale, then drew up a second stool and sat down alongside me. I had never noticed before how graceful all her movements were. 'I was very much in love with my husband when I married him. My friends and family advised me against going away to live in Hereford with a man I hardly knew, but nothing any of them said could have stopped me. I would have gone barefoot with Owen Juett to the world's end. He was a kind, gentle soul, the sort of man I'd always dreamed of, and I was certain that he loved me as much as I loved him. Oh, he liked me well enough, I'm sure of that, and he'd never been the object of so much adoration in his life before. Who can blame him if he was flattered? But at heart he was a cold man, a little afraid of all women – as he was of his old harridan of a mother, who was slowly dying of some wasting disease or other. What he really wanted was a housekeeper and a nurse for her, to make her last days comfortable. And when she died within three months of our marriage, his greatest need of me was gone. I'd realized by then, of course, that Owen didn't love me as I loved him, and I thought I should never recover from the pain. But I did, in a surprisingly short space of time. And so will you.'

Naturally, I didn't believe her, in spite of a lurking suspicion that she might be right. But just talking to her, just the act of sharing my unhappiness and burdening her with part of my sorrow, had in some strange way made me feel better. And when I eventually took my leave, we parted as friends in the deepest and truest meaning of the word. I kissed her lips, and she returned the salutation in the same passionless manner. Then I set out for Redcliffe and home.

During the next two weeks, I lay low, avoiding all contact with Alison and William Burnett.

On the first occasion when Mistress Burnett called at the house, I was fortunately from home, and although she left a message with my mother-in-law, requesting me to wait upon her as soon as possible, I ignored it. The second time, I was not so lucky, but Margaret, returning from the weaving sheds where she had deposited her basket of yarn, was able to warn me of Alison's approach. Elizabeth was spending the day with Adela and Nicholas Juett, so I was able to roll beneath the bed without any fear of my presence being innocently divulged by my little daughter. Mistress Burnett was invited by mother-in-law to enter the cottage and check for herself that I was nowhere to be seen.

Her message was peremptory. 'Tell the chapman that I want to know when he's setting out for London. It's high time he was thinking of going. I'm not in the mood to brook further delay.'

'You heard that,' Margaret remarked when the visitor had departed. 'I don't know what you're playing at, Roger,' she reproved me as I scrambled, dusty and dishevelled, from beneath the bed, 'but I won't tell lies for you again. As it is, I shall have to do penance for those I've already told on your behalf. If you don't want to continue poking your nose into Alderman Weaver's affairs, then just tell Mistress Burnett so and have done with it. You know you'll have my blessing.'

I hesitated, almost succumbing to an impulse that had become familiar to me over the past fortnight or so. But always, just as I was about to reach a definite decision to have nothing further to do with the case, I drew back from the brink. Even in the moments of my greatest despondency, I could not quite resist a mystery, and particularly not one with which I had been so closely connected in the past. I said, surprising myself as well as Margaret, 'I shall start for London in two days' time. But tomorrow is May Day and I've promised to go maying with Adela, if you'll look after the children for us.'

No such arrangement had been made between us, and I should now have to make good my lie in order not to disappoint my mother-in-law, whose delight at the news was palpable. She was immediately off to market to buy all those ingredients necessary for a May Day breakfast; parsley, lettuce, endive and fennel; cider, apples, cream and butter. Adela, when I explained what had happened, earned my lasting gratitude by agreeing to get up at the crack of dawn. She would be happy, she said, to accompany me into the surrounding countryside in order to bring in the branches of hawthorn, birch and rowan that were used to decorate the various maypoles set up around the city.

She and Nicholas slept with us in the cottage overnight, and as soon as the Redcliffe Gate was opened at sunrise, we were two of the first people to venture out into the open fields beyond. As we climbed Redcliffe Hill, William Canynges's great church rose out of the mist like a milky cloud, and to our right, the snaking line of the river glittered silver-grey in the uncertain morning light. The hem of Adela's gown was quickly saturated with dew, and my boots were wet almost to their tops. Birds shrilled the dawn chorus from the branches of the trees, daisies spangled the grass like snowflakes, and cobwebs, spun overnight between blades of grass, trembled with a myriad diamond drops. A distant orchard caught the first rays of the rising sun, a froth of pink and white foaming up through the mist to bewitch our eyes; and a flock of sheep, newly released from the fold, turned to watch us with their silly, vacuous faces.

'I think we must be the oldest couple here,' Adela protested, laughing, surveying our companions who did indeed seem young; boys and girls for the most part, hardly one of them above the age of sixteen and all in their holiday clothes. They cheered us on as though we were in our dotage, solicitously helping us over the rougher patches of ground and assisting us to gather our armfuls of rowan and may.

The young girl who had been chosen to be their Queen was carried home in triumph on my shoulders – for I, as the tallest man present, had been singled out for this honour – and I was physically exhausted as I settled down to the breakfast that Margaret had prepared. But I also felt curiously content, as though this morning's jaunt had purged me of the sadness that had plagued me for the past few weeks. While we ate, my mother-in-law decked the house with some of the boughs that we had brought back with us. She also decorated the children's hoops with garlands of trailing leaves and swags of ivy, adding bows of coloured ribbon and little bells, bought the previous day in the market, so that they flashed and twinkled as they were bowled along. Afterwards, the five of us went to join in the dancing around the nearest maypole, and later still, as the sun began to sink in a blaze of crimson glory, I accompanied Adela and Nicholas home to Lewin's Mead.

As we crossed the Frome Bridge, the river bloodied by the

sunset, I said quietly, 'You've been a good friend to me, Adela. Thank you. I shan't forget. If I can ever be of service . . .'

'You and Margaret have already been of great service to Nick and me,' she interrupted. 'You have nothing to thank me for. It's very little that I've been able to do in return.' She quickened her step as we passed beneath the archway of the gate. 'Look! There's Richard waiting for me. He must have finished his spell of duty at the castle.'

Not for the first time, the sight of Richard Manifold's smiling countenance made my hackles rise. There was nothing about him – not his red hair nor his bright blue eyes, not his stocky figure nor his aggressive stance – that commended itself to me. I had no idea why his appearance so irritated me; no notion why I wanted to wipe the smug, self-satisfied expression off his face each time we met. I gritted my teeth, gripped Nicholas's hand more firmly in mine, as though to emphasize my right of possession, and reluctantly followed Adela to the cottage door.

But for once, the Sheriff's Officer had not come to pass the time of day or to reminisce about times past, and he gave me none of his usual disapproving looks when I entered the cottage in Adela's wake. He was too full of news that had arrived at the castle earlier in the afternoon, while most of the population had been out celebrating.

Adela, ever the careful hostess, plied Richard with ale and offered him a seat before allowing him to proceed with his story.

'Now, what's happened?' she asked, but only when satisfied that he was comfortable.

'The King has arrested one of Clarence's household, a man called Thomas Burdet, and he's to be tried on a charge of attempting to procure the King's death by necromancy. The Sheriff reckons there's no doubt but he'll be hanged. A life for a life, even if it means another rigged jury.'

I sucked in my breath. 'Brother George won't stand for it,' I said, forgetting for a moment my dislike of Richard Manifold in my anxiety for his opinion. 'Does this mean civil war after all, do you think?'

He nodded portentously. 'It could lead to that. But the lord Sheriff is in two minds about it. He said it wasn't like King Edward to be so maladroit.'

'Nor is it.' I chewed my lower lip thoughtfully. 'He's up to something. But what? How did you come to hear of this development?'

'An Augustinian friar from All Hallows on the Wall, in London, has come to Bristol on business with his fellows at Temple Gate. This was one of the bits of news, amongst others, that he brought with him, and it was thought to be of sufficient importance, in view of its possible consequences, to pass on to the lord Sheriff.'

'Is there more to the story than you've told us?' Adela asked quietly, but with an edge of steel to her voice. 'Or has some poor unfortunate retainer in Clarence's employ simply been picked upon, as Ankaret Twynyho was picked on by Prince George, to be a scapegoat, in order to satisfy the Queen's desire for revenge?'

Richard Manifold swallowed the remainder of his ale and glanced hopefully at the barrel on the far side of the room. When Adela ignored this hint, he sighed and continued, 'He was apparently accused of sorcery by an Oxford clerk, whose name I can't at this moment recall – Blake, was it? Thomas Blake? – who, in his turn, had been named as a necromancer by another Oxford clerk called John Stacey, a caster of horoscopes. So you see, Adela, this man has *not* been picked at random by the King and his officers.'

Adela smiled grimly. 'And what, I wonder, have these other two, this John Stacey and Thomas Blake, been promised if they impeach some poor man of the Duke of Clarence's household?

Will they stand on the scaffold alongside him when he's hanged, or will they mysteriously be forgiven for their sins?'

Richard Manifold clucked his tongue disapprovingly. 'You're becoming far too cynical, my dear. It's not womanly. You're allowing yourself to be influenced by others.' He glared at me; and before a furious Adela could rebut his accusation, he had noticed the still damp, mud-streaked hem of her gown. 'Don't tell me you were gathering may this morning! No, no! This won't do at all! At your age you really should know better.'

The reproof was meant for me. He was angry because he guessed that I had been her companion on an expedition that he would have liked to have shared with her himself. He spoke without thinking of the effect of his words upon Adela, and stared at her in astonishment when she rose wrathfully to her feet and ordered him from the house.

'You forget yourself, Richard! I am not a child to be spoken to in such a fashion. I am twenty-six years of age, and I ask you to remember that. Nor am I answerable to you for any of my thoughts and feelings. Nor,' she added significantly, 'for my friends or the company that I keep. Please leave, and do not return until you are invited back.'

Like all red-haired people, he blushed easily, and the colour surged into his face in a fiery tide. 'Now look here!' he blustered, first thumping the table before standing up. 'There's absolutely no need . . .'

'Please leave,' Adela repeated in a quieter voice. Nicholas had crept to her side and was holding tightly to her hand, uneasy, as children always are, when their elders quarrel.

Richard Manifold looked like someone who had stepped into a quagmire where he had thought all to be firm ground. Then he jutted his chin belligerently. 'You were always a stubborn woman,' he taunted her. 'If you hadn't been, you'd never have married that weakling from Hereford, who died on you after

171

only seven years.' He drew himself up and puffed out his chest to demonstrate his own health and strength. 'All right! I'm going. But you'll soon be begging me to come back, see if you're not!' And on that valedictory note, he stalked to the door and let himself out into the soft May twilight.

Adela sucked in a deep breath and smiled tremulously at me. 'I've been looking for an excuse to do that for months,' she said. 'I never liked him very much, not even when I was young. There was always something about him, some touch of arrogance, of self-importance, that irritated me beyond endurance. I'm not surprised he hasn't married. No woman could put up with him.'

'If he bothers you again in the next few weeks,' I said firmly, 'let me know.'

She laughed. 'You won't be here. You'll be in London.'

Her words echoed the everlasting complaint of my mother-in-law, but they were uttered in a tone of amusement rather than reproach. Looking at her across the table, I remembered my first opinion of her as a self-contained and self-reliant woman, who, over the years, had taught herself to be emotionally as well as physically independent of other people. She would give her loyalty and her love without expecting too much in return. She would let a man go about the world and still welcome him back with open arms whenever he chose to come home. The man whom she eventually married would be extremely fortunate, and for a moment I felt almost jealous of him.

I only realized that I was staring at her when she lowered her eyes, obviously embarrassed by my steady scrutiny. 'You'd better be getting back to Margaret,' she said. 'She'll be waiting for you.' She looked up once more and smiled, having recovered her composure. 'I don't suppose I'll see you again before you set out for London. Take care. And God be with you.'

'And with you.' I kissed her proffered cheek and ruffled

Nicholas's hair. When I still hesitated, she laughed good-humouredly, anticipating my question.

'Of course I'll keep an eye on Margaret and Elizabeth for you. Nick would miss Bess if he didn't see her every day, wouldn't you, sweetheart?'

Nicholas nodded vigorously, understanding only the name and the fact that he was being asked to express his approval. 'Like Bess,' he affirmed. 'Like Bess.'

I thanked her and glanced towards the spinning wheel in the corner. 'All goes well with Alderman Weaver?'

'Very well. I've as much work as I can handle and he's a kind and considerate employer. I've seen him once or twice when collecting my daily supply of wool, and he always remembers my name and gives me a friendly word.'

I was interested. 'Is his so-called son ever with him?' I asked.

Adela clapped a hand to her forehead. 'There! I meant to tell you when I saw you again, and I quite forgot. I met them together one morning while you were away. I'd gone round by the rope-walk in order to get a breath of fresh air and to stretch my legs before returning to Margaret's to pick up Nicholas. Alderman Weaver was looking very unwell and leaning heavily on the young man's arm. But in spite of that, I thought how happy and contented he appeared.'

'How can he possibly be happy and contented,' I demanded angrily, 'when he's prepared to rob his daughter of her rights? How can he allow himself to be taken in by this impostor?'

'Well, that was the strange thing,' Adela answered slowly. 'The Alderman hadn't noticed me. It was a chilly morning with a nipping wind, and he had his hat pushed forward, over his eyes, against the cold. But the young man saw me. He was looking straight ahead, and as I drew abreast, he said, "Hello, Adela. I heard your husband had died and I'm sorry. You'd best marry a Bristol man next time."'

173

I shrugged. 'There's nothing in that. He could easily have heard the Alderman talking about you after you'd called to ask him for work.'

'But he knew me,' she insisted. 'He recognized me.'

'He must have seen you when you called at the Broad Street house. Of course! That would be how he and Alderman Weaver came to be talking about you. "Who was that?" our friend would have wanted to know, and then your history would have come tumbling out.'

Adela shook her head. 'You're forgetting,' she said. 'I didn't call in Broad Street. It was Margaret who went on my behalf. If this man is an impostor, we had never set eyes on one another before that morning by the rope-walk, but he knew me at once for who I am. And what is more, although my youthful memories of Clement Weaver are hazy, there's one thing about him that I do recall. Clement had a habit of looking you directly in the eyes when he spoke, as if everything he said was a challenge that he was expecting you to take up and contradict. This man looked at me in precisely the same fashion. You know, Roger, the more I think about it, the more I'm inclined to the view that he could well be who he claims he is.'

Chapter Fifteen

I have mentioned on at least two previous occasions in this narrative, the fact that throughout this strange case of Clement Weaver I was destined to be an observer of great events, simply because God decreed that I should be in the right place at the right moment. And so it was that during the last week of May, a few days after the execution of Thomas Burdet, I was passing through the city of Westminster when Clarence stormed his way into the palace council chamber to protest his henchman's innocence.

I had taken almost a month over the journey to London, not hurrying, going out of my way to visit the remoter communities of Wiltshire and Berkshire and the city approaches, allowing the quiet of the countryside to act as balm to my bruised and battered spirit. I had set out from Lawford's Gate still convinced of my undying passion for Rowena Honeyman, only to discover that by the time I reached the scattered hamlets and holdings of Savernake Forest, a whole day would go by without my once conjuring up her face. Indeed, as the fitful showers of early May gave way to more smiling weather, and as the white stars of the campion flowers began to displace primroses and sweet wild violets, I found that I might not think of her for several days together, until something happened to jog my memory. And even then, the sadness and regret did not last beyond an hour or two.

There was so much to be observed, and occasionally to be

done when my services could be of any use, that I had little spare time for repining. May is the month for rethatching roofs after the depredations of winter, when torn and loosened straw must be flattened down and stitched into place; for threshing grain when the weather is kind; for planting peas and weeding autumn-sown corn; for draining grassland. It is also the season for the start of the summer activities.

On Whit Sunday, after Mass, I clapped and cheered the Morris dancers on the green of some village whose name I have long since forgotten, although I shall never forget the mouthwatering taste of the Whitsun cheesecake given to me by one of the local Goodies. The pastry which encased it was light as thistledown, while the flavours of clove and mace were so skilfully blended with the curds and egg yolks that there was no bitterness or stinging of the tongue. And when I fell asleep that night, beside that same Goody's damped-down fire, I was undisturbed by dreams of a little, straight nose, periwinkle-blue eyes and a small, determined chin, all in a frame of silky fair hair. The following morning I awoke refreshed, and, if not entirely carefree, then certainly without that weight of misery that I had carried with me for so many miles at the beginning of my journey.

I was even prepared, when at last I reached it, to look with a tolerant eye upon the city of Westminster with its teeming streets full of aggressive Flemish merchants, not so much trying to sell their wares as to force them at knife-point on innocent passers-by. Lawyers, in their long striped gowns, and Sergeants-at-arms, in their silken hoods, strutted in and out of Westminster Hall with as much pomp and inconvenience to other people as they could possibly manage. Furthermore, the city, then as now, has always been a hotbed of thieves and pickpockets who can be out by the gate and halfway along the Strand towards London before their victims realize that anything is missing.

That particular morning, I pushed my way through the crowds, brandishing my cudgel as a warning, letting everyone know that I should defend myself if the need arose. The pack on my back also served as a handy weapon, for although it was not so heavy as when I first left Bristol, it was still weighty enough to give any rogue a hefty blow to arm or face if I swung my body in his direction. Coupled with my girth and height, this proved to be deterrent enough, and I was untroubled even by those most determined of cutpurses who operate the stretch of ground between the waterfront and the Abbey.

As I headed towards one of the many cookshops, their goods displayed enticingly on trestle tables set up in front of their booths, I recalled the last time I was in Westminster, two years previously, when, on the eve of the English invasion of France, I had seen the Duke of Gloucester, at the head of his retinue, ride by on his way to London. The thought was barely formed, before I and my fellow citizens found ourselves being unceremoniously pushed to one side in order to make room for another lordly procession, this time entering, not leaving, Westminster, its banners and pennons all bearing the insignia of the Duke of Clarence. The Duke himself led the cavalcade, his handsome, florid face contorted with an anger that was akin to hatred. In front of Westminster Hall, he reined in with a violence which must have torn at the delicate skin of his horse's mouth, and almost threw himself from the saddle, beckoning furiously to a man who rode just behind him. A palace official tried to bar his way, but was thrust roughly from his path.

'I must and will see my brother!' declared the Duke, his voice carrying clearly to our straining ears.

'His Highness has left for Windsor,' spluttered the outraged steward, still valiantly trying to prevent Clarence's entry.

'But the Council is still in session?'

'It is.' The affirmation was reluctant. 'But I have no authority to admit Your Grace.'

The Duke, however, balked of his chief prey, was in no mood to give in gracefully. 'I don't give a toss for your authority,' he snarled. 'Where are they sitting? Upstairs?' He addressed the hang-dog man at his elbow. 'Doctor, stay close and follow me.'

The palace official made one last attempt to halt this uninvited guest, but was immediately pinned back against the open door by two of Clarence's bravos, two whose faces I swore I could remember from the arrest of Ankaret Twynyho.

I turned to my neighbour who, judging by his bloodied apron and the cleaver fastened to his belt, was a butcher delivering meat to the pie-shops. 'What's it all about?' I asked him.

He shrugged. 'I don't know any more than you, friend, but I suspect it's to do with that man of the Duke's who was hanged on a charge of trying to procure the King's death by necromancy. I was told that before his execution, he read out a long statement on the scaffold, passionately protesting his innocence.'

'No doubt like the Widow Twynyho,' I commented bitterly.

'Who?' My companion was nonplussed. I explained and the butcher sighed. 'There's bad blood between those two brothers, no doubt about it. Small wonder really, when you consider how King Edward's had to put up with the Duke's carryings-on for all these years.'

'Who's the man with him, the one he called Doctor?' I wanted to know.

Neither the butcher nor anyone else in the immediate vicinity could enlighten me, but an elderly woman, standing just within earshot, said that he was that same Doctor Goddard who had proclaimed the late King Henry's right and title to the crown seven years earlier. 'You know! When the Duke of Clarence and the Earl of Warwick tried to oust King Edward and put King Henry back on the throne.'

This was disturbing news if Clarence were indeed stirring up old treacheries, and consorting with past comrades from those days of his greatest betrayal. I studied the rest of the Duke's retinue, patiently awaiting their master's reappearance, and saw with alarm that some of them wore breastplates and leg armour, and carried both sword and dagger at their belts. I wondered if others had also noticed.

The crowd began to disperse as people quickly grew bored with inactivity. It had been interesting for a moment or two while it seemed as if the Duke's retainers might start brawling in the street, with the hint of possible bloodshed to come. But all was now quiet and they started to drift away, anxious to pursue their own affairs once again. Just at that moment, however, the Duke of Clarence erupted from the hall, literally dragging the unfortunate Doctor Goddard behind him.

'Read it!' he screamed at the poor man, who was white-faced and shaking. 'Read it! Loudly, you stupid fool, so that everyone can hear you!'

What Doctor Goddard was being forced to declaim was Thomas Burdet's protestation of innocence, which, according to the butcher, the condemned man himself had proclaimed just before he was hanged. When the quavering voice eventually died away, the Duke cleared his throat and yelled, 'You all heard that! My man was not guilty! But that didn't protect him from the vengeance and spite of the Woodvilles. Let me inform you, however, that they are the ones who are exponents of the Black Arts, not Thomas Burdet! They are the ones who have put a spell upon my brother in order to turn him against me! They are the ones whose agents poisoned my wife and newborn child! They are the ones who, if they have their way, will consume me as a candle flame is consumed by the wind!' He paused for a moment, blinking, as though he had surprised himself by this flight of poetic imagery. Then he continued, 'But I shall not let them. I shall be requited. That creature who calls herself Queen of England shall be proved an impostor when the time is ripe! And that will be sooner than she thinks!' After which diatribe, he remounted his horse, wheeled it about and galloped off back to London, his retinue streaming in his wake.

This histrionic performance left his audience in two minds; some seemed to be genuinely worried at the prospect of renewed civil strife, while others merely sniggered.

'He's a windbag, that one,' laughed the butcher. 'He'll soon come to heel when the King whistles him up.'

'But suppose the King doesn't whistle him up this time,' I suggested. 'Suppose that, at long last, Edward's had enough.'

My companion considered this idea for a moment or two before confidently dismissing it. 'No, he'll forgive his brothers anything. Duchess Cicely's children have always been a closeknit brood.'

'So have the Woodvilles,' I retorted grimly.

But we parted friends, agreeing to differ, and when I had eaten my dinner, bought from a pieman's stall near the London Gate, I set out along the Strand, past the Chère Reine Cross, to the capital, where my first business would be to look up my old friend, Philip Lamprey, in his second-hand clothes shop, west of the Tun-upon-Cornhill.

The evening meal – a simple stew made special by some secret ingredient of Jeanne Lamprey's own – was finished, the dirty plates pushed aside and our cups brimming with ale. Sitting opposite me at table was my host, his small, pock-marked face, illuminated by the single rushlight, intent and interested. When I had first met him, six years earlier, he had been thin to the point of emaciation, a beggar on the London streets, deserted by his wife who had run off with another man while Philip was soldiering abroad. In those days, his friends, if they could be dignified by such a name, had been found among the dregs of humanity in East Cheap and Southwark. But between then and our second encounter, four years later, he had prospered, saving enough money from his begging to rent a stall in Cornhill, where he sold second-hand clothes, and was now living very happily with his second wife in the daub-and-wattle hut at its rear.

Jeanne Lamprey, a little, round, bustling body, with bright brown eyes and a mop of unruly black curls, was young enough to be Philip's daughter, being at this time, as far as she knew, some twenty years of age, compared with his forty-three. But in everything except years, she was far older than he. Her obvious love of him was not uncritical; she was not blind to his faults. She knew he was fond of strong liquor and therefore kept a wary eye on the amount he consumed, scolding him gently when he drank too much. Her business sense, too, was greater than his, although she was too partial and too clever to make him aware of it. Meeting her again, I was reminded of someone else, not in looks but in ways, and it was a long time before I realized that it was Adela.

'So,' breathed Philip, sighing with contentment at a well-filled belly, 'here's a puzzle. I can tell from your manner what you think, Roger, without even having to ask. You think this man who claims to be Clement Weaver is definitely an impostor. But he could have escaped in the way he says he did, you know.' My host spoke with all the authority of one who had played a part in the original mystery, and made a contribution, however small, to its unravelling. 'I knew a man once who struck his head a severe blow, and knew nothing of who he was, or where he came from, for months after he recovered consciousness.'

I shook my head. 'You haven't met this Irwin Peto. There's something about him I just don't trust.'

'Something you don't want to trust,' Philip surmised shrewdly, 'because, foolishly, you feel it to be somehow your fault that the Alderman has suffered his son's absence all these years. You blame yourself for not having thought of the possibility of escape and your failure to search further.'

'No,' I insisted stubbornly. 'The real Clement was fond of his sister, everyone who knew him says so. He wouldn't have allowed his father to rob Alison of her share of their inheritance, however badly she behaved. He wouldn't have been so unfair.' I wiped my forehead with my hand. The hut was small and the May nights were growing warmer.

Philip gulped more ale. 'Yet this friend of yours,' he continued in his rasping voice, 'this Widow Juett, is of the opinion that he *is* Clement Weaver. According to her account he recognized her without any prompting, although if he was an impostor, he couldn't have known her. What do you make of that?'

'I think Adela was pointed out, and her history made known to him at some time or another without her being aware of the fact. That seems to me the most likely answer.'

Philip grinned. 'All right,' he said. 'We won't waste time arguing. So what do you want of me?'

I glanced guiltily at Jeanne Lamprey as I answered, 'To help me find this Morwenna Peto who lives in the Southwark stews. I want to hear what she has to say; to see if her story tallies with Irwin's.'

Philip, too, looked towards his wife, as though asking for her approval, but Jeanne kept her eyes lowered, apparently absorbed in the task of picking at one of her nails. Denied her authority, my host said cautiously, 'I'm not sure . . . It's a long time since I was in those parts. I doubt I'd be remembered.'

'Bertha Mendip would remember you,' I insisted. 'And as far as Morwenna Peto's concerned, Bertha's a West-countrywoman herself, and would surely have heard of any other such in the neighbourhood.'

'That's possible,' Philip admitted, trying not to sound too enthusiastic. He knew from past experience that my appearance in his life invariably meant trouble, and that his wife also knew it.

Jeanne stopped picking her nail and looked up, fixing her big brown eyes sternly upon her husband. 'You must do what Roger asks, Philip,' she said, surprising both of us. 'He is a friend, and he needs our help. As long as you carry your knife with you and Roger takes his cudgel, you should come to no harm. Wear your oldest clothes. Better still, you can pick the worst items from the stall.'

Philip was unable to restrain the face-splitting grin which cut his sharp little features almost in two. I guessed that, just occasionally, he pined for the freedom of his old way of life and the companionship of his former comrades. Not for long and not very often, respectability had become too deeply ingrained in him by now to be lightly abandoned, but every now and then he needed some excitement in an existence which had become a little too humdrum.

'We'll go to Southwark tomorrow morning,' he said. 'Meanwhile, drink up and let's hear the rest of your news.'

So I recounted the episode I had witnessed at Keyford the preceding month, also the one at Westminster that selfsame morning, and the conversation immediately turned to the likelihood of renewed civil strife, this time not between Yorkist and Lancastrian, but the possibility of internecine war between two royal brothers.

'Timothy Plummer predicted it,' I said gloomily, 'when I saw him at Tewkesbury last January, after the funeral of Duchess Isabel and the news of Charles of Burgundy's death at Nancy. He said Clarence would propose himself for Mary's husband, and blame the Woodvilles if he were thwarted, and that's exactly what has happened. Either he or the Queen will eventually be destroyed in the process, but in the meantime, other innocents on both sides are being sacrificed.'

'That's all very well, but how d'you know they're innocents?' argued Philip, who liked to take the opposing view, often for no better reason than sheer cussedness. 'Take this clerk, this Stacey, who accused Blake and Burdet! I was chatting to a man in Leadenhall Market only yesterday morning. He was from Oxford, and he said Stacey's well-known among the undergraduates as a caster of horoscopes. His whole family's been involved in the business at one time or another.'

'Maybe, but that doesn't make Blake and Burdet equally guilty,' I insisted, started to get heated.

'No smoke without fire,' Philip countered belligerently, slapping his empty cup down hard on the table.

'Nonsense!' I snapped. 'I've seen plenty of smoking fires where there was never so much as a wisp of flame.'

'You'll tell lies just to win your point,' my host retorted, and was about to thump me, not altogether playfully, on the shoulder, when his wife leaned over and grasped his wrist.

'Stop it, the pair of you! Why can men never talk seriously without losing their tempers? In any case,' Jeanne added, 'it will soon be time for bed. Roger, you know you're welcome to share our quarters if you don't mind sleeping on the floor.'

'I've slept in far worse places,' I assured her heartily, while Philip, a little shamefaced, poured us both more ale, 'but tonight I'll walk as far as the Ald Gate and the Saracen's Head. I've stayed there before, two years since.'

Philip at once demurred, urging me to remain, but Jeanne was too sensible to contest my decision. She knew as well as I did that the hut was not big enough to be shared by a husband and wife, not yet out of love with one another, and a comparative stranger.

'You'll be comfortable at the Saracen's Head,' she agreed. 'But you must promise to return here for breakfast.'

I gave her my word and, leaving my pack in a corner of their room, but armed with my cudgel and also Philip's knife, which he insisted that I borrow, I set out eastward through the evening dusk for the inn which stood just inside the city gate, on the southern side of the wall.

It was an inn greatly favoured by travellers and merchants from East Anglia, being the first hostelry they happened across after entering the city, and consequently was always busy. That evening was no different from any other, and I was forced to share a room with a tailor from the Fens, who had come to London in search of a runaway daughter. I was compelled to listen to his unhappy chronicle of filial disobedience well into the night, and, when he did at last fall asleep through sheer exhaustion, to his snoring. However resolutely I closed my eyes or stuffed my fingers in my ears, I could not sleep, nor could I block out the noise. In the end, I stopped trying to do either, linking my hands behind my head and staring into the smoke-scented darkness.

As my body began to relax, and as I was at last able to ignore the snorts and snuffles coming from the opposite side of the bed, my vacant mind was suddenly preoccupied with another worry; one that I was familiar with and had experienced many times before. It was the feeling that something had been said by someone that should have had significance for me, if only I had had the wit to realize it at the time. I cudgelled my brain, trying to recollect my conversation with the butcher and the woman outside Westminster Hall. Was it something one of them had said? Or the Duke of Clarence? Or Doctor John Goddard? Or was it some words uttered by Jeanne or Philip Lamprey? But the more I thought, the more my head ached and the less I was able to recall.

At last, as I teetered on the brink of sleep, I was seized by the conviction that it was somehow something that all of them had said; that there was a thread linking the various conversations which was eluding me. And my final thought, as I tumbled into the pit of unconsciousness, was that this thread, if it could only be traced, would lead me straight to the heart of the mystery surrounding the impostor who claimed to be Clement Weaver. And even as this thought came to me and was lost again in the mists of sleep, Adela's face swam in front of my eyes. She was smiling and beckoning me forward, into her cottage . . .

I sat bolt upright in bed, wide awake, the tailor still snoring on the other side of the bolster which separated us. I had almost had the answer. It was there, somewhere, hovering in the darkness all around me. I had had it, but now it was gone, slipping away into the night like a puff of smoke when the candle flame is doused. I lay down again. Perhaps it would come back to me in the morning. Meanwhile, there was nothing else to do but give my companion a nudge and try once more to sleep.

Chapter Sixteen

Philip and I were rowed across to the Southwark side of the river early the following morning.

I was no wiser as to what was troubling me than I had been the previous evening. No great revelation had burst upon me when I awoke. My bed companion from the fen country was still snoring loudly, so I had dressed, paid my shot for the night's board, resisting the landlady's pressing invitation to stay to breakfast, and made my way back to Cornhill. There, Jeanne Lamprey, as neat and bright-eyed as ever, having offered me hot water to wash and shave in, regaled me with a meal of bread and salt bacon, washed down with ale. Philip, for a small man, had eaten and drunk with exceptional heartiness, and had then sat picking his teeth while Jeanne bustled about, getting the booth ready for opening. I had offered a helping hand, hoping to shame him, but he had only grinned. He knew his wife better than I did.

'No, no!' she had said, almost angrily, waving me to one side. 'You and Philip get on about your business and let me get on about mine. And, Roger, you'd best leave that leather jerkin behind. Both of you would do well to do as I suggested last night and borrow something from the stall.'

Now, as the oarsman rowed us across the river, skilfully riding the incoming tide, I thought to take notice of what Philip had on, and saw it to be an extremely old and disreputable camlet tunic, with tattered remnants of fur at neck and wrists. It might have been a garment of quality once, but I couldn't imagine anyone wanting to buy it in its present condition, and said as much.

Philip laughed. 'It isn't off the stall, you great lummox! Can you see my Jeanne selling anything as tattered and torn as this?' He leaned towards me from his seat in the stern. 'Don't you recognize it?' I shook my head, bewildered. 'Look closer,' he urged. He pointed to just below the collar; or rather to where the collar had once been, for it was now more than half ripped away. 'At one time, there were two initials there, worked in gold thread, but nothing's left of 'em now except the stitchmarks.'

Enlightenment dawned. 'CW,' I breathed. 'That's the tunic you bought all those years ago from Bertha Mendip, after she'd stripped it from a corpse she found in the river. It's Clement Weaver's tunic. Fancy you keeping it all this while!' I wrinkled my nose. 'Particularly as it still stinks of fish.'

Philip gave another of his raucous laughs. 'That's what my Jeanne says, but she knows better than to throw it away because it's always brought me good luck. Mind you, we never knew for certain that it belonged to Clement Weaver. We only thought it might have done because of the initials.'

'That's true enough,' I admitted grudgingly. 'And Alison Weaver, as she was then, confirmed that her brother had possessed such a garment and thought he might have been wearing it on the day that he disappeared. But come to think of it,' I added, 'a camlet tunic, trimmed with grey squirrel's fur, was mentioned to me not so long ago by none other than "Clement" himself. But he claims it was stolen from him by the thief who stripped and robbed him after he had swum ashore.'

The oarsman gently beached his craft on a narrow strip of sand and Philip and I disembarked. We climbed the flight of steps to the quayside above, but had barely reached the top before we were surrounded by half a dozen whores, immediately identifiable by their striped hoods. (Most of the Southwark stews are owned by the See of Winchester, whose yearly income is greatly enhanced by these women's earnings.) They seemed in no way deterred by our impoverished appearance, but turned violently abusive when Philip and I declined their services. For a moment, I was afraid for our safety, but my companion grabbed me by the arm and we took to our heels through a warren of narrow, filthy alleyways fringed by dark and desolate dwellings, whose inhabitants turned to stare suspiciously after us as we ran. I was thankful on more than one occasion for my good stout cudgel and the gleaming steel of Philip's unsheathed knife.

But finally, without mishap, we reached Angel Wharf, long since abandoned for all commercial purposes, and still looking much as it had done six years earlier. The same collection of hovels and near-derelict houses provided shelter of a sort for the tribe of beggars, thieves and vagabonds who lived and found sanctuary from the law there. As Philip and I got closer, shrill whistles gave warning of our approach, just as they had done on our first visit; and as we emerged on to the quayside, I noted again the little fleet of boats moored alongside the shallow flight of well-worn steps leading up from the river. The denizens of Angel Wharf took no chances: they made sure that they could escape by both land and water.

I could sense that Philip was far less at ease in such a community than he had once been, but he put on a good show of bravado, turning with a flourish to a little knot of onlookers who had gathered outside the door of one of the hovels. 'Can someone tell me where I can find Bertha Mendip?' he asked.

They all shuffled their feet and stared vacantly at him, as though he were speaking in Turkish instead of good plain English, and when he repeated his question, they looked even more bewildered.

'God's breeches, we're old friends of hers,' Philip said impatiently. 'Bertha knows us.'

A young man, so wizened and stunted in growth that he might have been any age from twelve to twenty, stepped forward. 'And what names shall we give these friends of hers?' he demanded.

Before either of us could reply, a voice from inside the nearest hut called out, 'It's all right, Matt! I know 'em. One of 'em, at least, and I think I remember the other.' Bertha Mendip emerged into the daylight, smaller and more emaciated than when we had last met, and with a skin like well-tanned leather. The elf locks that straggled, unkempt, about her shoulders had once been chestnut-brown, but were now almost completely grey. 'You're a pedlar,' she said, addressing me. 'Leastways, you were, although you look as if you've come down in the world since then.'

'We're in disguise, Ma,' Philip grinned, circling her waist with his arm and planting a smacking kiss on her unsavoury cheek. 'We were afraid that if we came smartly dressed, we might be set on by cutpurses and murderers, although I can't for the life of me think what should have given us that idea! Not when we're surrounded by so many honest faces.'

Bertha made a strange gargling noise in her throat which seemed to indicate amusement, for she punched him in the chest and protested, 'Get away with you, do! So why are you and the pedlar looking for me?'

'We're trying to trace a Morwenna Peto,' I said, 'and hoped that you might be able to tell us where to find her.'

'Morwenna Peto, eh?' The shrewd eyes, whose bright blue had clouded with the passing years, regarded me straitly. 'Now what would you be wanting with Morwenna?' But when I would have made shift to explain, Bertha held up her hand imperiously. 'If it's going to be a long story, you'd best come indoors. We don't want all these knuckleheads gawping at us. Matt!' she yelled to the young man who had first spoken to us, and jerked her head towards the door of the hovel immediately behind her. 'You remember my son, I expect,' she added as the three of us followed her inside, and I hadn't the heart to admit that I had failed to recognize him.

Bertha earned her living from 'corpsing'; fishing dead bodies out of the Thames, stripping them of their clothes and other belongings (which she then dried and sold) and tipping the denuded cadavers back into the river. The inside of the hut reeked with the stench of decaying flesh and salt water, as garments from her latest catch dried on poles hanging above a smoky, slow-burning fire. The smell was so unpleasant that I was forced, from a fear of being sick, to refuse her offer of ale, saying that I wasn't thirsty, but Philip accepted with alacrity. Little seemed to upset *his* stomach.

'Right,' she said, when she had discharged her duty as hostess and directed us to sit on a couple of very rickety stools, 'what's this about then?'

She listened carefully to all I had to say, sucking thoughtfully on the couple of good teeth still left to her, and, every now and then, spitting with remarkable accuracy into the fire, several feet away. When I had finished, she drank up the rest of her ale and said belligerently, 'Well, *I* never said the owner of that tunic Philip bought of me belonged to this Clement Weaver. *I* don't deal in names.'

'No, of course not,' I agreed hastily. 'But do you recollect anything about the body you took it from?'

'After all this while?' she asked scathingly. 'I expect he was too nibbled away by the fishes to be recognizable, anyway.'

I swallowed the bile that rose in my throat and shook my head. 'No, at the time you said he hadn't been in the water long enough for the fish to get at him.' I turned towards Philip, catching at his sleeve. 'This sorry-looking garment is the actual one, still preserved. Look at it carefully. It might bring back a memory or two.'

Bertha rose from her seat and peered closely at the tunic, fingering the cloth and examining it around the neck and down the seams, her face growing ever more lined as she furrowed her brow in concentration. 'I don't know how you expect me to remember anything,' she whined at last, 'considering the amount of garments I deal with in a twelvemonth. And this happened six years ago, you say?' She shook her head. 'No, I can tell you no more than what I've told you already.'

'You said, back then, that the man you took it from was young and had been stripped of all his valuables. He'd been caught in a fisherman's net, and he was one of three corpses you'd recovered from around the same spot in the river. Is it possible,' I went on, 'that this particular man was not dead, but only drugged, both when you dragged him out of the river and when you tipped him back in?'

Bertha furiously dismissed the notion. 'Do you think I don't know a stiffer when I see one? I've been doing this job since long before you were born, you young jackanapes!'

I had no wish to provoke her further. 'I'm sorry,' I said placatingly. 'Is there nothing more that you can recollect? Can you remember the two initials embroidered in gold thread on the tunic, here, just below the collar?'

But it was too much to hope for. There had been too many dead bodies between then and now for Bertha to distinguish one from the other. But we had at least established our bona fides as seekers after truth, and when she had recovered from the insult I had offered her, agreed with perfect readiness to direct us where to find Morwenna Peto. And without her goodwill, it could have been many weeks before we were able to track down the lady.

The thieves' kitchen, run by the Cornishwoman, was tucked into a noisome little alleyway behind the White Hart, the inn favoured as his headquarters by Jack Cade, when he and his army of rebels had marched on London seventeen years previously. Some of the damage inflicted on the buildings by the Kentishmen was still visible, and added to the general sense of decay and decrepitude. There were, and still are, some very fine mansions in the area, and the Priory church of Saint Mary Overy is always a pleasure to look at, but as London jurisdiction does not extend across the river into Southwark, and as there are more bear-baiting pits, cock-fighting rings and brothels to be found there than in the capital itself, it has always attracted rogues and vagabonds and harlots in vast numbers.

Morwenna Peto was not at all as I had imagined her, being large and fair, with a clear, unwrinkled skin despite the fact that she must have been well into her forties. I had been expecting someone more like Bertha Mendip, who, I suspected, was much of an age, but on whom hardship and deprivation had left their mark in no uncertain fashion. The Cornishwoman, on the other hand, appeared to have weathered the storms of life with little outward show of suffering, whatever her inward turmoil might have been.

Bertha had insisted that her son should accompany Philip and myself to Gibbet Lane and introduce us to Morwenna. This turned out to have been a wise precaution, for no sooner had we crossed the threshold of her house, than two of the most evil-looking men I have ever seen emerged from a door on the left-hand side of the narrow passageway to bar our progress. The fact that they uttered no word, merely standing there in stony silence, only served to make their presence the more menacing. I could feel the hairs rising on the nape of my neck, and Philip shuffled a step closer to me for protection. Matt was the only one of the three of us unaffected.

'It's me, you great zanies!' he apostrophized them crossly.

'Matt Mendip! Bertha Mendip's son! These men are her friends. They just want a word or two with Morwenna.'

I was aware that a second door, a little further along the passage, had opened slightly, and that someone was on the other side of it, listening intently. 'It's about her adopted son, Irwin,' I said loudly.

The door was pushed wide and this buxom, smooth-skinned woman emerged to stand, arms akimbo, looking at me with interest.

'I'm Morwenna Peto,' she announced. 'What do you mean, my *adopted* son? What do you know about Irwin?'

'I can tell you where he is and what he's doing,' I said, 'if, that is, you don't know already.'

She glanced towards Matt. 'Can you vouch for these two?'

'My mother can. Knows 'em of old.' He turned to go. 'I must be off. I've done my duty. Got things of my own need seeing to.'

Morwenna nodded and waved away the two bravos standing guard behind us. 'Off about your business, and make sure there's no fighting in the ale-room this dinner-time. One dead and three wounded already this week,' she went on, addressing Philip and myself, and indicating that we should follow her into what appeared to be her private lair at the back of the house. 'Now then,' she said, when the door was fast shut, 'what's this about Irwin? Ungrateful bastard that he is! After all I've done for him, he just ups and leaves one day without so much as a word.'

There was a bench beneath a horn-paned window, which looked out over a noisome courtyard, and Morwenna waved a hand in its direction. She herself sat regally on a backless stool with two rolled, carved arms and a padded velvet seat, now torn and faded, once the property, I guessed, of some noble household. When she was ready, she nodded at me to speak.

When I had finished my story, she pursed her lips. 'So that's what it was all about,' she muttered, more to herself than to us.

I waited for several seconds in mounting impatience before urging her to explain further. 'Irwin hadn't confided in you, then, about the sudden recovery of his memory?'

Morwenna shook her head. 'There wouldn't be any point,' she spat viciously. 'You say he's claiming to be my adopted son? The ungrateful whelp! After all I've done for him! How dare he repudiate his own mother! He's my own flesh and blood, fathered on me when I was working in one of the local stews. Oh, he wasn't the first I'd fallen pregnant with, nor he wouldn't be the last, but there are ways of ridding a woman of bastard children. But for some reason or another, I decided I wanted this one. God knows why, the thieving little toad! Maybe I was lonely. Maybe I needed someone to call my own. How can I tell, after all these years, why I made such a feckless decision? I was young, far from home, unhappy . . .' She lapsed into silence, looking back over the years to the green girl she had once been long ago.

I leaned forward eagerly. 'So you never had a son who died on the gallows? And Irwin wasn't washed up on the Southwark strand, unable to remember who he was or where he came from? And you didn't take him in out of pity?'

'No is the answer to all those questions,' Morwenna replied grimly. 'Although I suppose I might yet end up with a son who's hanged for a felon. Indeed, it seems to be more than likely, from what you tell me.' She sucked thoughtfully at the end of one of her little fingers. 'That man must have put him up to this,' she said, almost to herself. 'Irwin couldn't have dreamed up such a scheme on his own.'

'What man?' I asked, my voice trembling with excitement. 'Do you mean that you saw your son talking to someone?'

Morwenna nodded abstractedly. 'On several occasions.'

'When? What did he look like?' I demanded.

She stroked her chin. 'As to when, it would have been sometime last autumn; before Christmas, certainly. But I couldn't tell you what the man looked like. Irwin and he were never close enough for me to catch a proper glimpse of his face. When I questioned Irwin about him, he told me that the stranger was a potential client, and that he, Irwin, was pimping for some of the Winchester geese.' This I knew to be a local nickname for the prostitutes of the area, and inclined my head to show that I understood. Morwenna continued, 'So, naturally, I thought nothing of it. Irwin was often employed on such work. It was a job he did well.' She added hastily, 'Not that I mean to decry his pickpocketing skills. He was good at most things he turned his hand to.' She spoke with a simple pride, and I could see that Philip, for all his new-found respectability, sympathized with her.

'But this stranger,' I persisted, 'how old would you say he was?'

Morwenna Peto grimaced. 'I don't know. I didn't take much notice of him, not after Irwin's explanation. There are lots of men who return to the Southwark stews whenever they're in London. Irwin's father was such a one. He was from your part of the country, that I do remember.'

'Surely,' I pressed, 'you must have formed some idea as to whether this man was young or old, rich or poor, tall or short. Can you recollect nothing about him?'

She darted me a look of irritation. 'Neither young nor old, rich nor poor, tall nor short. And with that you'll have to be satisfied,' she finished waspishly, 'for it's the truth. I was at a distance on each occasion that I saw him and Irwin together, and there was nothing to distinguish him from anybody else.'

'Can't you recall any item of clothing that he was wearing?' I was growing desperate. 'A hat, a cloak, a tunic?'

Morwenna frowned. At length, she said, 'I think he may have had a scarlet lining to his cloak. Now you force me to it, I think I can remember a flash of colour as he turned.' Her face took on a grimmer expression. 'Why didn't Irwin tell me what he was up to?' She answered her own question. 'I suppose because he knew I'd advise him against it. He'll be out of his depth.'

'On the contrary,' I said, 'he managed to persuade Alderman Weaver that he is indeed his son, right from the start.'

An angry flush tinged Morwenna's cheeks and she compressed her lips tightly.

I had been aware for several minutes that Philip was growing restive, but I had attributed it to boredom, now that our quest was at an end. But suddenly he jumped to his feet, handed me my cudgel, at the same time ostentatiously fingering the haft of the knife tucked into his belt. 'Time we were going,' he said. There was an edge to his voice and the eyes which met and held mine were bright with urgency, willing me to agree.

I got to my feet with the utmost reluctance, for I felt sure that if I were to press Morwenna Peto further, she might recall something about the stranger which she had temporarily forgotten. But Philip had already opened the door and was halfway through it, and by the time I had taken a hasty farewell of our hostess, he was out in the street. As I joined him, he grabbed my arm and hissed, 'Walk normally to the corner, and then run as fast as you can back to the water stairs.'

'What's all this about?' I asked indignantly as we made our way out of Gibbet Lane, Philip's obvious desire to break into a trot showing plainly in the peculiar nature of his gait. 'For goodness' sake, why didn't you let me question her further?'

'I wonder about you sometimes,' my companion said, his grip tightening on my arm, 'I really do! Morwenna is this fellow's mother! Not his adopted mother, but his own flesh and blood; and she's got more cutthroats at her command than you and I have had hot dinners! And there are you, making it plain to her that you're going to put a noose around her son's neck, and you don't expect any reprisals? I was trembling in my shoes. I thought that at any moment she was going to shout for assistance and have us both carved up there and then. I think it's only because she's so angry at her precious son's betrayal, because she can't accept that he didn't confide in her, that what you're up to hasn't quite sunk in . . . Here's the corner. Now, run as if old Scratch himself is after you!'

He dropped my arm as he spoke and was off, weaving his way through the network of narrow alleyways, every now and again doubling back on his tracks, never pausing for breath until we came out on to the quay close by the Southwark gate of London Bridge. The strip of sand was now covered with water, but a boat was, fortunately, moored alongside the water stairs, waiting for custom. We sank, panting, into its stern, with hardly enough breath left to issue our instructions.

'You gentlemen seem to be in an almighty hurry,' the boatman observed. He nodded in the direction of the receding Southwark shore. 'Couple more there, by the looks of it, in as great a haste as you two, shouting and shaking their fists. Well,' he added comfortably, 'there'll be another boat along in a minute. Ah . . . Seems they can't wait. They're setting off across the bridge.'

Chapter Seventeen

By offering him an extra penny above the price of our fare, we persuaded the boatman to row a little way downriver and put us ashore at Saint Botolph's Wharf, instead of at Fish Wharf, which was adjacent to London Bridge. From there, we returned to Cornhill via Roper Lane, Hubbard Lane and Lime Street, glancing anxiously over our shoulders all the way. Fortunately, we seemed to have shaken off our pursuers, but we took a circuitous route, nonetheless, to the Old Clothes Market and the daub and wattle hut behind Philip's stall.

I could see, while we ate the dinner prepared for us by Jeanne, that my companion's enthusiasm of the morning was already on the wane. Philip's taste for adventure had faltered at the first hint of possible danger, and who could blame him? He had his wife and business to consider; and in any case, he knew as well as I did that he could be of no further use to me. He had helped me find both Bertha Mendip and Morwenna Peto: my visits to the Weaver family I must pay alone. As for himself, he would lie low for a week or two, and trust that after such a lapse of time the details of his appearance would fade from Morwenna's mind. (My height was against me, as always, when seeking anonymity, but, with luck, I should be gone from the capital within a very few days.)

'What I can't understand,' Jeanne said, serving me with a second helping of dried, salted fish fried in oatmeal, 'is why this Irwin Peto should hang on to any of his past life at all. Surely he might have expected Alderman Weaver to make enquiries of his own, and so discover the truth. He couldn't have known, as you say, Roger, how unquestioning would be his acceptance.'

'I've been thinking about that,' I said, wiping my mouth on the back of my hand. 'First of all, without Bertha Mendip's assistance, and Matt Mendip to guide us, we might never have traced Morwenna Peto. And without your husband, I should never have discovered Bertha again. In that part of Southwark, they're as close as oysters, and won't betray the whereabouts of any of their kind to outsiders; so unless the Alderman's envoys knew someone like Philip to begin with, it's more than probable that they would never have found her.

'Secondly, we have now established that Irwin Peto is indeed an impostor, and therefore there must be more than enough for him to remember, more than enough pitfalls strewn in his path, without having to make up a story about his life for the past six years, as well. And on those six years, he must be accurate; there must be no discrepancy between one account and another; no risk of being told "but last time you said so-and-so, although the time before that you said the other". There is a good excuse, you see, for his lapses of memory concerning his early life as Clement Weaver, but none at all for forgetting what happened to him as Irwin Peto. So it's much simpler for him to tell the truth whenever he can. The only thing he has to remember is to refer to Morwenna as his adoptive, and not his real, mother.'

Philip nodded his approval of this reasoning, agreeing that it was simpler and safer to tell the truth where possible; and even Jeanne, always harder to convince of anything than her husband, finally agreed that it might be so. 'What will you do now?' she asked me.

I swallowed my last morsel of fish and took a swig of ale. 'I must visit the rest of Alderman Weaver's family, and also the cousin of a certain Baldwin Lightfoot who lives near Saint Paul's.'

'You won't be needing my company, then?' Philip suggested anxiously, exchanging a somewhat shamefaced glance with his wife.

I shook my head and laughed. 'You've been more than helpful, Philip, and I couldn't have got this far without you. But henceforward what I have to do, I must do alone. I shall say my goodbyes after dinner, and you won't be troubled with me any further. I shall return to Bristol as soon as possible.'

They both looked relieved, and neither enquired what I should do for a bed for the next few nights, although I could see that the question was on the tip of Jeanne's tongue. Indeed, she had her mouth open to speak, when I saw Philip give an almost imperceptible shake of his head. What they did not know, they could not reveal, should anyone come knocking on the door for information.

I decided, upon reflection, to visit Baldwin Lightfoot's cousin first, as Saint Paul's was on my way to the Ward of Farringdon Without; but it was only as I approached the churchyard and the towering bulk of the church itself, topped by its great, gilt weathercock, that I realized I did not know the cousin's name. Throughout my life, I have, from time to time, been guilty of this kind of oversight, and although I am always ready to curse myself for my stupidity, I am perfectly well aware that it will happen again and again. As my mother used to say, periodic inattention to detail is one of my many failings.

I recollected that Alison Burnett had referred to Baldwin's cousin as a kinsman of his father; therefore there was a possibility that he, too, might be called Lightfoot. Consequently, I began knocking at every house in the vicinity of Saint Paul's churchyard, starting in Paternoster Row, proceeding along Old

Change and then turning west into Carter Lane, enquiring if one of the inhabitants was so named. And luck, or God, was with me, for at the third dwelling from the further end of Carter Lane, the young maid who answered the door said that if I'd wait, she'd see if the master was within. She disappeared, returning a few moments later to ask my name.

I told her, adding with a fine disregard for the truth, 'I'm a friend of your master's cousin, Baldwin Lightfoot.'

She eyed me askance. 'That won't be much of a recommendation,' she sniffed. Nevertheless, she departed for a second time, eventually reappearing with a request for me to follow her upstairs.

The small, first-floor parlour into which I was shown was snug and well furnished, with a fire burning on the hearth, for the May day was chilly, plenty of fresh, sweet-smelling rushes on the floor, a corner cupboard on whose shelves were displayed items of pewter, silver and latten tin, tapestry cushions liberally piled up on the windowseat, and two beautifully carved armchairs. In one of these, his knees covered by a hand-embroidered, fur-lined rug, was an elderly man wearing an old-fashioned woollen gown trimmed with budge, while a linen hood, with lappets and strings that tied beneath his chin, protected his head from the many draughts whistling about the room.

Master Lightfoot looked me appraisingly up and down with a pair of beady grey eyes. 'And who might you be? I don't recognize your name. Have you come to pilfer from me, like that wretched cousin of mine?'

'I, I'm sorry, sir,' I stammered, taken aback. 'I don't know what you mean.'

'I mean what I say,' he snapped. 'Baldwin came to stay with me last November, sponge off me would, I suppose, be nearer the mark – and after he'd gone I discovered that a silver-gilt cup was missing from that cupboard over there, and my housekeeper reported her best leather girdle had been taken from her room. There were some other odds and ends taken as well, a few trinkets that he purloined and has no doubt by now turned into cash, for Baldwin's always hard up. He's piddled away the money his father left him on women and strong drink, and has virtually nothing left. So if he's sent you as his emissary to touch me for a loan, then he's going to be disappointed. You may tell him from me that I know all about his thieving ways, and that he's lucky I don't set the law on his tail.' The old man continued grumpily, 'It's not that I haven't thought of doing so, believe me, but blood's thicker than water when all's said and done, and unluckily he's the only family I have left nowadays.' He raised his eyes to mine. 'Well! Speak up! Why did he send you here?'

'Er . . . Master Lightfoot didn't send me,' I faltered, trying desperately to find something to add, for I had really been told everything that I needed to know. I now felt almost certain that Baldwin's denial of being in London six months earlier had more to do with his shame at having stolen from his cousin than from any need to deny a meeting with Irwin Peto. 'He . . . er . . . He's talked of you so often that I . . . er . . . Being in London, I thought I'd call on you and see how you did.'

The elder Lightfoot snorted. 'Talked of me, has he? He might well do so if his conscience troubles him.' He gave me another long, deeply suspicious stare. 'You don't look like a friend of Baldwin's to me. In fact, you look more like a pedlar with that great pack on your back . . . What's going on, eh? Get out of my house! Go on! Get out of my house, before I send the maid for the law. Susan! Susan! Where is the dratted girl? Never about when I want her!'

'It's all right,' I assured him hastily. 'I mean you no harm. I'm going. Now, this minute!' And I left the room so fast that I collided with Susan, just outside the door.

'Oops!' she exclaimed, and giggled, looking up coyly into

my face. 'You're in a hurry. Upset him, have you? Well, that's nothing new. He's an ill-conditioned old codger, but I suppose I'd better see what it is he wants.'

'He wants me out of the house,' I said. 'He'll be all right now that I've gone.' She was nothing loath to be persuaded, not wishing to brave her employer's bad temper, and preceded me downstairs again. At the bottom of the flight, I caught her arm. 'Your master has a cousin who's an acquaintance of mine . . .'

'A friend, you said.' The girl laughed. 'I'm not surprised you weren't received with favour. There were things went missing after Master Baldwin's visit last November, and he –' she jerked her head upwards, indicating the room above – 'hasn't had a good word to say for him since.'

'How long did Baldwin stay?' I asked.

Susan shrugged. 'Three days, maybe four; I can't remember exactly. But it wasn't for any length of time. His visits are always short, but this one was shorter than usual.'

'And did he go out much?'

If the girl resented this interrogation, she gave no sign of it. 'He hardly left the house. It was very bad weather, raining and sleeting the whole three or four days. But when I sympathized with him, Master Baldwin said it didn't matter; he didn't have any money to spend anyway.' Susan gave a reminiscent chuckle. 'He's a one, that Baldwin! He never stopped trying to get me into bed with him all the time he was here.' She gave me a demure glance from beneath long dark eyelashes.

On impulse, I bent and kissed her lips, which were soft and pliant, and I felt the tip of her tongue brush mine. I backed away hastily. Apart from the fact that I had no time for dalliance, I found that I had no inclination for it, either. I assumed that it was because of my attachment to Rowena Honeyman, but the face that suddenly swam into my mind was not fair-skinned and blue-eyed, framed by corn-coloured hair, but of a sallow complexion with a pair of steady brown eyes and tendrils of dark hair escaping from beneath a widow's cap. The mind, I thought irritably, could play strange tricks at times.

Susan, pardonably angered by my recoil, opened the street door and indicated that I should leave. 'And don't bother coming back,' she called as she slammed it shut behind me.

I had no intention of returning, but neither did I immediately hurry away. At the end of the street was a stone water trough, and as no horses were drinking from it at that particular moment, I lowered my pack to the ground and sat on its rim to think. Was I now convinced of Baldwin Lightfoot's innocence in this matter of Irwin Peto? All in all, allowing for the fact that there could be no total certainty until the true culprit was exposed, I thought I was. He had stolen from his cousin and, being at heart an honest man and deeply ashamed of his action, was trying to persuade himself that he had never been in London last November. Indeed, he had by now probably convinced himself of the fact. Added to this was his assurance, backed up by that of Alison Burnett, that he had not seen Clement often enough in the years immediately preceding the latter's disappearance to recognize a double if he saw one. I felt reasonably confident, therefore, that I could rule out Baldwin Lightfoot as the instigator of this plot.

That left the Alderman's brother, John, and the various members of his family; his wife, Alice, his two sons, George and Edmund, and their wives, Bridget and Lucy. As I have already mentioned, I had met Dame Alice and George and Bridget Weaver six years earlier during my search for the real Clement, and I thought it almost impossible that the first of these three was capable of hatching such an elaborate piece of mischief on her own. She had seemed to me a compliant woman, submissive in all things to her husband's will and without a thought in her head that he had not put there. But that she would go along with anything of his devising, and think it right to do so, I could well believe. As for the others, I should have to suspend judgement until I saw them.

I remembered that although John Weaver lived in Farringdon Without, his looms and weaving sheds were in the Portsoken Ward, on the other side of the city. The three men, therefore, would probably be from home, thus giving me an opportunity to talk to their wives alone. I rose from my seat on the edge of the water trough and passed through the Lud Gate to make my way along Fleet Street, where the stink of the tanners' yard assaulted my nostrils and made me sneeze. As I approached the bridge over the River Fleet, I had to wait for a party of horsemen coming from the opposite direction, all wearing the badge of the Duke of Clarence and every one of them heavily armed. A carter, who had drawn up beside me, watched them pass with an impassive face, but once they had gone by he turned to me and grimaced.

'Trouble brewing,' he remarked succinctly, and spat before moving on.

I nodded in agreement at his departing back and swung into Shoe Lane, heading north across the Holborn highway into Golden Lane on its further side. Here, there was a cluster of some ten or twelve dwellings, those at present on my right having gardens at the rear which ran down to the Fleet; and if memory served me correctly, John Weaver's house was one of these, somewhere in the middle of the row. It was pointed out to me by a passer-by, who also, without being asked, informed me that George and Edmund Weaver lived on the opposite side of the street, adding gratuitously that the two wives were in and out of their mother-in-law's house all day long. 'You may well ask me when do they cook and clean?' the woman finished indignantly. 'And my answer to that is, I doubt very much if they do.'

In view of these neighbourly strictures, I was not surprised when, in reply to my knock at John Weaver's door, it was opened by a most attractive girl with deep blue eyes and fair curls that were loosely confined by a ribbon at the nape of her neck. Her gown, which was the same colour as her striking eyes, was of the best quality wool, trimmed with matching silk braid, an expensive garment for Golden Lane. This, I guessed, must be Lucy, Edmund Weaver's wife, and described to me by Alison as, 'as big a spendthrift as Bridget is a miser. . . Lucy gets rid of Edmund's money as fast as he can make it . . . so pretty that she can wind him round her little finger.' Well, there was no doubt that she *was* very pretty; equally as pretty as Rowena Honeyman.

I waited for my heart to give its customary lurch of misery at this conjuration of my true love's name, but nothing happened. In a perfectly calm and steady voice, I heard myself asking if I might come in and speak to Dame Alice. 'It's on behalf of her niece, Mistress Burnett.'

Lucy hesitated, eyeing me with caution, but she evidently liked what she saw, for she suddenly smiled and motioned me inside. The interior of the house was much as I remembered it. A long passage led to the back door and the garden, a narrow, twisting staircase rising halfway along its length and giving access to the upper storey, while doors on either side of it opened into various rooms. A faint, but all-pervasive smell of the cattle market at Smithfield hung in the air, borne on the wind and seeping through the building's numerous cracks and crannies.

Lucy Weaver ushered me into a small overcrowded room at the front of the house where Dame Alice and her other daughter-in-law, Bridget, sat yawning over their embroidery. They glanced up hopefully as Lucy announced, 'Here's a visitor.'

'I know you,' said Bridget. 'You've been here before.'

'Well!' exclaimed Dame Alice some time later, when my story was finally told. 'Here's a to-do! Clement alive, after all these years! And poor Alison cut out of her father's will! Not that she'll starve, mind. That husband of hers is as rich as Croesus.'

'That's not the point,' Bridget reminded her mother-in-law sharply. 'Uncle Alfred's money rightly belongs to her, but because he's a fool, she's being cheated of it by some impostor.'

I glanced across at her and asked, 'You feel certain then, Mistress, that this man *is* an impostor?' For the one piece of information I had kept to myself was the knowledge that Irwin Peto was indeed a fraud.

She seemed disconcerted by the question. 'Well . . . That is . . . I suppose him to be. I thought you said he was.' I shook my head and she shrugged. 'It's far too convenient, him turning up now, when Uncle Alfred is so ill.'

'You know that the Alderman is sick? I understood that you had not seen him in some while.'

'John and I visited him in Bristol last summer,' Dame Alice cut in. 'It was easy to see that he was in poor health then, and we told George and Edmund when we returned that their uncle couldn't be long for this world. The only wonder is that he's lasted until now.'

'But you've known nothing of what's been happening since Christmas? Mistress Burnett hasn't written to you? Or the Alderman? But now I come to think of it, I recall Dame Pernelle saying that she had sent you a message by a London-bound carter.'

'Well, it never reached us,' Lucy declared. 'And Alison hasn't written, as far as I know.' She turned with raised eyebrows to her mother- and sister-in-law, seeking confirmation, and they both shook their heads.

'What is *your* opinion, Master Chapman?' Dame Alice wanted to know. 'Do you think this man could possibly be my nephew?'

'No,' I answered. 'I don't. His story is plausible enough, except in one respect. The day Clement disappeared, he was wearing a camlet tunic edged with squirrel's fur, but Irwin Peto described a black frieze tunic trimmed with budge.'

But my bait wasn't taken. Not by so much as the flutter of an eyelid did any one of the three women betray that she knew my story to be a lie, or hint that it could not be so because Irwin Peto had been given the correct information. Indeed, my falsehood appeared to have no effect at all, and they continued chattering and speculating and exclaiming over the news I had brought with every indication that it was a completely fresh revelation to which they still could not come to terms.

I made a move to take my leave, but they detained me, begging me to remain until their husbands came home so that I should be on hand to supply the details that their memories lacked.

'You had best stay to supper,' Dame Alice decreed. 'John and my sons will surely wish to question you, and it would be as well if you remained to hand. We can make the stew go round if we scrape the pot.'

It was neither the most flattering nor the warmest invitation that I had ever received; moreover, the smell emanating from the kitchen at the back of the house was not one to make my mouth water. But it would save me a long walk to the Portsoken Ward, and ensure that I could observe all three men together instead of having to chase them from one weaving shed to another, while at least half their attention was elsewhere. So I thanked Dame Alice and said that I should be pleased to stay.

While the two younger women bustled about fetching plates and knives from a corner cupboard and bread and ale from the pantry, and while Dame Alice disappeared into the kitchen to attend to her broth, I sat quietly with my thoughts. The house was not large, and boasted only one maidservant, but I suspected that this was due far more to parsimony than to poverty. Both Alison Burnett and Dame Pernelle had insisted that John Weaver was comfortably off, even if he were not as wealthy as his brother. If, therefore, he deliberately chose to live in this modest fashion, why should he want more money? Why should he covet half the

Alderman's fortune? Not to spend it, that was certain, but then, misers did not want to spend their money, only to know that it was there, in a hole in the wall or under the floorboards.

And yet I could not bring myself to believe that even if one or all of the Weaver men had hatched this plot their womenfolk were party to it. Total innocence is very hard to simulate, and amongst three people I should have expected at least one unguarded look or word that would have indicated their complicity. But Dame Alice and her daughters-in-law had acquitted themselves without faltering. I must wait patiently, therefore, for their husbands in the hope that either John Weaver or one of his sons might supply me with a clue . . .

And if they didn't? If I was convinced of their innocence as well as that of their wives, what then? I knew, at least, that Irwin Peto was an impostor, but not who else stood to gain from this fraud. And without that second, shadowy figure being unmasked, there was little chance of convincing the Alderman that he had been grossly and cruelly cheated.

Chapter Eighteen

The May days were growing longer, and it was well into the evening before the three Weaver men returned home from the Portsoken Ward, tired, hungry and none too pleased to find a stranger at their table. John Weaver demanded roughly, 'Who's this?'

When all was explained, however, and he and his two sons had blunted their appetites with generous platefuls of stew, I sensed the same sort of excited curiosity in their questioning and general demeanour as their womenfolk had shown, and which, to me, betokened innocence. They were either accomplished dissemblers, with long practice in the art of deception, or they had nothing to hide. Again, as with their wives, there was no momentary hesitation, no surreptitious glance at another member of the family, no feeling on my part that any one of them had been caught out by my unexpected visit. Once more, I dangled my bait of a black frieze tunic, trimmed with budge, and once more it remained untaken.

After an hour or so, I was ready to swear that no one present had been party to Irwin Peto's masquerade, but was I being too credulous? Was one of their number, after all, the person whom I sought? Lucy Weaver could be exonerated as the instigator of the plot, for she had not known Clement, but there still remained the other five. If, however, either Dame Alice or Bridget were involved, then their husbands must be also, for Morwenna Peto was certain that the person she had seen with Irwin was a man. But I had been offered no evidence of collusion between any of the couples. That left the possibility that one of the men, or maybe two, or even all three of them together, had hatched this evil plan, yet the same objection remained. So far, there had not been a single indication of conspiracy amongst them; not one sign of guilt, however fleeting, on any of their faces.

'My brother always was a gullible fool,' John Weaver declared, embarking on a summary of the Alderman's character that tallied with those I had heard before. 'Oh, a shrewd enough businessman, I grant you, and not above a few shady dealings where he thought it worth his while. He's a true Bristolian in not putting God before profit! But my nephew was his weakness: he loved Clement to distraction and the boy's death hit him hard. I'm not saying Alfred isn't fond of Alison, leastwise, he always has been until now, but the girl is more of a de Courcy than her brother ever was. Her mother's blood runs strongly in her veins and now and then makes her a bit imperious. I used to have the feeling that Alfred wasn't altogether comfortable in her presence, and he certainly grew to dislike her husband; called him a numskull and a popinjay within our hearing when my wife and I were staying with him in Bristol last summer. Didn't he, Alice!'

'Yes, my dear,' the dame dutifully agreed.

'So I don't find it at all surprising,' her husband continued, 'that my brother has taken this young man to his heart without making any enquiries as to his bona fides. Sort of damn stupid thing he would do. Sort of damn stupid thing anyone who knows him well would *know* he'd do, if you take my meaning.'

I glanced sharply at my host, but the face, so reminiscent of the Alderman's, was as bland and as guileless as before. And the subject of Clement, however intriguing, was temporarily played out. The conversation turned to other matters; what had happened that day in the Portsoken weaving sheds and tenting grounds; how well the woollen cloth was taking a new purple dye that used a greater proportion of crushed blackberries to bilberries than heretofore; and, more generally, the growing sense of unease throughout the capital and its suburbs as increasing numbers of the Duke of Clarence's men took to the streets bearing arms.

'There's going to be trouble,' Edmund Weaver opined, echoing the carter's sentiments.

'The King ought to do something about Prince George,' his father added tersely.

'It would upset Prince Richard,' Dame Alice objected. 'You know how fond they say he is of both his brothers.'

'He's a good, loyal lad,' her husband concurred, 'but even he won't be able to keep the Queen's family from Clarence's throat for ever. If he's any sense, he'll stay on his own estates, up there in the north, and let the rest of 'em fight it out without him.'

There was no way in which I could prolong my stay, and reluctantly I rose from my seat. As I did so, the bells began to ring for curfew. The city gates would now be shut against me, and I must find lodgings for the night outside the walls. To my surprise, the same thought seemed to have struck John Weaver, for he said, 'You'd better stay here, Chapman, if you don't mind a bed on the kitchen floor.'

'Th-thank you, sir,' I stuttered, and glanced towards Dame Alice for confirmation.

But whatever her husband's wishes, they were hers also, and she acquiesced willingly, promising to find blankets and a pillow after the dirty pans and dishes had been cleared away. In both these chores she and the maid were assisted by her daughters-in-law, while their husbands remained drinking ale and chatting in the parlour. I tried to make my presence as unobtrusive as possible, but occasionally they remembered that I was there and revived the subject of 'Clement' and his reappearance. For the

213

most part, however, they seemed to have lost interest in the matter.

When their wives rejoined them, they sat companionably together until the candles had burned low in their holders and it was time for the younger members of the family to return to their own homes across the street. Goodnights were said and I was shown to my makeshift bed in the kitchen by my hostess, who also indicated the water-barrel, in case I should want to wash my hands and face, and told me that the privy was in the garden. The fire now was little more than a pile of ashes, but some warmth still emanated from both the wall ovens, and the night itself was mild. I took off my boots and jerkin, cleaned my teeth with the piece of willow bark I always carried in my pouch, and lay down beneath the blanket provided by Dame Alice. All the same, I kept my cudgel within easy reach of my right hand, being somewhat suspicious of why I had been invited to stay. My general feeling was that there had been no ulterior motive, and that it was simple good-heartedness on the part of John Weaver, but I couldn't let myself be too sure.

I lay on my back, staring up into the smoky darkness, and realized that in spite of the less than complimentary pictures painted by Alison Burnett of her kinsfolk, I liked them. More importantly for my purpose, however, was the sense that the six of them made up a strongly united family, and that it was extremely unlikely that they had secrets from each other. In short, I was convinced that if one was behind this plot to palm off Irwin Peto as Clement Weaver, then they would all be in it. And yet the knowledge that I might be wrong kept me wakeful, tossing from side to side, unable to settle. Eventually, I got up and walked around the kitchen, then into the passageway in order to stretch my legs and rid them of the twitchy feeling that always possesses them when I'm restless. It was there, standing beside the stairs, that I saw a chink of light on the upper floor and heard the muted sound of voices. John and Alice Weaver were still awake; so, cautiously, and trespassing against all the rules of hospitality, I crept up the twisting flight in my stockinged feet. As I reached the top, their voices came clearly to my ears.

'A strange business! A strange business!' John Weaver was saying. 'And if the man's not genuine, as the chapman hinted, then who, in God's Name, has put him up to it? Who's made him free of all the facts he needs to know?'

'I'm sure I couldn't guess,' said Dame Alice's voice, now growing sleepy. 'But it's very unfair on Alison.' She yawned. 'D'you think you should go to Bristol, my dear, and try to shake some sense into Alfred?'

There was a momentary silence while, presumably, her husband considered her proposition. Then he, too, yawned loudly. 'My niece has a husband to protect her interests. My interference might do more harm than good, and could well do further damage to her cause.'

'My sentiments exactly,' Dame Alice murmured placidly. 'Goodnight, my love. God bless you.'

John Weaver held forth a little longer on the folly of his brother, but as his only answer was his wife's gentle snoring, he was forced to give up. Silently, I crept downstairs again.

I now felt as certain as I possibly could be that neither John nor Alice Weaver was the person whom I sought. And if not them, then not their sons nor daughter-in-law, Bridget, either. I slid beneath my blanket on the rush-strewn floor, the musty, stale scent of the dried flowers and grasses irritating the back of my nose, and resumed my sightless contemplation of the ceiling. I seemed to have eliminated Baldwin Lightfoot and all John Weaver's family as suspects, so who was there left?

If, at that moment, I had still been in any doubt as to whether or not Irwin Peto was a fraud, I might very well have decided in his favour; for without someone to coach him in all the aspects of his former life, who could he be but Clement? The trouble was, however, that I now knew him to be an impostor, therefore there had to be someone who had primed him. But who? Who else was there, apart from the Weaver family and Baldwin Lightfoot, who would know enough details about Clement's childhood to have such information at his, or her, fingertips?

Common sense whispered that of course there were many others. As far as servants went, both Ned Stoner and Rob Short had been eliminated by Mistress Burnett herself, but there was still Dame Pernelle who, on her own admission, had known both Clement and Alison as children and was, moreover, the sister of Alice Weaver. But when would she have had any opportunity for meeting Irwin Peto? What, then, of former servants? What of neighbours? What of friends? My head began to spin as I realized that even if I discounted members of the Alderman's family, the possibilities were endless, and that my investigation had barely begun. There might be half of Bristol to choose from . . .

Yet, I could not rid myself of the notion that the answer was there, somewhere, almost within my grasp; a feeling that I had all the pieces of the picture to hand if only I knew how to fit them together. Perhaps if I could get to sleep, I might dream; one of those strange dreams which, periodically, I had experienced from childhood and which, if interpreted correctly, smacked of second sight, a gift that I had inherited from my mother. (Although my mother, conscious of the dangers of such a claim, had always been loath to own to more than womanly intuition.) But when at last I did fall asleep, my dreams were just the usual jumble of worthless nonsense, immediately forgotten on waking, and deservedly so.

I was roused the following morning by the activities of the little maid-of-all-work as she set about rekindling the fire, putting water on to boil and heating the ovens ready to take the first of the day's batch of loaves, that had been left standing on a marble slab overnight. I visited the privy in the garden, washed under the pump and then, whilst waiting for some hot water in which to shave, wandered down to the banks of the Fleet.

The gardens of the houses in Golden Lane were separated one from another by nothing more than a few trees and bushes, and all gave access to a footpath that, to the right, led as far as the Holborn Highway, and, to the left, beyond the entrance to Chicken Lane on the opposite bank, dwindled into an overgrown track. It was a quiet, peaceful scene in the early morning light, mist rising from the river and clumps of golden kingcups standing sentinel along the water's edge. Willows bent to stare at their reflections, and the lilac heads of Lady's Smock swayed in a gentle breeze. The flowers of the butterbur nestled among their heart-shaped, hairy leaves . . .

I felt a great shove between my shoulder blades, and the next moment I was in the river. Someone leapt in after me and was forcing my head beneath the water, trying to drown me in the Fleet. I had been taken so completely by surprise that the shock rendered me helpless for several precious seconds; but eventually my senses cleared enough to make me start to fight back. My lungs felt as though they were bursting from holding my breath, but I kicked out violently, at the same time raising my arms clear of the water and, by great good fortune, managing to catch my assailant around the neck. As my fingers tightened about his throat, he was forced to let go of my head in order to prise my hands loose, and I came up, gasping for air.

To my surprise, I did not know him; for in the very few seconds of rational thought afforded me since my unexpected immersion, I had decided that my attacker was either John Weaver or one of his sons. But this was a stranger, a rough-looking man with a tangled, bushy, black beard, broken teeth and of an enormous ox-like strength. 'What do you want of me?' I demanded, coughing and spluttering.

He had by now freed himself and lunged at me again. Luckily, I saw the blow coming and managed to seize his wrist in mid-air, exerting all my own strength to prevent his fist crashing into my jaw and rendering me unconscious. With both of us treading water, it now became a trial of strength, but I suspected my assailant to be even stronger than I was; and how it might have ended I still shudder to think, had not the maidservant come running down the garden, shouting at the top of her voice. The man swore, dragged himself on to the bank and loped away, as fast as his girth and his sodden clothes would permit, in the direction of the Holborn Highway.

With the assistance of the girl and some willow roots, I managed to climb out of the water, and sat for several minutes on the path in order to get my breath. Meantime, John Weaver and his wife, awakened by the noise and still in their nightclothes, had come out to see what was happening, and, when they knew, to inveigh against the prevalence of footpads in the area.

'It used to be such a respectable neighbourhood,' lamented Dame Alice.

They accompanied me back indoors, leant me some of John Weaver's clothes to put on while my own were drying and invited me to remain beneath their roof for as long as was necessary. I assured them that with the good fire now blazing on the kitchen hearth, I should have no need to trouble them for more than an hour or two; and indeed everything except my boots was dry well before the ten o'clock dinner hour. I was just wondering if I could impose on Dame Alice for another meal, when there was a knock at the back door. The maid went to answer it and returned with Philip Lamprey at her heels.

'Someone to see you, Chapman.'

I rose from my stool by the fire. 'Philip! How on earth did you find me?'

'Never mind that.' He gripped my arm. 'I'm not the only one out looking for you, but thank God it seems I'm the first who's run you to ground. Word has it that Morwenna Peto's men are still searching for you, and I wouldn't give a fig for your chances if one of them finds you. Get out of London as fast as you can.'

When Philip gave such advice it was not to be taken lightly. I knew that 'word has it' meant that some of his old Southwark friends had been in touch with him and issued a warning.

'I've already had one encounter,' I said, and told Philip what had occurred that morning.

'Then go now! This instant!' he urged. 'You've not a moment to lose.'

I began pulling on my boots, although they were still damp and squeaked a little in protest when I walked. 'Won't Morwenna send her bloodhounds after me to Bristol?'

Philip shook his head. 'It's doubtful. These people don't like venturing so far outside their own territory.'

'And you?' I asked, stamping my feet to make the boots fit more comfortably. 'Will you and Jeanne be safe?'

'We'll be all right,' he assured me confidently. 'Morwenna will have forgotten what I look like by now, and there are plenty of people who'll stand my friend. Come on, lad! Come on! Grab your pack and cudgel and get on your way!'

I said a brief farewell to John and Alice Weaver, tendered my thanks for their hospitality and went; an unceremonious departure that must have left them thinking me ungrateful and extremely impolite. But there was no time to worry about such niceties. I parted from Philip at the bottom of Golden Lane and turned westwards along the Holborn road.

For the first few days of my journey, I walked at a steady pace, not stopping to sell the remainder of my wares, and staying as far as possible on the open highways, where I was able to keep an eye on the road at my back. I also travelled in the company of others whenever I could, and being late spring and the weather fine, there were many people, clerks, friars, pardoners, troops of mummers and jongleurs, out and about. Close to London, and heading towards it, I encountered more companies of armed men, all wearing the Duke of Clarence's livery; and on one occasion, a wet evening when I felt extravagant enough to take a bed at an inn, I fell in with a courier of Robert Stillington, the Bishop of Bath and Wells, who was returning home after carrying a message from his master to His Grace of Clarence. And once again, I reflected on how often the names of those two malcontents seemed to be linked.

As the days passed, however, and the number of miles between myself and the capital increased, I began to feel safe, seeking out the more remote villages and hamlets in order to sell my goods. Consequently, the month of June was well advanced by the time I reached Bristol, to receive a warm welcome from my mother-in-law and daughter. It so happened that Adela Juett and her son were paying them a visit on the afternoon of my arrival home, and I was astonished at the pleasure I felt on seeing them both again, so much so that I was moved to slip an arm about Adela's waist and kiss her thin, pale cheek. Nicholas, I threw up into the air, catching him as he fell, rough treatment which delighted him and which Elizabeth immediately clamoured to share.

'No, no!' I protested. 'I must wash and change my shirt and then be off to see Master and Mistress Burnett.'

As usual, my mother-in-law was inclined to be offended by my going out again almost as soon as I had come in, but Adela only laughed. As I went outside to the pump, I overheard her say, 'It's no good being cross, Margaret. Surely you must know by now that Roger's not the man to be kept on a chain. It's one of the reasons why I like him.' And suddenly, as I ducked my head beneath the pump's clear jet of water, it seemed not enough that Adela should merely like me. I realized that I wanted more than that.

'So!' Alison Burnett's eyes glittered feverishly in a face that was now a skeletal mask. 'You say you know this Irwin Peto to be an impostor, but you have no evidence that would convince my father. Also, by reasoning that I find flawed and feeble in the extreme, you have decided that Uncle John, Aunt Alice and all my cousins are innocent of concocting this plot to rob me of my inheritance. The same goes for Baldwin Lightfoot.' The claw-like hands tightened on the arms of her chair and her voice grew shrill. 'How dare you come back here to report a job half done! Why didn't you stay in London and search for proof against my uncle and his family?' She beat her hands together and rose abruptly, pacing the floor. She was plainly growing hysterical, and I glanced anxiously at William Burnett for guidance.

He got up and went to his wife, trying to soothe her. 'If the chapman says there's no proof to be found, then there is none, and at least we have the satisfaction of knowing that we are right as regards to this impostor and your father wrong. Let us be satisfied with that. After all, we have no need of his money.'

'No *need*? What has that to do with anything?' Alison Burnett was growing yet more frenzied, lashing out at her husband and beating him about the face and head. 'Why are you all against me?' she screamed. 'First my father and now you! What have I done to be treated like this? *Your* stupidity deprived me of *all* my inheritance instead of only half, and now you say that it doesn't matter! Why should I be forced to give up what's mine just because my father's a wicked old fool and you're an incompetent nincompoop?'

William opened the parlour door and yelled for Dame Pernelle to come to his assistance, but Alison, biting and kicking and scratching, now seemed beyond all control. It was obvious that during the months of my absence her emotional state had sadly deteriorated, and I decided that it was high time I left. I could return another day when things might be quieter, and Mistress Burnett less agitated. I therefore slipped unobtrusively out of the room and crossed the hall, letting myself out though the front door.

The afternoon was still warm, the sun riding high in the sky. I guessed that Adela would have returned to her own home by now, for she had been talking of going before I left, and I was seized with a sudden, seemingly irrational desire to see her again. I therefore walked down Small Street, turned right into Bell Land and made my way under Saint John's Arch, across the Frome Bridge and out by the Frome Gate into Lewin's Mead. As I glanced across at Adela's cottage, I thought I saw a slight movement in the shadows cast by one wall, and the hairs on the nape of my neck began to rise; but after waiting several minutes in the shelter of the Gate, I could detect nothing further and told myself not to be a fool.

I advanced rapidly across the open space in front of the row of cottages and had raised a hand to knock on Adela's door when someone gripped my shoulder. Without even glancing behind me, I bunched my right hand and swung about, smashing my fish into the unknown's face and felling him to the ground with a single blow.

Chapter Nineteen

Timothy Plummer sat at the table in Adela Juett's cottage looking extremely sorry for himself. In front of him was a bowl of bloodstained water, and pressed to his nose a rag on which Adela had smeared some of her home-made sicklewort ointment in order to staunch the bleeding.

'Master Plummer, I must apologize,' I said, for what seemed like the twentieth time.

'So you should,' he grunted, deigning to speak at last. 'All I did was touch your shoulder.' He raised his head and regarded me shrewdly. 'You're as jumpy as a cat, Roger. In trouble again? To do, I suppose, with the business you told me about that day in Frome. No!' He flung up a hand. 'I don't want to know. I've problems enough of my own.' He lowered the compress and took a long draught of the ale that Adela had thoughtfully set before him.

His mood was improving, so I drew up another stool to sit opposite him at the table. 'What are you doing in Bristol?' I asked. 'More importantly, what are you doing skulking around this cottage?'

'I was not skulking,' he replied indignantly. 'I was about to knock when I saw you approaching. If you must know, I'm looking for an Imelda Bracegirdle.' He glanced sideways at Adela.

'This is the Widow Juett,' I said quickly. 'The lady you want is dead. Unhappily, she was murdered last January, and Mistress

Juett has been renting the cottage from the Priory ever since.'

Timothy swore softly. '*Dead?* And since the beginning of the year?' He chewed his underlip, adding, 'This will be bad news for the Duke.'

'For Duke Richard, do you mean?' I asked, and he nodded. 'But of what possible concern can it be to His Grace?'

Once again, Timothy glanced at Adela, and she, quick on the uptake as always, took hold of Nicholas's hand. 'I've promised to visit a neighbour,' she said, 'but please don't disturb yourself, Master Plummer. Stay here as long as you wish; until you feel recovered enough to move.' She smiled at me and went out, dragging her reluctant son behind her and gently closing the door.

'Well?' I demanded impatiently, looking at Timothy.

He swallowed more ale before asking gloomily, 'You've heard the news about Brother George, of course?'

'What about him? I've heard nothing, but then I've been on the road for weeks.'

'I've told you before, you just don't keep your ears open. That's the trouble with you, Chapman!' Timothy exclaimed in exasperation. 'I should have thought that everyone knew by now that the Duke of Clarence was arrested at the beginning of the month and is a prisoner in the Tower. Do you really mean to say you haven't heard?'

I shook my head, my jaw hanging slack. 'Not a word,' I breathed, when finally I could find my voice. 'I knew that he was arming his retainers. I met whole troops of them when I was in London, in May. And I happened to be at Westminster the day he proclaimed Burdet's innocence. But the King has forgiven his brother on so many occasions in the past, that I never thought he'd do more than try to reason with him and calm him down. What's happened to make His Highness behave differently this time?'

My companion grunted. 'Perhaps Clarence has gone that one step too far. Perhaps the King's patience has finally run out.' He lowered his voice. 'Or perhaps, and I tell you this in the strictest secrecy, Roger, because of the great service you once rendered my master, it's because King Louis has written to King Edward informing him that Clarence's bid for the Duchess of Burgundy's hand was just the first step in an attempt to seize the English crown. Louis says he has this information from his Burgundian spies, who, he maintains, are absolutely to be relied upon. King Edward told my master, who told me in my capacity as his Spy-Master General. So you see, it comes straight from the horse's mouth.'

I didn't argue the point, for I had no doubt at all that the Duke of Clarence was perfectly capable of such treachery, judging by his previous conduct. 'But,' I cavilled, 'on what grounds could he possibly depose his elder brother? He'd have to advance some reason, and what could it be? And as well as King Edward, there are the Prince of Wales, the Duke of York and the five Princesses who all have a claim to the throne after their father.'

Timothy propped his elbows on the table and dabbed at his nose, where a thin trickle of blood was beginning to ooze again from his left nostril. 'As to that, I can't speculate. Duke Richard is sure that King Louis is lying, in order to make bad blood between his brothers. He might even be right, but he's been prejudiced against the French ever since the Treaty of Picquigny. But it's also true that King Louis detests my master. However, whatever the truth of the accusation, Kind Edward thought it serious enough to summon Brother George to Westminster and then order his arrest on a charge of "subverting the laws of the realm and of taking the administration of justice into his own hands." Members of the Royal Guard were called and Clarence is now safely tucked away in the Tower.'

'Will there be a trial?'

'If the King doesn't decide to pardon him first, then yes, there's bound to be one sometime or another. And if the Duke's found guilty, what can the sentence possibly be, other than death?'

'Edward wouldn't allow it,' I predicted confidently. 'If that happened, he'd reprieve Clarence. Anyway, he's probably only imprisoned him to give him a fright.'

Timothy pursed his lips. 'My master isn't so certain. There are rumours flying about that Clarence employed the Oxford clerk, John Stacey, to cast the King's horoscope, which prophesied His Highness's early death.'

'Is there any substance to these rumours?'

'Not yet. But there are also whispers that the damning evidence was parcelled up by Stacey and entrusted to a kinsman to bring to a cousin here in Bristol. If that should prove to be the case, then Duke Richard is anxious to get his hands on it before any of the Woodvilles do, so that it can be disposed of.'

If I was shocked at the idea of the Duke of Gloucester destroying evidence that might be used to incriminate his brother, it was an emotion largely suppressed by the tumult of ideas suddenly spinning around in my head.

'The cousin you mention must have been Imelda Bracegirdle,' I said. 'I'd forgotten it until now, but somebody once told me that her mother's name was Stacey and that she came from Oxford.' Now at last I knew what it was that had been nagging at me ever since I first heard the name of John Stacey. 'But why would he want his papers lodged with a kinswoman? Why didn't he simply burn them? Surely that would have been the safer, easier way?'

'Maybe they were too valuable. Maybe they represented too many hours' hard work.' Timothy drained his cup and wiped his mouth on his sleeve. 'There's another rumour that says this cousin is, or was, herself a caster of horoscopes. Perhaps he wished to bequeath her his secrets.'

226

'Wait a minute,' I interrupted. 'A man did come to this cottage a month or so ago, looking for Mistress Bracegirdle and carrying a bundle of some sort under his arm. I arrived here just as he was leaving, but according to Mistress Juett, he'd claimed to be a kinsman of Imelda. He seemed most put out to discover she was dead.'

Timothy sighed. 'There you are, then. And if she hadn't been dead, she'd probably have relieved him of the parcel and hidden it somewhere.' He glanced disparagingly around the cottage. 'But it's difficult to see exactly where.'

'No, it's not!' I cried excitedly, and rose from my stool to fetch the hooked iron bar from its resting place in a corner of the room. I then cleared the rushes from the necessary portion of the floor and raised the flagstone. 'Come and look at this,' I invited.

Timothy joined me, kneeling down and staring thoughtfully into the cavity. 'Undoubtedly this is where Mistress Bracegirdle kept her own charts,' he said. 'You see how the bottom is lined with waxed cloth to keep them dry and stop the parchment from mildewing.'

'Of course!' I breathed. 'We thought it must have contained a secret hoard of money that was stolen by her murderer, but why would she have gone to so much trouble just to store coins? The bare earth would have sufficed.'

Timothy sighed regretfully. 'Well, there's nothing here now.' He lapsed into silence for a few moments, before adding, 'I must return to Duke Richard at once and tell him that we'll have to search elsewhere for John Stacey's papers. Let's pray to God that the Queen's or Earl Rivers's spies don't locate them before we do!'

He had risen to his feet and was making ready to leave even as he spoke. For the sake of politeness, I urged him to stay a little longer and have some refreshment before setting out, but he refused. There could be no delay: he had to get back as soon as possible to London, where Duke Richard was on a brief visit from the north, to remonstrate with the King and comfort his mother, and decide what was now best to be done.

I did not argue, for I was as anxious to see him gone as he was to go. My mind was whirling. All those scraps of knowledge that had been in my possession for days, weeks, months, had begun to make sense, and I could not wait to start piecing them together.

Adela sat in the place that Timothy Plummer had so recently occupied and I sat opposite her, our hands almost, but not quite, touching in the middle of the table. Nicholas had been sent to play with his toys at the back of the room, but, childlike, was happier cradling an old leather water bottle in his arms and talking to it in his own baby language.

Having engaged Adela's pledge of secrecy, I had told her not only what I had found out in London during my visit to Morwenna Peto, but also everything that had passed between Timothy and myself this afternoon, for I knew she was to be trusted, even if he did not. She was intrigued by the notion that Imelda Bracegirdle had been a caster of horoscopes, and readily agreed that the underfloor cavity could have been the hiding place for her charts and predictions.

'But who would have taken them?' Adela asked. 'Who would have known that they were there?'

'Someone who had asked her to cast a horoscope. Someone who had either noticed that iron bar in the corner and worked out what it could be for, or who had seen her use it. And when she was dead, that someone opened up the hiding place and took the charts away.'

Adela frowned. 'But to what purpose? Are you saying that they were the reason she was murdered? Not her money?'

'I doubt if she had any money other than what she earned from spinning, and the little extra she made in secret by her horoscopes. But after Irwin Peto turned up, claiming to be Clement Weaver, she may have been sharp enough to put two and two together and realize how she could extort more money in return for keeping her mouth shut. If that is what happened, she signed her own death warrant.'

My companion's frown deepened. 'I don't understand. How can Mistress Bracegirdle's murder and Irwin Peto's impersonation, as you now assure me it is, be linked?'

'By the murderer,' I answered simply. 'Do you remember when we first looked at the iron bar, we discovered some threads attached to it?'

'Two black threads and a red; yes, I remember. They were silk.'

'And do you also remember, on an earlier occasion, a woman, outside her father's house, calling and calling for her husband, who made no answer? And why didn't he answer? Probably because he wasn't there; probably because he had slipped out earlier, across the Frome Bridge, and was busy about his own murderous business.'

Adela passed her tongue between her lips. 'You're talking about William Burnett,' she said, 'unless I'm very much mistaken.'

'I am.'

She gave an incredulous laugh. 'But that's nonsensical! If Mistress Burnett is disinherited, then he is too. If she gets no money, then neither does he. What would be the point of it?'

I didn't reply directly. 'A few days before Margaret received your letter from Hereford,' I said, 'I saw Alderman Weaver and Mistress Burnett coming out of his house together. Now, everybody says that Alison is like her mother, that she looks like the de Courcys more than the Weavers, but that day it struck me that she bore a stronger resemblance to her father than I had previously imagined. At the same time, I thought how sickly the Alderman appeared.' I leaned a little closer, and suddenly my hands were holding hers. 'Don't you see, the similarity lay in the fact that they are both unwell; that both are suffering from some wasting disease? Alison Burnett was ill long before the quarrel over the will. That has aggravated it, accelerated it, *but it's not the cause.*'

Adela followed my reasoning without any prompting, as I had known she would. 'And you think that William Burnett, realizing this, had Imelda Bracegirdle cast his wife's horoscope. And if that horoscope predicted Alison would die before her father . . .' Her voice tailed off and she looked at me with startled speculation in her eyes.

'Yes! Yes!' I breathed, tightening my grip on her hands. 'If Mistress Burnett were to die before the Alderman, then her husband would never get a penny of her father's money. I've been told that Alfred Weaver has grown to dislike his son-in-law, so he would be extremely unlikely to make a new will that provided for William.'

'But Master Burnett doesn't need the Alderman's money. He has a very substantial fortune of his own.'

'So we are led to believe. But has he? Firstly, *did* he inherit as much from his father as everyone thought? I've been told that both old Alderman Burnett and his father before him were gamblers; and only three months after the Alderman's death, William merged the business with that of his father-in-law. Why? Simply because it made good sense to do so, or because he realized that it was the only way to keep it going? And secondly, there's the matter of his own gambling debts.'

'Does he have any?' Gently Adela freed her hands from mine and rose to fetch us both more ale.

I swivelled round to watch her as she crossed the room, and

thought, not for the first time, how gracefully she moved.

'According to Nick Brimble and Jack Nym, William Burnett is a frequent visitor to the upper room of the New Inn, which is apparently given over to games of hazard. Nick Brimble told me that William owed money to Jasper Fairbrother, and he and Jack reckoned it was a couple of Jasper's bravos who attacked William that night outside Saint Werburgh's Church, because he had delayed paying Fairbrother his money. But why had he delayed, knowing what might happen to him? I don't think it was out of meanness or cussedness as Jack and Nick believe, but because he couldn't afford to honour the debt.'

Adela handed me my cup of ale and sat down again, sipping her own. 'But why, in that case, when he must have guessed who his assailants were, did he try to throw suspicion on Irwin Peto?' She answered her own question. 'To put Alison off the scent, I suppose.'

'Partly for that reason, maybe, but also because he knew she was only too eager to believe everything bad about Irwin, and that, with a little encouragement, which he no doubt subsequently gave her, Alison would quarrel even more bitterly with her father on the subject. One of the things,' I went on, 'that has always bothered me about that quarrel is the apparently maladroit way in which William Burnett handled the affair, making the rift between the Alderman and his daughter even greater than it need have been by his arrogant and insulting behaviour.'

'With the result,' Adela said slowly, 'that Alison was cut out of the will altogether.' She tidied away a stray lock of hair that had escaped from beneath her linen hood. 'Now, let me see if I have this aright. You're accusing William Burnett of being the instigator of this plot, the man who stumbled across Irwin Peto, recognized his likeness to Clement Weaver and persuaded him to impersonate his dead brother-in-law. But when could this have happened?'

'Listen! When Timothy Plummer and I were talking, that evening in Tewkesbury, he mentioned, quite by chance, that a deputation of Bristol weavers had been in London last October, demanding a higher price for their cloth. William may well have been one of them, and that could have been when Irwin Peto crossed his path. He was immediately struck by the likeness to Clement, and saw a way by which he could try to secure at least a portion of the Alderman's fortune for himself after Alison's death. No doubt, he and Irwin Peto arranged to split the inheritance in half. The state of Alfred Weaver's health had probably convinced William that they wouldn't have long to wait.'

Adela regarded me with consternation. 'Roger, are you sure you're not letting your imagination run away with you? I can see that William Burnett would know enough of his wife's past, and enough details of Clement's disappearance, to make him a good instructor; but how could he possibly rely on the word of a man such as Irwin Peto? What's to prevent Peto hanging on to all the inheritance once it's his?'

'I have no doubt at all that William Burnett has foreseen that situation, and holds some sort of written, legally witnessed document, allowing him to claim half of any monies that come to Irwin. And with such a paper in William's possession, Irwin would be a fool to withhold his share, unless he's willing to risk getting his neck stretched.'

Adela rubbed her nose. 'But why would William murder Imelda Bracegirdle?'

'For the reason I've already given you. When Clement turned up just after Christmas, and the city was buzzing with the news, she was astute enough to suspect some underhand dealing on William's part, and threaten him with exposure. He panicked, because she held the only proof that might connect him to such a plot, Alison's horoscope, predicting her death before her father's. So he killed Mistress Bracegirdle and removed the evidence. What he did with it, heaven alone knows. Burnt it, most like.'

Adela said nothing for a minute or two, turning over what I had said in her mind. At last she asked, 'The black and red silk threads, where do you think they came from?'

'The day William Burnett visited Margaret's cottage with his wife, he was wearing a black and red silk girdle. He could have been wearing it the night of the murder.'

Adela still appeared dubious. 'If all you say is founded in fact and isn't a product of your imagination, and presuming that William Burnett believes the horoscope cast by Mistress Bracegirdle to be true, then why did he seek to widen the breach between Alison and her father? If she dies first, the Alderman will leave everything to Clement anyway.'

I shrugged. 'I can't say for certain, but probably to make it plain to Alison that he was taking her part against her father, and to make absolutely sure that all the money goes to his partner in crime when the Alderman is dead.'

'But supposing Imelda Bracegirdle's prophecy is wrong and Mistress Burnett *doesn't* die before her father, then Master Burnett will have robbed himself of half of Alfred Weaver's fortune.' Adela finished her ale, propped her elbows on the table, cupped her chin in her hands and regarded me challengingly.

I returned her look resentfully. I was growing irritated by her constant questioning of my theory. To me, it all seemed as clear as day. 'You have to try to think like he does,' I protested. 'You have to think with his thoughts, not your own. He must know enough of his wife's state of health to believe implicitly in Mistress Bracegirdle's forecast. Most likely, all he sought from her was confirmation of his own worst fears. At that time, he couldn't see what to do about it; indeed, he may well have reconciled himself to the idea that there was nothing *to* be done.

It was only when he chanced across Irwin Peto and recognized his likeness to Clement Weaver that he saw a possible remedy for the situation.'

'So, what do you propose doing now?' Adela asked. 'As far as I can see, you have no proof for any of these accusations. And it's doubtful if anyone will credit your story without it.'

'I can only go to Mistress Burnett and Alderman Weaver and tell them what I think happened,' I answered.

My companion shook her head. 'Neither will believe you,' she warned. 'Neither will want to.'

I sighed. 'Nevertheless, I must try. I might rattle either William Burnett or Irwin Peto enough to make one of them do something foolish. The realization that I know the truth . . .'

'If it *is* the truth,' Adela murmured.

I continued as if she had not spoken, '. . . could make them panic. Or I might plant a seed of doubt in the mind of either Mistress Burnett or the Alderman. It's in God's hands.'

It was Adela's turn to sigh. I rose to my feet and she rose with me, coming round the table to embrace me. 'Take care, Roger. If you're right, both William Burnett and this Irwin Peto are dangerous men.'

'I'll be as careful as I can,' I promised, before gently kissing her goodbye.

I left the cottage and set out in the direction of the Frome Gate, so intent on my errand that I failed to notice I was being followed.

Chapter Twenty

It must by now have been approaching four o'clock and supper-time; but although it was many hours since I had eaten dinner at an inn on the heights above Bath, so much had happened since my arrival home that I was feeling none of the pangs of hunger usual after so long an abstinence.

Traffic was thin at the Frome Gate, and the Porter would willingly have exchanged a few words with me had I not pushed my way past him, intent only on confronting first Alison and William Burnett, then Alderman Weaver and Irwin Peto, before my courage failed me. My rudeness was greeted with a sniff, and I was vaguely aware that the Porter, with a resolution to match my own, had waylaid the man behind me, determined to alleviate the tedium of a slack afternoon with a little conversation. On such slender threads of chance does human life depend, for I am certain that had my pursuer not been detained, a knife would have been slipped between my ribs once we were across the bridge and within the shadows of Saint John's Arch. As it was, I had walked out into the sunshine of Broad Street before he could shake off the unwelcome attentions of the Porter. (This is surmise, of course, but well-founded surmise, given subsequent events.)

My eyes were momentarily dazzled as I stepped from darkness into light, and for a second or two I was unable to see what was happening. My ears, however, told me that a very public quarrel was taking place, and that the chief protagonist was a woman. Indeed, I instantly recognized the voice as that of Alison Burnett, her vituperations carrying loudly in the still, summer air.

My sight cleared and I could see the tableau ahead of me. Alison, her face livid and damp with sweat beneath her blue silk hood, her eyes wild and staring, was so beside herself with rage that she was behaving like any fishwife from Billingsgate Market. Her language, as she heaped abuse on her father's head, was worse than anything I have ever heard used by a man, and how she came to know such expressions is a mystery. (Although Adela always used to laugh when I said as much.) Behind her hovered William, gesturing ineffectually and apparently incapable of restraining her excesses.

The opposing group consisted of Alderman Weaver, dressed in one of his old-fashioned velvet gowns and looking more ill and fatigued than he had done at any time since Irwin Peto's arrival, six months earlier; Ned Stoner and Rob Short, together with a horrified Dame Pernelle, who had followed their master outside to ensure, if necessary, his safety; and, lurking in the doorway, the impostor himself, his face wearing a strange expression compounded in almost equal measure of defiance and guilt, or so, at least, it seemed to me.

It was obvious that Mistress Burnett, incensed beyond reason by what I had told her concerning Irwin Peto, had been unable to contain her fury, and, sometime after my departure, had marched round from Small Street to Broad Street to vent her fury upon her father. Whether she had refused to step across his polluted threshold, or whether the Alderman had forbidden her contaminating presence in his house, I had no means of knowing, but for whatever reason, the bitter confrontation, rapidly deteriorating into a brawl, was taking place in the middle of the street. Faces, some eager, some shocked, were appearing at neighbouring windows, and one or two people had already ventured out of doors to stand and gape. Such a display of paternal foolishness and filial condemnation was a rare enough sight, and one not to be missed. But it would not be long, I hoped, before someone notified the Sheriff and his Officers at the castle, and a patrol arrived to deal with this flagrant breach of the peace, before physical harm was done.

'So now you know,' Alison was screaming at the top of her voice, her finger pointing accusingly at Irwin Peto, 'that that *creature*, that *thing*, is not your son! I demand that you hand him over to the law immediately!'

While she paused to draw breath and ease her aching throat, the Alderman was able to storm into battle. 'How dare you come here,' he demanded furiously, 'with some trumped-up story, concocted between you and that paid lackey of a chapman, trying to pretend that this isn't Clement! Can you really believe that I don't know my own son?' He glared fiercely at William. 'Get her away from here, now, at once! Haven't you more authority over your wife than this? Although, on second thoughts, perhaps you haven't. I've thought for years that you're a weak, inept sort of being, whose only talent is for empty boasting.'

'Be quiet, you stupid old goat!' Alison had got her second wind. 'Don't you ever speak to William like that again!' She looked round and saw me, falling upon me with claw-like hands, urging me to tell her father all I had learned from Morwenna Peto.

I hesitated, not from any reluctance to blacken Irwin Peto's name, but because I was wondering just how I was going to disclose my suspicions concerning her husband. I hadn't bargained on such a public venue or an audience of anyone but the people most closely concerned in the matter. But the crowd of neighbours venturing into the street was growing by the minute.

'Go on!' screamed Alison, shaking my arm. 'Tell him! Shout it from the rooftops so that everyone can hear! That man is *not* my brother!'

I cleared my throat. 'Can't we all go somewhere more private?' I begged.

But before anyone could answer my question or comply with my wishes, Irwin Peto suddenly started out of the shelter of his doorway, crying, 'No, Jude, no!' There was an urgency in his voice that, because of the previous attempt on my life, alerted me to present danger. Moreover, his eyes were fixed on something, or somebody, immediately behind me. And in that split second, I recollected the shadowy figure I had seen skulking around Adela's cottage, and which, mistakenly no doubt, I had later assumed to have been Timothy Plummer. Resisting the very natural impulse to glance over my shoulder, I dropped to the ground and rolled sideways.

There was a gasp from the onlookers, a shriek from Mistress Burnett and a terrible groan of protest and despair from her father. Seconds later, Irwin Peto pitched down beside me, measuring his length on the cobbles, the knife that had been intended for my back embedded in his chest up to the hilt. The person he had addressed as Jude, and whom I recognized at once as the man who had tried to drown me in the Fleet, fled up the street towards the High Cross, running straight into the arms of Richard Manifold as he rounded the corner, four other Sheriff's Officers hard on his heels.

Irwin Peto was still conscious, although breathing stertorously, when Ned Stoner and Rob Short carried him into the Alderman's house; but death was not far off, and I could see the knowledge in his eyes. His unintentional murderer, arrested and pinioned by Richard Manifold and his fellow officers of the law, had been hustled in after him, and I had followed with

William and Alison Burnett, a horrified Dame Pernelle and a distraught Alfred Weaver bringing up the rear. The street door being firmly shut against prying eyes, Ned and Rob laid their burden down on the floor of the hall, propping up Irwin's head with a cushion. The rushes beneath him were soon soaked with his blood.

'Ned, run for the physician as fast as you can!' the Alderman quavered. And when Ned hesitated, realizing that such an errand was futile, his master shouted, 'Go, man! Go! Hurry, for God's sake!' He knelt down beside Irwin, holding one of his hands. 'Clement,' he moaned. 'Clement! Don't die. I can't bear to lose you again.'

At these words, the dying man opened his eyes and seemed to summon up all his remaining strength. 'I'm . . . not . . . your son,' he breathed. 'I'm not . . . Clement.'

I glanced at William Burnett and saw him start, then stand as though turned to stone, a sudden desperate, hunted look on his face. And I knew that all my suspicions of him had been correct, at least where Irwin Peto was concerned. A moment later, in a sudden torrent of words, Irwin himself confirmed William's complicity in the affair; a confession gasped out with an urgency that made it obvious time was running out for him, and that he wished to make amends before he died. How much Alison and the Alderman were able to understand immediately, while that fading voice rasped and rattled in their ears, I cannot be certain; but in the long silence that succeeded his final words and his soul's departure from this world, I saw the gradual dawn of comprehension in their eyes.

William Burnett saw it, too, and made a sudden rush for the street door; but one of the Sheriff's men was before him, standing with his back to it, arms outspread and a drawn sword in his hand. He wasn't yet sure exactly what was happening, but he recognized someone trying to escape and acted accordingly. He glanced for instructions at Richard Manifold, who, in his turn, looked at me.

'You seem to be embroiled in this affair up to your neck, Roger Chapman,' he said, 'so I'll hear from you next.' He then demanded testily that the wildly protesting William Burnett should be silent, at the same time indicating that another of his men should guard the hall entrance that led into the kitchen. 'We don't want anyone getting out through the back of the house,' he warned. 'Right, I'm waiting.' He stared down at the dead body at his feet. 'Perhaps, for the sake of the women, it would be better if we went elsewhere.'

So, except for the two officers keeping watch on the doors, we all crowded into the parlour, where I told my story; a story which was corroborated in part by Irwin Peto's dying testimony. But my theory that William Burnett was the murderer of Imelda Bracegirdle was more difficult to sustain, for I had no real evidence.

Alderman Weaver, however, seemed to need no proof. Fixing his eyes on his son-in-law, his breathing rapid and shallow, he panted, 'You! *You've* played this dastardly trick on me! *You've* given me false hope that Clement was still alive! I wouldn't put murder past you! I wouldn't put any sort of villainy past you!' And suddenly he launched himself at William, the force of his weight, and the unexpectedness of the attack, bearing the younger man to the ground.

Richard Manifold, who had heard the crack of William's skull as it hit the flagstones as well as I had, started forward and, with the help of another of the Sheriff's Officers, managed to prise Alfred Weaver's fingers from his victim's throat and haul him to his feet.

'Let me alone! I— I'll kill him!' panted the Alderman, now shaking violently from head to foot and looking rather blue about the mouth.

'I think you already have,' Richard Manifold retorted grimly, going down on one knee beside the inert body lying on the floor and leaning forward to listen for a heartbeat. After a moment or two, he glanced up and slowly shook his head.

Alison gave a great sob and covered her face with her hands, but she made no attempt to touch her husband. Indeed, she seemed rather to withdraw a pace or two; and suddenly, without any words being spoken, she and her father were clasped in each other's arms.

I looked from the horrified Dame Pernelle to Ned Stoner and Rob Short and, finally, from Richard Manifold to his fellow officers. 'As far as I'm concerned,' I said, quietly but distinctly, 'William Burnett fell and hit his head while trying to escape. The Alderman was nowhere near him.'

'That's right,' Ned agreed, while Rob and Dame Pernelle nodded vehemently. 'We'll all testify to that.'

Richard Manifold pursed his lips, but he recognized an easy way out of an unpleasant situation. He looked at his fellows, both of whom shrugged and indicated their willingness to take their lead from him. 'Very well,' he conceded at last. 'If you're all determined to corrupt the course of justice, there's nothing I or Jack Gload or Peter Littleman here can do about it.' But I had a strong impression that he was not as reluctant to accept our decision as he sounded. 'At least,' he went on, brightening a little, 'we have one villain in custody. Can anyone explain why he killed this young man who was pretending to be Clement Weaver?'

'He meant to kill me,' I said. 'He'd already tried to murder me last month, in London, by drowning me in the Fleet. He's a member of Morwenna Peto's gang. Morwenna had no notion why her son had disappeared or what he was up to, and was very angry with him when I put her wise. But she was, after all, Irwin's mother, and she didn't want him exposed and turned over to the law for punishment by me. When she realized that she had carelessly revealed the truth, and what my mission was, that, in fact, my enquiries were being made on behalf of Alderman Weaver's daughter, then she did her utmost to prevent me returning to Bristol.'

'This man followed you here?' asked the Sheriff's Officer named as Jack Gload.

'Not exactly. When I escaped from him in London and, later, gave him the slip, he was presumably sent on ahead of me, to Bristol, to lie in wait. Unfortunately for him, but the time he found me, I had already told Mistress Burnett all that I had learned. He didn't know that, however, so he made another attempt to kill me by stabbing me in the back. I should conjecture that he was afraid to go back to Morwenna Peto without having accomplished his mission, and was desperate to stop me bearing witness against Irwin.'

Richard Manifold sighed: it was a complicated story. He was coming to the end of a long and tiring day, and there were still reports to be made, bodies to be disposed of, depositions to be taken down. 'And do you really believe,' he asked me, 'that Master Burnett murdered Imelda Bracegirdle in order to steal a horoscope you think she may have cast for his wife?'

I nodded. 'I do. But as he probably burned it straight away, I doubt if we'll ever really know.'

But I was wrong. A search of William Burnett's papers revealed all Mistress Bracegirdle's charts and predictions, including both Alison's and her father's horoscopes, the latter plainly showing that Alison would die four months before the Alderman.

My mother-in-law, hastily crossing herself, said with a shiver, 'To know when you are going to die must be very frightening.'

'Only if you truly believe that such events can be foretold,' Adela reproved her. 'But that's expressly against the teaching of the Church. Only God can determine the hour of each person's death.'

A few days had elapsed and she and Nicholas were paying their customary visit on their way home from the weaving sheds, where they had deposited Adela's newly spun yarn and collected more raw wool for spinning. Elizabeth and Nicholas had settled down to play like the familiar friends they had become, laughing and quarrelling and rolling around the floor, instantly comfortable in one another's company. I saw my mother-in-law glance at them and then at me, as if to make sure that I was aware how happy the two of them were together. She valiantly forbore to comment, however, merely wondering aloud what the Alderman and Mistress Burnett would do, now that each had been rudely deprived of a dream, betrayed by those in whom they had most trusted.

'Oh,' said Adela, 'I meant to tell you as soon as I came in. The weaving sheds are buzzing with the news this morning that Mistress Burnett has closed her house in Small Street and is going to sell it. She's moved back to Broad Street to live with her father, for as long as they both have on this earth. And the Alderman has rewritten his will, leaving everything to her, just as before.'

My mother-in-law sighed sentimentally. 'I do so like a happy ending.'

Adela looked at me, quirking one eyebrow, and I knew what she was thinking. Was it really possible for two people to forgive and forget the hurts that lay between them; the betrayal, the bitter insults, the realization on Alison's part that her father had always loved her less than her brother? And I realized that Adela and I often did know what the other one was thinking, because our minds were so much in tune. Like our children, we were comfortable together: we had no need to explain things. Nor would Adela ever demand to know where I was going, where I had been, or why I hadn't come home when I said I would. There would be no silent reproaches as there were with my mother-in-law. She wouldn't cling to me and refuse to let me out of her sight as Lillis had done, during our brief married life together. And I remembered Rowena Honeyman as I had last seen her, hanging on the arm of her country swain, and knew suddenly that she was another such, needing constant attention and reassurance, uneasy when her man was not at her side.

I heaved a secret sigh of relief as though I had had a lucky escape, even though, the next moment, honesty forced me to admit that I had never stood a chance with her. I could not help smiling in self-deprecation, only to become aware that both women were watching me, my mother-in-law with a certain amount of puzzlement, Adela with a mocking tilt to her lips.

I rose hastily to my feet and offered to escort our guest and her son home, if they were ready to leave. Margaret, who, womanlike, must have divined something of my intentions from my general demeanour, hustled us on our way without even offering Adela any refreshment, a most serious lapse in her code of hospitality. Elizabeth, protesting vociferously at being robbed of her playmate so soon, was told sharply to be quiet; and was so surprised at being spoken to in such a manner by her grandmother that she did as she was bidden.

Adela, too, was unusually tongue-tied as we walked back to Lewin's Mead, and our journey was saved from embarrassment only by Nicholas's artless prattle. Once inside the cottage, I decided that I must waste no more time in order to save us from further awkwardness.

'Adela,' I said, turning her about to face me, 'will you marry me?'

'As second best?' she asked levelly, holding my eyes with hers.

I shook my head. 'No. Over the last few months, I've come to realize that what I thought was love was nothing more than moonshine; a foolish dream. But my love for you has grown steadily, against the odds, against my own resistance to it, because Margaret made it so plain from the start that our marriage was what she wanted '

Adela smiled. 'I know. I know I could see it in your eyes. It was why I encouraged Richard Manifold for a time, hoping to cure myself of loving you, which I have done almost from the first moment we met.'

I took her in my arms then and kissed her, and went on kissing her until I thought I should never stop. Nicholas must have thought so, too, and, annoyed at being ignored for so long, he came across and tugged furiously at his mother's skirts. Adela broke free, laughing, and scooped him up into her arms. 'Will you mind having a son as well as a daughter?'

'No.' I managed to embrace them both. 'And I promise you, most solemnly, that Nicholas will be as my own son to me. You need have no fears on that score.'

She raised her mouth to be kissed again. 'I haven't,' she answered. 'If I had, as much as I love you, I wouldn't marry you. But I've always known you for a good, kind man. And now,' she added with a chuckle, 'before all this flattery turns your head and makes you utterly unbearable, you'd better go back to Redcliffe and tell Margaret the news.'

Adela and I were married in the porch of Saint Thomas's Church early in July, and received our nuptial blessing at the altar. Together with Elizabeth, I went to live in the cottage in Lewin's Mead, leaving Margaret to enjoy the freedom of being on her own without the responsibility of a young child to look after. But, of course, we saw her every day, and she rapidly became grandmother to Nicholas as well as to my daughter. And as Adela was an orphan, I continued to think of, and refer to, Margaret as my mother-in-law, a title which she retained for me until the end of her life.

Alderman Weaver didn't outlive his daughter, dying three weeks before her, at the beginning of September, which meant that all William Burnett's evil scheming had been for nothing. Had he not believed in Imelda Bracegirdle's ability to forecast the future, he would have inherited the Weaver fortune through Alison, and been a widower very shortly afterwards. But Margaret's faith in horoscopes wasn't shaken, as she argued that had Irwin Peto not been introduced into their lives, matters might have fallen out differently.

There was an odd postscript to the affair. One evening in August, when I returned home after a day's peddling in the surrounding villages, Adela told me that she had had a visit from Dame Pernelle.

'Poor soul! Now that John Weaver has inherited the Alderman's fortune and sold the Broad Street house, she's very lonely. She stayed talking for what seemed like hours. I think I listened to the whole of her life's history, and the history of everyone connected with her, as well. Sometimes I had difficulty keeping awake. But one thing she did tell me which struck me as rather significant. Apparently, when he was younger, Alfred Weaver had a reputation amongst his family as something of a libertine. It wasn't generally known, and I gather he didn't visit the whore-houses here, in his own home town. But when he went to London on business, he used to frequent the Southwark stews. He confided this information to his brother, who, in his turn, told his wife, who passed it on to her sister, Dame Pernelle.' Adela leaned forward and rested her elbows on the table, where she had spread our supper. 'Do you think it possible that he and Morwenna Peto, once . . . a long time ago . . .?' She didn't finish the sentence.

We looked at one another, a long, speculative stare. At last I said, 'Perhaps. Who knows? After all, it would explain Irwin's likeness to Clement. And didn't Alderman Weaver always declare that a man couldn't fail to know his own son?'

The Brothers of Glastonbury

Kate Sedley

August, 1476: Roger the travelling chapman – whose
sharp wit and tender heart have been involved in
affairs touching the mightiest and humblest in the
land – ought to be on his way home to Bristol after a
peaceful summer's peddling. But a request from the
Duke of Clarence to escort a young bride travelling to
meet her betrothed takes him instead to Wells – and
an extraordinary adventure. For the bridegroom has
vanished, and his brother soon follows.

Roger links the disappearances to the discovery of an
ancient manuscript written in a strange language. But
as he gradually deciphers the manuscript's meaning,
he concludes that a greater mystery still may lie at the
heart of the brothers' disappearance . . .

'Weaves a compelling puzzle into the vividly
coloured tapestry of medieval life' *Publishers Weekly*

'An attractive hero and effective scene-setting'
Liverpool Daily Post

0 7472 5877 5

HEADLINE

The Wildcats of Exeter

Edward Marston

His business completed, Nicholas Picard rides home in the gathering dusk of the Devonshire countryside. Lost in his thoughts, he does not see the danger ahead. And by the time he is aware of the snarling wildcat it is too late. They find his body in the woods – the claw marks on his face a hideous indication of his attacker. But the laceration to his throat is the work of a human hand.

The discovery of Picard's death complicates an already difficult task for Ralph Delchard and Gervase Bret. The murdered man was involved in one of the land disputes they are in Exeter to adjudicate and new claims are now made on the property in question. Picard's wife, Catherine, views herself as the obvious benefactor, but his mistress and the mother of a previous owner have other ideas. So determined is each woman to prove her claim that the commissioners soon begin to wonder if this piece of land could have driven one of them to murder. But the root of the mystery lies far deeper than avarice . . .

'Delchard and Bret make an enterprising pair of sleuths' *Sunday Telegraph*

0 7472 6055 9

HEADLINE